THE GLOVE

THE GLOVE

JEAN EDWARDS

This work of fiction based on the life of Adelene Sullivan Oakes is written of possibilities; what might have been, or could have been. Although much history is included, be aware that it is a work of fiction, of imagination and supposition. Personality traits are mere conjecture, and fabricated to accommodate events as depicted. Of the major characters, only Randolph, Borden, Heralda, Tug and Dora are fictitious. The information given to me by Donald Burke, current owner of the mansion, genealogy and research by Dr. Royce Miller, newspaper articles and reports from Mr. Robert Fuller, Appleton town reports, records supplied by Appleton historian Mary Gurney from the Appleton Historical Society, The Illustrated History of the Civil War, by William C. Davis, the Encyclopedia Americana and various magazines, along with photo enhancement by computer guru Ed Kennedy, have all aided in the writing of this novel about the life of an extraordinary Maine heroine.

This book was printed in the United States of America.

To order additional copies of this book, contact:
Xlibris Corporation
1-888-795-4274
www.Xlibris.com
Orders@Xlibris.com
28346

PROLOGUE

The ageless mansion sits upon the rocky berry hill,
And in the quiet of the night one hears the laughter still,
Of one of timeless beauty, whose life and love came there,
To the mansion on the hilltop, her joys and tears to share
The loneliness that came from loss of love and life.
How harsh the world would come to be, how dark would be her nights.
But struggle on, brave lonely heart, fight on with head held high,
Your mansion will bear vigil as many years roll by,
And all who pass those turrets high, and diamond windows wide,
Will know by its mere presence of jeweled days gone by,
And history will write the book for all the world to see.
Dear Adelene, brave Addie, your home still honors thee.

PART I
1834

CHAPTER 1

The Blackwater River bubbled along towards Waterford as though this spring was the same as any other, but the world of Ireland was not the same. The political unrest had not been settled in spite of the penny collections to which the poor so sacrificially contributed in hopes that peace was a purchasable commodity. The population was increasing so rapidly many predicted job shortages to soon be a problem, and neighboring countries were struggling with a new plague, a potato blight, which, if it reached Ireland would be a catastrophe of unheard of proportions. Millions of Irish poor lived almost wholly on potatoes. A winter without potatoes would be a winter completely over for at least a half million poor Irish hill people.

Being convinced the blight would surely reach the shores of the Emerald Isles in the very near future, with low moans of skeletal mothers mourning for their lost children, (lost children with whom they would soon rejoin), sounded in the back of Daniel Sullivan's mind, pushing him forward. He could leave Ireland behind, not for the adventure of going to America, as was the case of many young Irishmen, but because of simple economics. His chosen profession of a butcher would not be realized in this land if there were no potatoes to feed the hogs. A shortage of animals to butcher and too many butchers would leave families without means of support. His family was fortunate. Being reasonably well off they could escape the famine, cholera, typhus and associated illnesses such a famine would bring, but he was eighteen years old, and the time had come for him to move on and find his own way. He'd heard men at Gerald's pub saying Ireland might lose its potatoes but in America gold was tumbling out of the hills.

Daniel felt he truly held the luck of the Irish. His father had been able to feed his family and give them many comforts, and he had taught Daniel butchering, that he might follow in his footsteps. One less mouth to feed would be the best gift he could give his father, and his own footsteps were leading him to a new life in a new country. With his few possessions in a small leather sack slung over his shoulder, his only suit on his back, and with newly soled shoes on his feet that had been made sturdy with hides from his father's shop, his well shod feet were taking him across Cork to Queenstown.

The walk to the embarkation point gave Daniel time to store up all the sights and sounds and smells of his homeland. He hoped to return one day, to visit and celebrate his success in America.

Resting on a stone, he put his hand down by his side and touched the small petals of an arbutus, a tiny wood flower valiantly holding its own against the elements of a harsh spring. Plucking it from its tough stem he held it to his nostrils and inhaled its sweet fragrance, wondering if this small flower would be found in America. Would he lose contact with everything Irish? Would anyone hire a rough Irishman, or would he starve in the city streets? He never believed the "streets paved with gold" tales, but he did feel it was his destiny to cross the ocean and give his all to building a life there. The few coins sewn into the hem of his undershirt had been a great sacrifice on his fathers' part, his last gift to a son he was never to see again.

His father's eyes reddened as he hugged Daniel before his son climbed onto the rough boards of Finnian Dale's farm cart for the lift as far as Midleton. He would have only a ten-mile walk from Midleton to Queenstown, where he would work his passage on the clipper "James Baines" to New York.

Young Sullivan had read of all the cattle in the West; he was sure to find work there, or even New England, perhaps a small town in the hills. Hills with streams and bogs and Irish looking land—where potatoes would grow unblighted. The thought of the conditions that threatened his homeland, the threat of starving hordes, would forever drive him to labor long and hard, and someday he would repay his father for helping him charge to his future. God bless him, forever and ever and ever.

CHAPTER 2

Blisters, running, weeping blisters. He couldn't sleep because of his torn flesh. How could it be that the handles of the butchering knives and cleavers hadn't hardened his palms enough to prevent this ravaging of his hands? The rough lines of the sails rubbed any overnight healing he had accomplished on the swollen heel of his palm; even his wrists were raw and bleeding. What the lines didn't rip loose, the wind and sun reddened and blistered. His fair Irish complexion was freckled and splotched and the back of his neck burned and ached. Well, his whole body ached, but it seemed to be lessening as the days went by. This working one's passage was harder than he had ever imagined, but his pride wouldn't let him complain. At least he had enjoyed the comfort of his tin whistle, and the sweet thin melodies he played on the aft deck in the moonlight soothed his aching body and his unsettled mind. Even his stiff fingers rallied and gently caressed that small Irish instrument of sound, bringing back the green hills and tiny blooms among the rocks in that homeland he had left behind. It strengthened him and firmed his resolve to make his father proud. By Glory, maybe he could make the States after all!

The old cook had noticed the condition of his hands and had him soak them in seawater, then gave him a small pot of fat renderings to rub on his wrists and neck. He ripped off strips of old sail and showed him how to put the strip around his middle finger, cross over the palm and after a single knot at the base of his wrist, tie it securely with a knot on the back of his hand. It was an amazing piece of equipment. Simple as it was, it had enabled him to make it through the day in spite of his wounds—yes, and it would get him through tomorrow and the day after. His hands would gradually heal and toughen, and by the time he reached America he would be hardened and ready to go to work.

When they were a few days out of New York he tied his shirts and underwear to a rope and threw them overboard to wash in the frothy sea (tightly, so he wouldn't lose them), with the end of the rope secured to the rail. Some had tried it and lost their clothes, but they were the ones that had been seasick and the smell was so bad he doubted they would have come clean anyway. He was determined to arrive in port as clean as possible and without the stench of the hold. The ship's beer was bad, but safer than drinking the water, though he hadn't been able to become used to the sour breath and sweat it caused. It was beyond his understanding how some men seemed able to ignore the awful foul odor of sweat, vomit, urine and feces that clung to their clothing, bedding and bodies.

Nor were they bothered by the fetid breath of old sailors howling with toothaches that no amount of ground cloves or tobacco packed in their jaws would abate. If it continued long enough someone would eventually send for the cook to bring down the tongs and remove the troublesome ivory, well, not really ivory, usually black with decay. They had never learned to pick their teeth with straws and splinters after every meal to save their teeth, so most were snaggle-toothed, which was most obvious at mealtimes when they ripped their meat and bread with the side of their mouths that had the most teeth. Daniel felt it would be a miracle if he could get settled in America whole, but a miracle worth working toward.

The old salts were tough scrappers so he had been careful not to let himself become embroiled in any arguments with the regular crew. Maybe they thought he was a weakling, but that was all right. His short stature didn't make him a threat to anyone and he felt that a plus in his situation. He wanted to start his new life in one piece with all his teeth, not one eyed, toothless and crippled, so he steered clear of trouble. Getting along was the way to go. Maybe he was no Morrissey, but he could fisticuff with the best of them, but not now, no, not now. No matter how teased and agitated he might be, he must keep his eyes on the goal. There were worst things than being called "Stubby", and it was becoming a friendly tag since he had done his work and not complained no matter how painful his hands and muscles had become. He had passed the test of all they had given without a whimper and seemed to have earned some respect. He must make a success of his life in America, he owed it to his father and he owed it to himself.

CHAPTER 3

One more day and they would be at the mouth of the Hudson. One more day of the constant roar of the ocean, but now the shriek of gulls was added to the cacophony. He hadn't slept much the night before, not only from the excitement (and relief) that the journey was nearly over, but the celebration in the hold had kept him awake—and on guard. Nearing port might make some men anxious to find any coins they could, and anyone sleeping soundly was a perfect target. They had been at sea a long time and there would be available women ashore, and every extra coin meant more availability more often, and beer to go with it.

Then the two Frenchmen, Jean Oulette and Phillippe LeFountaine were at it again. Jean was rough and tough, skin like leather from years on the ocean, and missing the end of one finger. He was always pointing with the stump when he could have used the other hand or at least a different finger, but he used it as a badge of honor. He claimed a chinawoman had bitten it off while he was making passionate love to her in a brothel in Hong Kong. Daniel figured he probably lost it in a fight over the last piece of bread when all the crew was becoming testy nearing the end of an ocean voyage, or else while making a grab for someone else's beer.

'And poor Phillippe. He was a tender looking sort with greasy blond hair thinning at the temples and hanging in strands over his slender shoulders, a perfect target for anyone as indiscriminate as Jean. They "shared" a bunk, but the noises he heard sounded like they didn't always "swap" sleeping hours between watches. But that was their business. Daniel's penchant for minding his own affairs had gained him respect on the journey and he hoped he could always remain non-judgmental, even into his old age if it be granted him.

Be thankful to my God. Loving merciful God—and he saw
the land burst over the horizon.

With the salted breeze on his face, Daniel held onto the fore-
studdingsail lines and leaned forward, looking down into the
swirling depths of the sea below. What world was down there?
That dismal world of fishes, where the big fish eat the little fish,
the little fish swimming frantically in their attempt to survive.
The same world as Ireland, he supposed. The little men struggling
through the generations trying to get ahead, raise their families,
barely surviving, (let alone really living), while the powerful could
decree who could hunt what and where, taking the most and best
for themselves. They wouldn't suffer from failed potato crops, they
would always have plenty of meat and other vegetables on their
tables, and they could afford imported potatoes. Oh, they would
grumble and pretend hardship, but they would have plenty even
if the poor went without their potato soup.

Yes, the world of fishes was the same as Ireland. If only this
new country was as fair and equal as its declaration, his dreams
could come true. This was his destiny. His family in Ireland would
survive, being of strong and hardy stock, and his father's profession
was one needed by the better off. If the poor died like flies, the
moneyed would not be concerned as long as it didn't affect them
too much. Being well fed, the plagues wouldn't hit them too hard.
Many would be spared as they could leave for healthier climates
until the siege of a plague passed; some would survive with only
weakness or scars because of their healthy bodies and the availability
of the best medical treatment. The short but sturdy Sullivans had
strong constitutions, they would be all right.

America, from all he had heard, seemed a healthier place,
probably because it was less crowded. Those coming from plague-
ridden ports headed for the so-called "wide open spaces," where
measles and colds were the common maladies. Not so good for the
Indians, he'd heard. Perhaps the savages were not as tough as the
wild muscular warriors looked to be in the pictures he had seen.
The word was that the Indians were dying by the hundreds in

their encampments, dying from simple diseases that were commonly mere childhood inconveniences in the rest of the world. Surely some doctor or apothecary somewhere would discover the cause of the plagues of the world and find a cure. Better yet, they should discover a preventive measure, and determine whether the cause be something poisoning the water or air, an animal or bug—perhaps a handshake or a kiss? Oh, well, let those who worked with medicines and herbs figure it all out.

Many ailments came and seemed to grab the unsuspecting mysteriously in the night, as the poor fellow that began moaning in the night the second day out from Queenstown, clutching his side and burning with fever. His moans had become screams of pain by the third day, followed by pitiful whimpering the fourth day, only to stop completely the fifth with the cessation of his breathing. There was no choice but to tie him in a sack of old sail and prayerfully launch him into the deep. How terrible a message the ship would be taking on its return trip to Ireland, to the poor relatives who had cheered him off to seek his fortune. Now they would receive the news that he had found his Heavenly reward instead, in his ceremonious plunge to the bottom of the sea.

At least Daniel felt robust and by the Grace of God had not suffered from the stomach upheavals and bowel complications so prevalent on ocean crossings, and the land emerging before him was a welcome sight.

CHAPTER 4

Daniel's disappointment with New York was a big surprise. He was properly impressed with the buildings and the hustle and bustle of the active port. It was fine for a day, but too noisy and confusing to make him want to stay. He considered taking the new train to Lake Erie where he could look for work. Western beef was processed in Chicago and some live beef might even make its way east to Buffalo, but the cost of the fare was more than he felt he could safely spend.

There seemed to be a lot of talk about pleasant summers in New England making up for harsh winters. Freezing temperatures would not be discouraging to a butcher, as meat would keep until it was smoked or salted down. After looking over all the posted work opportunities Daniel joined the migration north, applying for a job as driver for a sugar delivery company. Being one of the few sober men disembarking from the "James Baines," he was hired immediately. The horses were well trained, and the convoy of wagons supplying sugar, coffee, and spices to states in the North East gave him free passage to his destination as well as good food, and a small stipend for his work. If living in the United States continued with this kind of good fortune he would be lucky, indeed. Having saved all his money, gambling none, and now adding to it, he had already exceeded all his expectations. Arriving in Boston, he was tempted to stay but was lured on to Maine for the extra money it would bring; all to be saved to purchase land, HIS land, HIS future.

How fortunate he had been to work all the way to Rockland, where he turned the team and wagon over to the driver who would be making the return trip south with a load of salted cod, then walking inland sixteen miles, past glimmering lakes and ponds, crossing hills and valleys to a place on the Saint George River, "McLain's Mills." The land in the valley was too expensive, but the land on the ridge overlooking the river could be purchased with what he had brought and saved. There were plenty of trees with which to cut and build, . . . and cut and build, he did.

Meeting Ellen Driscoll had been the fulfillment of all his dreams, his true Irish lass. He could hardly believe his good fortune in finding a girl in this far off land that had been born in Ireland, and together they had walked over twenty miles for a wedding blessed by the church. It had been worth every step, and he knew Ellen felt the same. It was a good wife she was, and no better cook in the valley. The girls had come in quick succession; Mary, Margaret, Celestia, Sarah, then in 1844, a boy, Dennis, followed by Julia, Ella, Clara, and lastly, Adelaide Estelle.

CHAPTER 5

"Ma, Ma, she's doing it again! She's chasing old Rooster Tom to pull his tail feathers. She'll have him too upset to do his duty and soon we won't have any eggs for breakfast!"

"Dennis! You don't have to tell Ma EVERYTHING! You always have to tattle! You should respect me because maybe someday I will be a lighthouse keeper. I'll live on Monhegan and tend the light, washing all the lenses and cleaning the windows every single day until my hands are all red and raw. And because of me being so brave, all the sailors on ALL the ships will be saved, and probably I'll get an award for my great bravery, (placing her hand over her heart and putting on a dreamy look).—And perhaps Captain Pendleton will bring me fine silks from China to make grand dresses and I'll be invited to parties and balls in Searsport because I'll be a heroine, and then if you respect me maybe I will get you invited, too!"

Stopping to catch her breath so she could continue her rambling dissertation gave Dennis a chance to cut in. "Adelaide, if you were a lighthouse keeper the ships would sail away, not because of the light but to keep away from your pomposity. You'd probably starve and freeze out there and we'd be rid of you forever!"

"Ma! Dennis is being mean again!"

Ellen ran to the door and called, "Adelaide! You leave Old Tom alone! You hear? Leave him alone!" And Dennis, you leave Adelaide alone!"

Wiping her floury hands on her apron, upset that she had been forced to leave her bread making, Ellen sighed and then returned to the kitchen where she began kneading the soft dough on the floured board again. Adelaide. What could you do with a child like that! She had played dress up since she could walk and put on airs since she could talk, always play-acting. Now that she was six she was becoming more elaborate with her fancy dreams, making hats of bits of cloth stretched over cardboard after seeing the latest Paris styles in the newspaper. Poor old Tom's tail feathers were no longer safe when they could be used to decorate Adelaide's bonnets.

With a chuckle she thought back to when Addie was four, and Lucy McLain had come for tea and in strolled Addie being a grand lady, their collie, Sadie, by her side. Glancing around the room and seeing she had an audience, in a sudden impulse, Adelaide had reached down, grabbed the dog's tail and wrapped it about her neck like a fur collar, and stood there with one hand on a slender hip in a grand stage pose. Poor Sadie simply rolled her eyes sadly over this latest atrocity but withstood it bravely, as she worshipped Adelaide and followed her diminutive mistress everywhere.

And just last week the child had been play acting again, getting into the cornstarch and powdering her face white, playing "Geisha." Ellen had caught her burning matches to make charcoal tips to wet and draw slanty eyes and flared eyebrows. Saints be! If she hadn't smelled the burning sulfur the child might have burned the house down!

They all missed old Sadie since she died last winter. Addie had tossed her head when she heard the news and said, "Well, Papa, everyone has to go sometime," and marched bravely out of the room. Ellen was not fooled. She heard the muffled sobs late in the night and knew her daughter was in pain, but also knew her little actress would want to bear it alone. That tough little bugger! Old Tom might be losing a few tail feathers, but he would eventually be in a stew anyway, and less for her to pluck when the time came. Let Adelaide be. One day she would be married to some farmer or mill worker and have a babe every year—let her dream while she could.

Dennis was a little disgruntled when he saw she was not going to be punished. It was always that way. Adelaide was spoiled. The way she had screamed all afternoon when they came home from church last Sunday made him sick.

"Heralda is a liar! She goes to church and she acts all holy and then she takes things and says she hasn't got them. Mama, she has my little book about the monkey and she won't give it back! It was my favorite and she says she never borrowed it! I want it back, Mama!"

"Adelaide, I spoke to her mother and she says you are mistaken. She never had it."

"But Mama, she's lying. She really is lying! She's a thief and a burglar and a liar because she really does have it!"

Tears started rolling down Adelaides' cheeks as she realized the futility of her pleas. Was church something a thief could use as a shield?—An excuse for doing wrong? What an easy way to ignore one's selfishness! That was what it seemed. Heralda had taken her book and everyone was acting as though she, Adelaide, was the transgressor for accusing poor righteous Heralda of a wrongdoing. It was a great mystery but she had learned a lesson. She might be considered selfish and uppity, but she would hold onto her own possessions from now on. She may as well be selfish since she was considered so, anyway. Adelaide had been branded as a wrongful accuser. With resolve, she wiped her tears and haughtily left the room.

Ellen thoughtfully placed the supper biscuits in the pan, dipping the edge of each cut disc into the cup of melted lard before placing it in the neat row in the biscuit pan. Without a doubt, Heralda had taken Adelaide's book, but there was no proof, and sad as it was, she could not think of a way to retrieve it for her daughter. The Jensens were good customers, having their butchering done every fall, and a big fuss over a small book would not be a wise business move.

It was strange, the things that formed a child's outlook, and she was sure this injustice would be a factor in Adelaide's emerging personality. She wished there were a good Irish Catholic Church near by. The truth of the matter would be told to the priest in her confession, and Adelaide would calm down once she felt that at least someone believed her. Perhaps this injustice wouldn't have a bad effect, it might make her stronger, and she would need strength to go along with her willful ways. With a sigh she finished placing the last biscuit in the pan, popped it into the waiting oven and scraped the breadboard clean with her wooden spatula.

The next morning after breakfast Ellen called to her daughter who had wandered back to her bedroom as soon as the breakfast dishes had been washed and put away.

"Adelaide! Adelaide! Come help me with these greens. I need them carried to the brook for washing." Adelaide put down the hairbrush she had been pulling through her thick hair, grabbed a ribbon from the drawer and quickly tied her chestnut tresses back from her face.

How un-glamorous a name she had been saddled with. A common, ugly, unmusical name! It sounded so German, or Swiss or something. Borden had suggested she call herself "Heidi," short for Adelaide, as they did in Europe, but even that was not pleasing to her ears. Her sister Sarah had suggested changing Sullivan to "Sylvane," and went about chanting, "Sarah Sylvane from Jefferson, Maine" (not that they were from anywhere else but McLains Mills, or Appleton, as they now called it), it just had a nice rhyme.

Perhaps Mama's feelings wouldn't be hurt if she just changed it a little, to Adeline or Adelene—just to make it more musical, and if her friend would use it as her pet name, soon everyone would catch on. Mama was so sweet and understanding. "Adelene," that's what it would be—Adelene!

Happily, she ran down to the kitchen, fetched the kettle of freshly dug dandelion greens and carried it out to the brook. To Adelene, washing the greens was no longer a chore, and she began to sing,—sweetly, softly, happily. Draining the water from the kettle to get every bit of grit from the bottom of the pan, then filling it part way with fresh water, she gaily carried it back to the kitchen, still humming a tune, setting it on the black iron stove. Turning about she rushed to her mother who was busy at the sink. Throwing her arms about her, she exclaimed, "Oh, Ma, I'm so happy! Someday I'll build you a mansion, and there'll be water right in the house, and lace curtains on every window and velvet covered chairs, just for you!"

"Now, Addie, dear, your father has given me everything I want and need, you are playing with your dreams again!"

Adelaide continued her embrace, thinking, "Someday soon she will be calling me "Adelene." Perhaps it was dream playing to Ma, but she knew in her heart, that someday she would make those dreams come true.

Dennis felt frustrated and angry. How could such a little snip of a sister evoke such emotion in him?—In everyone! Julia or Ella or Clara didn't give him any trouble. They were usually unconcerned with his business, but Adelaide always seemed to bring out the worst in him.

He decided it was about time for him to leave home, make his own mark in the world. Perhaps he would sign up to assist at the Portland Observatory to make sure Mainers weren't attacked from Casco Bay. He could learn flag signals as good as anyone. Imagine what a hero he would be if he were the one to warn of an impending attack, like Paul Revere. "Dennis Sullivan, the hero of the day!" Everyone would cheer when the city was saved because of his early warning. There would be newspaper stories about his bravery and heroism, and maybe even a picture of him standing by the rail of the tower waving the signal flags! Girls that used to snub him and call him "Fatty" and "Porky" would now be vying for his attention. Poor things, they would have to cry themselves to sleep with longing, with their hearts aching for just one kind word, one passionate glance from him. What a pity. He would be just too famous and popular for mere ordinary damsels. Ah, fame. It was worth thinking about, applying for a job at the observatory. How everyone would miss him when he went to Portland!

It was maddening to have to put up with Adelaide's foolishness. The memory of "the bird thing" was still vivid. He had spent days making a bow and arrows, and had whittled the alder branches into straight shafts with fine sharp points, and Addie had begged him to let her use it. He had been sure she would shoot it once and see how hard it was to use, and he'd be rid of her begging. Right away she aimed at a goldfinch twittering happily on a bough and as luck would have it, she shot it dead on the first try. She was always so lucky in everything she did, but this was not so lucky for him. He'd be in big trouble if his father or mother found out he had let Adelaide play with a boy's weapon. She'd cried and carried on so about the "poor dead birdie" he convinced her it would be all right if they had a funeral for it, because if it had lived probably a cat would have caught it. Then it would have had a horrible death, and this way it had not suffered and also had a beautiful funeral like no cat-eaten bird would ever have. An appeal to the dramatic always worked with her. Ella, Julia, and Clara never had to try everything that came along. They had ignored his bow making as so much foolishness, but not Adelaide.

The funeral had gone well, and Adelaide had even pulled herself together and sung "Olde Lang Syne," and all was fine until hours later at the supper table when she burst into tears and blurted out, "I killed a poor little birdie," and the whole thing had to be explained. He had been chastised and lectured and given extra chores for giving Adelaide a "dangerous weapon" to play with. She was always getting him in trouble, just her nature, and he hoped she would outgrow it. His mother had said, "Some day you'll love and admire each other when you are all grown." He could hardly wait.

"Dennis! Do you have that pile of wood split yet?" his father's voice boomed from the shed.

"Yes, Sir. I mean no, Sir, but I'm working on it, Papa. I'm working on it,"—and he placed another stick on the block and went back to splitting the stove wood as the afternoon sun began to sink behind the western ridge.

CHAPTER 6

The following weeks presented a spell of clear crisp autumn weather. School had proved to be quite dull for Dennis Sullivan. The boredom was relieved by the presence of one "Annie Hicks." Her fragile beauty and gentle ways tugged at his heart, and was a balm for his agitation with his young sister. He felt he could stand just about any aggravation by Adelaide as long as Annie smiled his way occasionally. And now today was just perfect. The sun was glinting off the Sennebec, birds were chirping happily from the branches of the sugar maples, and butterflies were fluttering about late blossoms, celebrating their freedom from their silken cocoons. The sky was at its bluest with only a puff or two of white lazily floating on slow moving air currents, and Dennis was joyous. It was the day of the big debate, and he could hardly wait to get to school.

Kicking a rounded gray "lucky rock" along the dirt road, watching its white stripe rotate with each flight as he kicked it airborne, he suddenly wished he had worn his Sunday shirt, thinking, "One should always look one's best on a day like this." It was going to be the day of days. When the schoolmaster had called for volunteers for a debate he hadn't planned to raise his hand, but the subject was just too inviting to pass up such an opportunity—"Resolved: that women should be allowed to vote."

After volunteering to be one of the debaters he had a moment of panic when he thought he might be chosen to be on the affirmative team. He would have backed out then and there if luck had tricked him into that. He was not only relieved to be on the negative team, he was elated. Too many girls were becoming interested in politics (as though they could possibly understand the ways of the world). Here was his chance to define his manhood. His brief contained all the truths on the subject he could find, and he was prepared for any and all questions that the opposition could possibly fire at him. How Charlie and Maynard could agree to speak for the affirmative he'd never understand. He'd heard them bragging at recess that although they were on the ridiculous side of the question they were going to win the debate because they were smarter than Dennis and Elmer. Just wait. They'd find out who was smart! Certainly hundreds of years of men running things proved their case. Of course the favor of the rest of the boys was on Dennis' side, so Charlie and Maynard didn't have anyone on their side—except the girls. The GIRLS! That was why they took the affirmative so happily! To get on the good side of the girls!! That was the reason for their smug attitude! Well, they deserved the trouncing they were going to get. It was dishonorable to debate a question on the side one didn't believe in!

Kicking the rock to the side of the road Dennis walked across the field to the schoolhouse and entered just as the schoolmaster turned from the steps after ringing the bell to begin the school day.

The students quickly left their little groups and took seats in the neat rows of desks, desks built on black iron filigree frames with each frame holding a seat to the front and a desk cubicle to the back. Pencils were retrieved from the shelves under the desktops and placed in the groove above the writing surface; books were placed neatly within.

Mr. Carleton looked over the top of his glasses and scrutinized the group before him—kindergarten through tenth grades. It was not an easy job, but it was his chosen profession. With outstretched arms he placed his large hands on either sides of his desk and gripped the edge, then announced, "We've been waiting for this day and it is here at last. You have worked diligently to prepare your briefs and we will commence the debate shortly. The debate will be followed by a picnic lunch supplied by the girls, which I am sure you will all enjoy. With no more fuss, let us proceed."

Dennis was stunned. No one told him about a lunch prepared by the girls. That was their job, cooking and baking, not politics. But—but now if he really lambasted the girls in his arguments it might not go over so well with them. And he smelled chicken and ham, and chocolate cake. What if . . . .

"Dennis, Dennis Sullivan. Are you listening? Please come forward with your colleague."

Jumping back to the job at hand he stammered. "Yes, yes, Sir," and slowly rose and took his place at the front of the schoolroom.

Dennis sickened. If he gave his brief as written, all the girls would be angry. He had worked so hard to find every fault he could think of to present women as inept, ignorant and hysterical and therefore unfit to vote with any wisdom, and so should be kept in their place as obedient wives and mothers . . . and cooks. His stomach began to growl. Loudly, telling all those close to him that the picnic lunch was anticipated. But, would HE get any of it? That was a good question!! He felt that if he won the debate he was still going to be a loser. Nothing hurt like someone else getting the last laugh. Damn that Maynard and Charlie! They were going to lose the debate and be heroes to all the girls. He knew in that moment that he could win the battle but the war would be lost.

By the time the noon hour struck his day was ruined. He had delivered his well-planned arguments with all the gusto he could muster, which wasn't much. He felt as though some fog had drifted in and enveloped his whole being, setting him apart from the real world. He had been forced to strain and stammer his way through his presentation, and the cross-examination was even worse. When Charlie had asked if he thought girls were really inferior he had looked across the room to where a wide-eyed Annie Hicks was sitting awaiting his answer. "Just different," was all he could manage to say, and Elmer had glared at him, knowing they would lose the debate with evasive answers. Dennis knew he did not wish to sacrifice his future with Annie by proclaiming his real beliefs. Everyone knew girls were weak and needed to be taken care of, and his confusion over being trapped was reflected in his hesitant answers.

And they lost, bitterly, utterly and completely. Mr. Carleton successfully hid his amusement over the youth succumbing to the urging of his stomach and his heart and graciously explained the defeat, declaring, "Not on merits of the proposition, but on delivery of the presentation, the winning team of Charlie and Maynard receive the ribbon of victory."

And in the third row sat the smirking Adelaide. He could kill her. Her obvious delight irked him more than losing. The only good thing to come out of the whole affair was the gentle compassion with which Annie shared her lunch with him. Perhaps all was not lost, after all.

CHAPTER 7

1861

THE BALL GAME, THE BALL GAME
I WANT TO GO DOWN THERE
THERE WON'T BE A FROWN THERE
JUST LET ME GO DOWN THERE
AND JOIN THE BALL GAME.
THEY'RE RUNNING THE BASES
THEY'E MAKING SOME ACES
THEY MAY EVEN PLUG YOU
IT'S THERE ON THEIR FACES
I JUST WANT TO BE THERE
THERE'S SO MUCH TO SEE THERE
COME JOIN IN THE CHEER THERE
DOWN AT THE TOWN BALL GAME.

Dennis was feeling like the cock of the walk. He had been batting rocks with small limbs since he had been able to walk and he could hit a bird in the head with a stone at fifty paces any time he wanted to, and now at the age of seventeen he was on the McLain's Mills baseball team. Most of the men were much older than he was, so Dennis was elated to be chosen. Just let "Adelene" try to out-do that. It galled him the way she seemed to get away with her highfalutin', persnickety ways. And now everyone was calling her Adelene instead of Adelaide. His father even had a private talk with him about it, how it was to his own advantage to help keep dear Adelaide happy.

His father's words were, "Dennis, she has convinced her friends to call her "Adelene," and half the townspeople as well. She is very determined and persuasive, and we may as well go along with her wishes. We will call her "Adelene" in this house, Dennis, whether you like it or not. You can make it difficult or you can make it easy. But I advise the latter. I don't understand women much, son, but I've lived long enough to know that sometimes the easier tack is a man's best advantage, especially when it's within reason. She is unhappy with the name "Adelaide," and this is an easy compromise. An unhappy female seems able to make unhappy males. You should remember that women are able to stand a lot of physical pain, but as you will learn, when their vanity suffers, you suffer. It is their one most vulnerable spot, at least it is Adelene's."

Dennis had protested. "But Pa, she always gets her way!"

"Son, some women have less spirit than Adelaide, and are easier to control, but the spirited ones are very difficult. Having lived with Addie, I'm sure you will find a quieter, softer girl for yourself some day, but Adelene is your sister, and you can make this easy or you can make it hard."

Daniel knew Dennis had a lot to learn about women. A lot.

Although Dennis had resented giving in, she did seem a little easier to get along with these days, but it just didn't feel right. Maybe she would outgrow it someday, but he was sick of the way she was always stealing the show.

He was happy that the family was going to the game today, and he was confident of his ability, although since they changed the rule from four strikes to three, it sort of took some of the fun out of the game. A fellow was just getting warmed up at three strikes, and since it wasn't an out any longer if the ball was caught on the first bounce, it made it a lot more of a running field game. How could anyone get there before a pop hit the ground? Things were bound to get messy because they had taken away the twenty-five cent fine for leaving the feet and throwing themselves on the ground to catch a fly ball. By the end of the game they would all look like ragamuffins instead of gentlemen. Those two rule changes could ruin the whole class of the game. At least tennis and golf were still gentlemen's sports.

McLain's Mills was so hilly, space for a ball field had been difficult to obtain, but Lowly Sherman had offered the use of a pasture near the river. The problem with the meadow was spring flooding, and with the men all primed for spring baseball as soon as town meeting was over, (those who were still speaking to each other after said meeting), it always seemed a long wait until the flooding passed and the meadows dried out.

When Albert Perry offered his pasture just off Peabody Road, they were really excited, as the rocks were few, spring flooding was not a factor, and it looked like they would have a trump of a ballpark close to town. What's more, they could begin practice as soon as the snow left the field.

The trek to the old field had limited the spectators, and now, with the easy access, even the old folks would be able to enjoy the games, and they were starting to sell peanuts and lemonade. It was becoming one of the favorite ballparks around, but they had needed some softer bases than the wooden ones from the old park, especially if they were going to do all that ungentlemanly sliding in the dirt. If they couldn't play refined, at least they could play safely. He had mentioned it at supper one night and Ma had made them some dandies from old canvas, and stuffed them with hay. She would be thanked at the picnic following the game today, and the fellows had all pitched in and bought her the brooch she'd been admiring in the glass case at Gushee's store in the village. Every woman in town had yearned for that brooch, but it was more than one man could afford. Ma had worked hard, even made a pad for A. H.'s stomach when he played catcher, so they all pitched in. He had fudged a little on his pelts last spring, not telling his father the complete truth about the amount of money he received for his skins, saving out some money for himself. He had felt guilty ever since so he put the whole hoarded amount in the kitty for the brooch.

Today would be his day. He would shine on the field and then his Ma would be the center of attention after the game. Not "Adelene."

Dennis laced his boots, folded down the cuffs of his black socks that were more than tall enough to reach his game knickers and smoothed his shirt into his waistband. A fine figger of a man, he noted. His body was maturing nicely, no more little boy parts, and even a few hairs on his upper lip that he oiled with a little lard in an effort to make himself look more generously endowed. Yes, a fine figger he was!

CHAPTER 8

The cirrus clouds were pulling their trails of combed cotton across a light blue sky above her, and a slight wind rattled the leaves of the nearby trees. Looking to the East, ominous dark clouds were advancing westward with fierce determination. Gathering her skirts, Adelene began to sprint for the house. The heels of her newly cobbled shoes sank into the soft earth. Looking down at their neat points below the hooks and laces, the new brown soles showed at the edges below the polished black uppers that reached above her ankles. Her father had "rebuilt" them just last night, dragging his last to the kitchen and setting up his cobbler tools, with her mother fussing about the mess he invariably made when he worked in the kitchen. He claimed the light was better there, but she was sure he just wanted to be with the family in the evening after a long day's work.

He didn't mind working at night, actually he took pride in doing a lot of tasks in the evening as long as he could be with his family in the house. He had chosen the small iron foot and placed it on the last, and after carefully cutting the sole and heel replacement pieces from the stiff tanned cowhide he attached them to her worn shoes with neat rows of copper tacks around the edge of the soles and heels. Calling Adelene to try them on and feel for any tacks that might have penetrated to the inside, she told him they were "perfect," and he had smilingly taken them from her and polished them until they glowed. Today they felt like new shoes, but they were not. She loved her father, and she appreciated his time, talent and effort, and the rasping sound the nail heads made when she walked across a wood floor would always be a part of her memories of home. Still, she vowed that someday she would be able to buy new shoes of any color she might choose, any style she liked, perhaps even satin slippers with suede soles that would move soundlessly wherever she might walk.

Although she was small for her age, climbing the rock-strewn ridge and keeping pace with her brother had given her strong legs, a firm body and incredible wind. No wonder people marveled at the power of her young voice. Rich and resonant to be coming from the throat of such a small girl, practice had taught her to control the force of her healthy lungs. As her feminism developed, soft tones crept in to give a unique bell-like quality to her singing that demanded to be heard. Her renditions of old Irish ballads brought tears to the eyes of the toughest old farmers and loggers lucky enough to attend any gathering at which she agreed to perform, and today she had been asked to sing after the game, at a ceremony of some kind.

A. H. Newbert had asked Ella to request Adelene to sing, and Ella had told her to keep it a secret from Ma. Adelene knew A. H. had his eye on Ella and was waiting for her to get grown. Everyone thought a girl Adelene's age was blind and deaf, but Adelene knew what was going on. If Ella wanted to get married and run after children all her life, it was all right with Adelene, but for herself, she hoped better things awaited.

"Adelene, come take this basket to the buggy, we must be aleavin' now."

"Always the last one ready," Ellen grumbled, but when Adelene approached, she quickly forgot her impatience with her daughter. All her girls had been beautiful, but her youngest had a sparkle that she could not describe. The four oldest girls were married, and Ella, just four years older than Adelene, had a quiet beauty all her own. She noticed that A. H. Newbert was taken with Ella, while boys seemed to be intimidated by Adelene. She wondered if her youngest daughter would ever marry. Such an independent spirit was not an admirable quality to any men she had ever known, not that she had known that many. Oh, well, leave it to the Lord.

Daniel and Dennis sat in the front of the buggy, and the women in the back for the ride to the Mills, across the river and up the lower East Ridge to the ball field. There was much excitement because the Liberty Rounders team was reported to be the best in the area. They had matching shirts and striped socks, and all wore long moustaches defining their masculinity, making the Mills team look like a scruffy rag tag outfit.

Approaching the field, Dennis jumped from the buggy before Daniel could get the horse tied to a tree in the adjoining field. Having watered the animal from the leather bucket he had brought, Daniel assisted the rest of his family down from the buggy and carrying a rolled quilt soon had them safely ensconced in the shade of a wild cherry, having first checked it thoroughly for poison ivy before settling them in. Ella was nervous and kept jumping up, fluffing her skirts and twirling her parasol. "Trying to attract A. H., no doubt," Adelene mused. She stayed back on the pieced quilt and fussed with her bag and its contents. "Adelene, what in the world are you fussing with?"

"My glove, Ma. I've lost a glove. My favorite gray kid ones Aunt Mary gave me for Christmas. I can't run around with just one glove! You know how nervous I get when I don't look my best."

"Adelene, you will be fine. No one will notice you have only one glove if you hold it in your hand as you hold your parasol!"

"Lord have mercy," Ellen sighed. "This fussy child will drive me to distraction yet!" "Here, Darlin', have a sip of lemonade and relax, they'll be a'startin' soon."

The gathering of the McLains Mills Rollers opposite the first base was unusual. The Liberty team, dressed in all its splendor, was warming up and they were a handsome and confident bunch. The fuss was over a new boy in town who had shown up to try for a spot on the team. Pudgy built with bandy legs, he claimed he was strong and could hit the ball a mile. This seemed doubtful.

He was a barrel-chested feller and Dennis thought it looked more like belly than chest, and his wide face gave him a baby look, the missing front tooth doing nothing to enhance his countenance. Maddocks, the coach, told him to come to the next practice to try out. With his pitiful toed-in stance he pleaded, "Please, Sir, just let me warm up with the team. You'll see I can hit the ball a mile. I've batted off O'Brien before and I can hit offa him. I may not look like a runner, but I don't hafta. I can hit anything he throws right into the trees. Just try me once before the game starts. I don't know what you've heard about us boys from Portland, but I promise you, Sir, if you just let me play,—well,—well, if you let me play I promise I won't fart!"

Maddocks gave a helpless look, and someone sniggered, then chuckles broke out until finally the whole team broke into laughter, slapping the boy on his back until one of them gave the kid's hat a tug down over his eyes. Then the whole team chimed in with, "Come on, coach, give "Tug" a chance!"

After fifteen minutes of warm-up "Tug" Edgecomb was on the team. Dennis felt some of his thunder might be stolen, but when Maddocks changed the batting order to place him third in the line-up and Tug in the clean-up position, he knew he had been trusted to get on base. If his thunder was going to be stolen it would be worth it to beat the Liberty Rounders. This game of three old cat would be theirs.

The game was everything Dennis could have dreamed. He had hit two doubles and a single and a line to short with such force the short stop couldn't handle it, in fact, had to be substituted and spent the remainder of the game with his hand on a block of ice that had been meant to cool lemonade. What a waste of good Mirror Lake ice. But Dennis had gotten on base four times, a record, and good old Tug had batted him in each time. He had even enjoyed watching Tug puff and trot around the bases, slowing down as he rounded third, with the crowd roaring when he crossed home plate making his ace. The shocked Liberty Rounders gave a lesson in accepting defeat graciously, and the picnic afterward was well on its way when Franklin Gushee stood and requested attention. With much eloquence he thanked the Rounders and their coach for an exciting game of town ball, then changed the subject.

"Ladies and Gentlemen, I hope you have found today as exciting as I. It has been a privilege to host this great team from our neighboring town of Liberty, and we offer our boys thanks and congratulations on a hard fought victory against a most talented town ball team. The new rules have made the game somewhat more difficult than before but we in McLain's Mills were up to the challenge, as was our most worthy opponents. Perhaps you have noticed, a safety feature has been added for the protection of our players. One of our citizens has made the new safe bases, and also an innovative piece of equipment for our catcher, A. H. Newbert. We hope to see this protective gear adopted for all catchers in the future. Many a rib will be saved from harm due to the efforts of our heroine, Mrs. Daniel Sullivan. Will she please step forward?"

Ellen's face reddened as she slowly rose from her seat beneath the cherry tree. Feeling as though she would surely faint, she gave an appealing look at Daniel, then Dennis, and they stepped forward, each taking an arm. Dennis leaned over and whispered, "It's all right, Ma, you'll be all right." Until that moment, Ellen had not noticed that Dennis had grown into a man, taller than his father, though not as thick in the chest and shoulders. Her boy, her only boy was a man, and soon he would leave home and find his way in life.

These thoughts filled her mind until she had made her way to the circle gathered by home plate, and extended her gloved hand to Mr. Gushee. She shyly turned to the sea of people whose faces swam before her tear filled eyes.

"Mrs. Sullivan, the boys have gotten together a small token of their esteem and appreciation. We hope you will wear this brooch in good health. We thank you."

Ellen's eyes sparkled as her son took the brooch from Franklin and pinned it to the lace collar at her shoulder. A cheer went up from the crowd and hats were thrown and much hand shaking followed.

"And now, before we leave we have one more event. Miss Adelene Sullivan will render the new hymn, "Battle Hymn of the Republic." At this time of political unrest we must think of the possibility that many of our young men may soon be leaving to keep together this republic we hold so dear. Let us all hold hands and bind our hearts in support of freedom and justice. Adelene?"

It would never be determined whether it was the anthem or the richness of Adelene's voice that hushed the crowd, but there was no disappointment in Appleton that cloudy spring day.

It was a day that would be eternally etched in Dennis' mind. It had been perfect, not easy, but perfect. Something had happened that he felt would leave him forever changed. He had learned to overcome jealousy, been accepted by his peers, had accomplished his goals, and had even seen in Adelene something he had not noticed before or accepted. She was beautiful, and her extraordinary voice more compelling than he had ever realized. She had a rare talent, and perhaps her independent ways would be necessary for her to make her life as she wished, and if the stage was her desire, then he would support her.

The dark clouds moving in over the ridge had chased away the friendlier strands of white. The sky had held itself to threats throughout the afternoon, so he left his place and went to the carriage and put the flaps down. They might have a wet drive home. Dennis had some thinking to do; it was time to make some decisions. This day had been one a man could carry in his heart always. Somehow the clouds seemed to be a warning that perhaps a day like this would never come to him again, so he would seize it and hold it in his heart forever.

CHAPTER 9

1861
Fort Sumter
Charleston, South Carolina

The situation in Charleston was tenuous. To Francis J. Oakes all the fuss was ridiculous. Slavery was on its way out and the heated political debates between the North and South seemed to be cooling; even large numbers of Southern slaveholders had freed their slaves, and North Carolina in particular seemed to agree that bondage was unchristian. All the States needed now was a confrontation to blow all the diplomacy apart. Major Anderson had made the announcement of the South Carolina secession. Any situation was repairable as long as hotheads didn't rule, but now Governor Pickens had demanded they turn the Fort over to the Confederates, and that was not going to happen without a fight. Bringing the guns and manpower over to Sumter from Moultrie in the night last Christmas had delayed the action, at least for the time being.

If he ever got back home again he would make some changes in his life. He didn't plan to be a pauper forever and he had no intention of making the military a career. A business, that was what he planned. He would save all he could and borrow all the banks would let him, and start his own company; something in manufacturing. He had another two years to go, and Eliza was waiting for him. She was a good woman and they planned a large family, but that would be after he had made his mark in the business world.

Oakes looked across the channel. The troops were to remain alert throughout their watches. Rumor had it that a bunch of drunken ruffians at Jeb's tavern had been bragging that they could lick the whole Union army by themselves if given half a chance. There was always a bunch of ignorant drunks starting trouble in town. Francis was sick of the confines of the fort, but he took his duty seriously. James and Lonnie, the new recruits, reported the attitude of the Charlestonians in general and their tales of the talk and goings on in town convinced them that the precautions instituted by Major Anderson were warranted.

It was not a good feeling, knowing the forces across the water were better than theirs. The federal batteries were incomplete, and he didn't like the idea of being in less than full readiness. Many guns were not yet mounted on the parapets, in fact, they were still in their crates. Hell, even their barracks weren't finished. Roughing it didn't bother him, it was just the whole condition of unreadiness that got to him. With old Edmond Ruffin in Charleston gloating over getting his way in South Carolina's secession, it was just a matter of time before that victory paled and he'd be looking for more meat to grind. Francis hoped it wouldn't be his.

It would be a sad day if war came. Fanatics like Ruffin stirred men up, making them crazy until they believed a flowing scarf and a charging horse could win their freedom from the Union. Well, he and others wouldn't let that happen. It would take more than flair and confidence to earn their release, and feeding the southern youth the idea that it would be easy to "whup the Yanks", was a crime. Those rugged New England farm boys were tough. They worked summer and winter, through heat and forty below and were used to miserable conditions, but neither should the North assume the porch-sitters would be pushovers. No, war would be hell, and every time someone starts calling for the government to "send in the troops", they should be reminded that "troops" are made up of their sons, fathers, brothers and husbands. It seemed every generation had to make its own discovery that war is hell. Rabble-rousers like Ruffin and Louis Wigfall (who would enjoy profit from a conflict, being in the business of supply), should be shot before a war got started, in his opinion.

It was a good thing they left Fort Moultrie and rowed the eighty-seven men over to command Fort Sumter. Maybe it was small and built on a pile of rubble in Charleston Harbor, but at least it was more defensible that Moultrie. It must be tough on Major Anderson. Everyone knew he was a Kentucky slaveholder, but he was standing true to his uniform. Having spiked the guns at Moultrie the Major hoped to hold out at Sumter until reinforcements arrived.

Francis swore to himself that if he ever got through this enlistment he would study war no more. When he started his business it wouldn't be on the backs of the less fortunate, he would not be an opportunist. He'd be head of a business that would give jobs to those who wanted to work for a living and he'd give a fair day's pay for a fair day's work. His uncle had always called him his favorite and he was growing old. If he should receive an inheritance he would invest it all in his own company. That's what he would do.

Word of mouth came that the reinforcements would not be there as promised. It had leaked out in spite of the command's attempt to keep the bad news quiet as not to impair the morale of the men. Now their nerves were on edge, making sleep difficult when they were off duty. Ever since they had rowed over to Sumter on Christmas night they had been on the alert, but nothing had happened. Nothing, all right. No help, no new troops, and a lot of the men had come down with colds and fever. Sick bay was full of the sneezing snuffing bunch. They had no fresh fruit and they expected to come down with scurvy any day; they might as well be on a ship at sea. And now it was April of sixty-one, and they were still sleeping by their guns.

Suddenly the arc of a sputtering shell streaked overhead and exploded. It was only a signal shell, but the signal shot was soon followed by the fire of fifty cannon and mortars. Anderson decided not to fire back, his hope being that his resistance might prevent full-scale war. The barrage continued as morning came and went, until finally the Major made the inevitable choice—man the guns. Only thirty-two were operational, and Francis and Peter Hart manned their smoothbores side by side, with Abner Doubleday in charge of their section. When the order came from Doubleday— "Fire!" Francis put the flame to his cannon, as did Peter, but only one shot rang out as Peter's weapon misfired. They both reloaded and the war had begun.

THE HALLOWED GROUND

STANDING ON THIS GROUND WHERE ONCE THEY STOOD
SHOULDER TO SHOULDER, BROTHER AGAINST BROTHER
THE STONES CRY OUT
DEATH
DESTRUCTION
FREEDOM
EQUALITY
CRYING FOR THE LOST ONES
THE YOUTH OF AN EMBATTLED NATION
WRESTLING WITH THE CONSCIENCES OF THEIR DIVERSE
     HERITAGES
GIVING UP THEIR SOULS FOR THE CAUSES OF OLD MEN
WHEN THEY WANTED TO MAKE LOVE, NOT WAR
WEEP FOR THEM
SOME FOUGHT FOR THE RIGHT TO DO AS THEY PLEASED
SOME FOUGHT TO BRING SLAVERY DOWN TO ITS KNEES
AND THEY BLED
AND THEIR WOMENS' WAILS RODE ON THE WIND
AND THE EARTH CRIED

The war! The bloody, damnable war! How many lives were lost? Those who died on the battlefield, calling for their mothers, those who made it home with their infected wounds torturing them until they succumbed, those whose lives were forever changed by the loss of their only financial support. Widows lost their homes because their husbands were the legal owners, driven out with their children to the streets to wander and perish either by hunger or disease or crazed minds because of the only occupation left to enable them to feed their young. Children sold to bondage, taking every manner of abuse for their scraps of bread, save the lucky few taken in by relatives out of pity, a pity that was thrown up to them by words or action of peer family members. Enduring the pitying glances and sighs of the adults, living with it, sleeping with it, giving in to it. Hopelessness devoured them and only the dream of someday escaping and making their own way in the world sustaining them; youths of eleven "going to sea" as cabin boys and cooks' assistants, working their way to dignity. Girls knowing there was no fairy tale coming true for them and no prince would be coming to save them. What did come were babies to maidens, further removing them from any hope of a fulfilled life. They could only take pleasure in the smiles of their suckling children, grabbing any small pleasure, knowing it was all they would ever have of goodness.

These souls thrilled at the opportunity to go west on wagon trains. They were more than willing to accept the probable risks of dying of thirst in the desert, of freezing or starving to death in the mountains or dying a torturous death by savages who would show no mercy to those who would steal their land.

From the East would come these brave souls, pushing their way to the western coast—those who sought to make sense of their shambled lives. These survivors would transform the West. They would use their sweat and ability to withstand adversity to form a civility that had been unknown to them in their war-torn land, and they would build a society molded from many nationalities, different cultural backgrounds, and struggle to erase prejudices that would haunt the country for generations. Each color, each ethnic group working to establish its place in a world they wished to untangle from hate. In their attempt to find their own niche, they made the West a better place.

Not so, east of the Mississippi, where opportunists on so-called missions to reform the South used that opportunity to further their own fortune-seeking. They used the opportunity to take advantage of the vanquished, moving in with the carpetbags in which they carried their belongings, (as well as their self-serving ideas for expanding their own fortunes under the guise of good intentions.)

Would the South forget they started the war at Sumter and then hate the North for ravaging their land and destroying their way of life, or hate it because of those who exploited the remnants of their fortunes afterwards? Although they were free to make their own decisions, they were in a crushed and weakened state, an easy mark for swindlers.

The genteel were forced to work to survive, character building in some sense, but very painful. "Whupping the Yanks" was not the easy task they had expected. The aristocratic southerners were accustomed to slaves doing the hard labor and therefore had been no match for the stalwart farmers, loggers, trappers and factory workers who grew up fighting for every crumb that passed their lips. Also, they had not anticipated the binding force of uniform poverty. Yankee soldiers would not give up. They would march as long as they had legs, shoot as long as they had arms, and "Hurrah" as long as they had voice, because their cause was Freedom. Those who fight for freedom, be it their own or for those they deem their brothers, are the most ferocious fighters of all, because they are not looking for glory, nor are they fighting specifically to beat down another culture. They fight for a cause, and God pity those who become sidetracked in a search for glory, because the dog soldiers will take them and their vanity down.

The most pitiful part of the whole conflict was that soldiers from both sides would hold church together, share a meal on Sunday and then resume their battle-lives on Monday. Young men had been sucked into the skirmish by calls to patriotism, young men who were too youthful and idealistic to understand the commitment they were making, a commitment to offer up their lives to a war that could have been avoided if only old men had used diplomacy instead of sending young men to their deaths.

Lincoln had tried to help by giving the defeated army their horses and rifles, but they were small tokens, what they needed was new hearts. A hundred years would pass before the problems would be sorted out and the South would become whole again as it grudgingly gave in to equality. The whole damn mess was all because the North and South were divided, not over slavery specifically, but a division built from not knowing each other's way of thinking. Bloodshed could have been avoided had the South recognized the strength of the North and had the North been more understanding of the genteel lives to which the Southerners had been bred. Zeal, self-righteousness and overconfidence made a disastrous mixture that could have been prevented from coagulating if cool heads had ruled. It was a no-fault situation that became explosive when a few hot heads became the fuse. Many went south, many went west, and some went back up North, as did Francis J. Oakes of Boston.

CHAPTER 10

1871

In the little town of McLain's Mills, Maine, far from the battlefields that now lay silent, daily life bustled on. The sawmills were in full operation, houses were being built at a rapid rate, families were growing and the grocery stores in the village, North Appleton, and Burkettville were all doing thriving business. Only a few reminders of the conflict that had torn the country apart remained. Surviving veterans returned, many weakened or crippled, but those able to stand behind a plow did so. Those who were permanently injured either lay fighting lingering infections or valiantly founded businesses or learned trades to survive the peace as they had survived the conflict, with grit and determination.

Some had dreams that relived their agony. Visions of Rebels with their "yip, yip, yip," charging up the hills; remembering, dreaming, and the fight for survival never left their minds. Hearing the moaning of a dying comrade, and discovering that it was not a friend but a rebel, crying for his maw just like a kid, crying that the Yanks were killing him, and realizing he was just a kid and the fight was brother against brother. Coming to terms that war is a useless waste of life and limb, and then having to accept the awful realization that it is too late for so many. The zeal with which they enlisted had vanished in the horror of war. Knowing, now that the conflict was over, that the fight had been avoidable, convinced them that generation after generation the same mistakes would be repeated. Rulers had always given up on settling differences peacefully (preferring instead to rattle their sabers) until all the young march off bravely to their deaths and ruination, with never a thought to listen to grizzled old soldiers who had been there before them. How sad is Man.

To the relief of the Sullivan family Dennis had come home safely, and now his grocery business in Portland was booming, and his family was growing. The Sullivan girls were all married, except Adelene. Ella had married A.H. back in May, and his political career had given many opportunities for Adelene to enjoy a busy social life. She seemed to have changed little from her early childhood, always spending time fussing with her clothing, and her mother continually frustrated with her daughter's lack of interest in the domesticity so important to Ellen.

When Adelene needed to think about her life as it was, she would take walks along the ridge, stopping on her favorite gray slate ledge, looking down at the church spires in the valley below. There were so many springs on the ridge. It was one of the magical things about the ridge besides the spectacular view; sweet, crystal clear water in abundance, much better than any in the valley. The townsfolk were always having difficulty with their wells from the time they cut a cherry limb for a divining rod to finding someone with the "gift" to use it, the digging, the rocking up and then the disappointment when it went dry in mid July. But here, here on the ridge, cold sparkling water fairly jumped from the rock. There were so many springs just a quarter of a mile North from the house she often wondered why no one ever thought to dig a large hole connecting the pools. It would be marvelous to have a big spring fed pond on the mountaintop.

Probably the boys would all skinny dip and would cause it to be forbidden to girls. So many things seemed to be "for men only." It didn't seem fair. Men could go anywhere they liked and never be told it was improper, drive horses as fast as they wanted, or even ride them barebacked and no one complained. She would be in big trouble if she ever straddled a horse, even with a saddle. Then there was the vote. There was a real slap in the face. She was as smart as any boy in her class and they would be able to vote in a few years, and help run the town, and she would be forbidden. She was sure she was more capable of making intelligent decisions that most of them, but she would be denied. All her growing up years she had watched Dennis mimic everything he heard Papa say, nothing he had reasoned by himself, yet he had been empowered with the vote. Of course now he was a big businessman in Portland, and she was proud of him, but she certainly thought she was at least, probably more, politically aware than he was at eighteen. Someday she would show them all. Someday she would be somebody, somebody famous.

Leaving the ridge and heading for the house Adelene was still fuming. Meetings! Men were always holding meetings; meetings about taxes, meetings about this, meetings about that. Men meeting. Men voting! Men deciding what everyone should do! She knew if she voiced her real thoughts on the matter her father would be furious and she would be derided. Men! Who made them boss? Somehow, someday she would find a way to make some changes. Men decide indeed!

After the evening meal Adelene asked to be excused and went to the stool by the fire. Her basket of rag strips with the large wooden crochet hook standing point down in the beginnings of a rag rug sat between her and the glowing embers of the fireplace. Grabbing the hook, she quickly wound a strip on her finger and pushed the hook through a woven hole and jerked a loop of cloth through the opening, then looped the strip and brought it through again.

Ellen tried not to notice the displeasure Adelene was crocheting into every stitch. Adelene had voiced her disapproval of the dominance of men to her mother privately before the evening meal and she was sure it was still on her mind. Would this girl ever learn to trust the men to make the decisions that were their due? Where had Adelene ever gotten the notion that she could control her own destiny and even that of others? That was a job for men. A girl should have it inbred to let them lead, but this child refused to accept the way of the world. She wondered if she had done something wrong while Adelene was a babe in the womb, that she so lacked the ability to see things as they should be. Maybe someday when she was through her teen years she would settle down.

When the light broke in the east the following day Adelene rose early to begin her chores. As soon as she was dressed she made her way to the shed where the toilet was located at the end of the corridor. She thoughtfully walked past the grain bins and the big water-streaked grindstone used to hone the scythes and blades; on by the workbench where her father's tools were neatly hung. There sat the vise she had learned not to play with after catching her finger in the screw mechanism, causing her to run frantically to her mother as the blood spurted from under her fingernail. Luckily, her nail was not permanently lost. How could she have borne such a disfigurement?

The door of the outhouse closet creaked as she pushed it open, and she stood for a moment and sighed. There must be a different kind of toilet, she reasoned. No matter how often Papa put ashes down the holes it still stunk. A lady shouldn't have to take care of her needs in such a smelly place. The wooden covers Papa had built helped some, but when she grasped the small board handle on the top that held the two half circles together and removed it from its place over the hole, the smell she hated surged upward, stinging her nose and insulting her sensibilities. Once she had gathered wildflowers and had thrown them down before sitting but even that hadn't seemed to help. Someday she would figure something out, if someone else didn't. It should be something smooth and clean, with no splinters, something befitting a lady. Yes, when she became a grand lady the first thing she would plan would be a little room, clean and fresh and maybe a bathtub in the same room, and a mirror . . . Yes! It was all forming in her mind—but the toilet in the same room as the bathtub? Well, why not?—as long as it wasn't a wooden two-holer like this. Someday she would figure it all out and even make a drawing.

Adeline took care of her needs, returned the cover to the seat and marched determinedly back into the main house. When the day's work was finished she would have time to visit with Borden. Borden had some strange ideas. She had been using lard on her face to make her skin soft when she decided washing it was drying it out. She had a daily ritual of smearing her face and neck with the grease, letting it "soak in" and then wiping it off. Adelene had to admit it seemed like a good idea except Borden had a lot of black tipped pimples ruining her complexion. Whether it was the grease or just a fault in Borden's constitution, it convinced Adelene to continue her ritual of washing with the gentle soap her mother had made for her and using just the tiniest drop of sweet oil patted around her eyes. Sometimes it seeped into her eyes and although it blurred her vision somewhat she thought it gave her eyes a luminous look, making her feel very dramatic. She could envision herself in a large house someday, with a winding staircase to descend like a princess, her hair piled high on her head and her eyes shining. Yes!

With a light gait Adelene slipped in through the kitchen door. Ellen looked at her daughter's face. With its set look her eyes seemed to be seeing something beyond ordinary vision.

"Bring in an armload of wood from the shed, Adelene, the wood box is running low," her mother called.

Coming back to the real world from her busy thoughts, Adelene returned to the shed. She missed Dennis. Keeping the wood box filled had been one of his jobs. She remembered how angry she had been when they were younger, thinking about how one day he would be a man and be making decisions for her—decisions for her! She didn't think so. She would be a grand lady far away before she would let that happen. Being a woman was almost like being a slave as far as she could see. Even then, she was sure of one thing, she didn't want Dennis or anyone else making her decisions for her, but Dennis was good at bringing in wood.

Some things he used to do still made her stomach churn. Every spring he went looking for frogs and he'd pull a leg off and turn it loose, and the next year he'd be down at the spring looking for him. He had announced that a frog could live missing one leg but wouldn't survive when he pulled off two. She could have figured that out without hurting a poor innocent frog.

It always amazed her that people could do such repulsive things. When she was younger Borden had described the gross things she had seen watching through the cracks between the boards in the barn when a cow was being bred. She had gleefully told Adelene all the lurid details and asserted that all creatures were made from such an act, even humans, but Adelene couldn't imagine it being true. Her mother couldn't ever have allowed Papa to do a thing like that, and besides, she had seen Dennis naked when they were younger so she knew what men were like, and no little wormy thing like that could be forced into any woman's body. She had determined that Borden had a big imagination and told things that couldn't possibly be true. Of course now she knew it was mostly true, but she didn't have to approve and it still seemed like an unpleasant way to create life. It was hard to imagine her parents engaging in such a practice. They must have wanted children so very badly they were willing to do the deed.

She wished she could be more like her mother, so sweet and patient, so content being a wife and mother, doing all Papa asked and always putting aside anything she was doing to accommodate someone else. She even seemed pleased when someone asked for her assistance, and only rarely did Papa show her any affection. She had caught them once in the kitchen, Papa standing behind her back with his arms crossed over her ample bosom, and when they heard her step they had pulled apart abruptly and seemed unable to speak for embarrassment.

Filling the wood box to the top she hesitated a moment to see if her mother needed anything else and then went up to her small bedroom on the second floor of the Sullivan's neat cape. Peering in her mirror on the oak dresser she pulled back her lips and inspected her teeth. Using a thread from her sewing box and pulling it between her teeth after meals had paid off. It was a trick her mother had shown her when she was very young, that and rinsing afterwards with baking soda water. Borden's teeth already had black spots near the roots, even in front. She had tried to convince her friend to adopt the thread method of cleaning her teeth, but to no avail. Borden had called her foolish and vain (probably true), but she had never had a toothache while Borden suffered miserably. She had visited her one time when she hadn't been to school for several days and had found her suffering, with her jaw all swollen and her breath reeking from the ground cloves packed in the cavity and her cheek. The strength of the spice had stripped the skin from her lips and she was still in pain from the decaying molar. Adeline could hardly stand to look at the teary, bloodshot eyes, knowing it all could have been prevented. Adelene had all her teeth and they were white and shiny. Yes, her Mama was a special lady and her advice was to be respected.

Returning to the kitchen, Addie looked at her mother's busy worn hands, and felt a rush of love and compassion for the woman who bore her. She never heard her complain, even when she was visibly fatigued. Sometimes she looked pale and her eyes looked red and dry after a long day of snapping beans and keeping the wood burning stove stoked and roaring to can them for winter. The days she salted down greens tired her also. Adeline helped her with the picking and carried them to the brook to wash them. She scoured the heavy crocks with gravel, then lugged them back to the house and layered the salt with the greens to the top with a final layer of salt before the lid was clamped down. Yes, her mother worked hard to care for them all, and the dry split knuckles and crumbled fingernails were proof of the love she held for those God had given her.

She went to her mother and stood behind her, wrapping her arms about the stout body. "Ma, I love you, Ma. Some day I want to build you a mansion, with lots of rooms and a wide hall and staircase and someone to wait on you so you can just sit in a soft chair and rest your head on a silk cushion. Someday, Ma."

"Adelene, Oh, Adelene, what shall we do with a dreamer like you? This little house is all I need. My mansion is here, with you children and your father; all I need, Dearie, all I need." She turned and kissed her daughter on the forehead. "Now run along," and she gave Addie a little spank on the derriere as she left the room. Turning back to the sink and picking up another potato, she began to peel it for the evening meal, then hesitated—"and someone to wait on me"—what an imagination that girl had—head on a silk pillow, indeed!

CHAPTER 11

Daniel Sullivan leaned on the rough handle of his hoe and looked out over the Georges Valley. This had been a lucky shot, coming to Massachusetts, now called "Maine." His schooling in Ireland hadn't kept up with the times. Everyone had always spoken of America as one vast continent, open and free, with very little thought of it being broken into small provinces. New York was a city and all north of that New England, with Massachusetts at the most northerly tip of the country, but when he had arrived at this green valley it was Maine, and had been a state in its own right for over twenty years. Indeed, the people certainly were deserving of their own state. Hardy and tough, determined to the point of bullheadedness, they ran their local government with confidence. At their rousing yearly town meetings issues were thrashed and rehashed with many a side fight outside the town hall, and many a former friendship dissolved, not to be reestablished until summer. It was as though being cooped up through the harsh winter had caused them to store up explosive energy, and by the time town meeting came in March it erupted with a vengeance. The final determinations were usually fair and even the most avid grumblers were calmed by June.

Heifers were born, fields were plowed, seeds were planted, and the earth continued its endless revolutions, and these New England hills reminded him of home. Even though the Georges River was small it rushed more violently than the Blackwater. After the spring rains washed over the land from the northwest, it stopped to rest awhile in the Sennebec before rushing on to its meeting with the sea.

How vast an ocean between Ireland and himself—but at least he could dream of the Georges' flow pushing and roiling its way east to his homeland. He didn't dream he'd ever see the emerald shores of Ireland again, but perhaps his children might someday visit there and raise a mug to him in Gerald's Pub. That's what McLain's Mills needed—a good pub, a place where a man could amble in at the end of a long day and be handed a foam-dripping mug of warm amber. But he guessed that would never happen. The straight-laced Protestants here imagined hell-fire lurked within that satisfying liquid, and that it tainted any man that raised it to his lips, and their description of fire and brimstone was certainly enough to stay any man's arm from tipping the mug. No, probably a pub was out of the question. There did seem to be a lot of trafficking in hard cider. Most houses had a barrel of cider in the cellar that was intended to become vinegar for pickling purposes, but most barrels were only half full by the time it was ready for use, and the women seemed to believe it had "evaporated." One could always find a few sweet apple breath tipsters in every crowd.

Hard cider was a sneaky brew. It never tasted or looked strong and a little went a long way. He tried it once and wandered into the kitchen, embracing Ellen and giving her a pinch here and a rub there and it hadn't worked to his advantage. Ellen had whirled on him and with great disgust had said, "You're drunk, Daniel. Ye ought to be ashamed of yerself, a grown man with children, drunk as a common wastrel. You can just take your fruity breath and sweaty body away from me and don't be about me until it's clean and sober ye are!" Daniel had skulked away from the rebuff and slept it off in the barn. He wouldn't try that again. Ellen had claimed she had a headache for three weeks after that. But that was when he was younger. A pub. What a blessing that would be!

Taking a small sharpening stone from his pocket he leaned to the bank beside him and rubbed it on the wet grass, decided it still wasn't wet enough, so he spat on it twice. He thoughtfully began sharpening the edge of the hoe, the rasping sound making a rhythm as his steady swipes across the edge changed the sound from a rough grumble to a smoother tone as the edge began to shine. Then he turned his head toward another sound, a melody of such sweetness he at first thought he was dreaming. It came fuller and stronger, not the high timbre of the voices of maidens in Ireland, but lower, more resounding, but so melodious and echoing he stood entranced by its magic. Adelene. If the world could hear her joyous voice she would be taken from him and be made a queen. He must do something to bind her here. She had spurned every suitor and she had been a very difficult young lady. He remembered back when she was five and they had donned their Sunday best and hitched up the buggy to attend the funeral of Horace Sprague. What a handful she had been! Horace had died of the dropsy and nothing could have been done to save him, but Adelene could not bear it that her friends, Azuba and Elmer, had lost their father. She had stood by the hand hewn pine casket where the elder Sprague rested and stared at the pale face of their neighbor.

Fidgeting with the ribbons that held her bonnet tightly over her curls she had said, "Pa, what does he see? Pa, see how his eyes sparkle, like they see something we can't. What does he see, Papa?"

"Along with ye, Addie."

"Papa."

"Move along and be quiet, now girl."

"But, Papa, see his eyes," pointing at the partly opened eyes. "He sees something wonderful, see how they sparkle."

Grasping his child's shoulders he moved her along past the coffin to their seat in the second row of pews.

"It's all right, Addie, but ye must be quiet. He sees the Gates of Heaven opened for him and all the Glory beyond. But we'll speak no more of it."

Addie had taken her place between her parents and quietly thought it over. Perhaps dying wasn't a bad thing, especially if life had been hard and cruel. She'd never seen Horace's eyes shine so brightly when he was alive. She'd have to think more about that when she had time to sort it all out.

Daniel had cursed poverty. He had personally gone to the Spragues' as quickly as possible when he heard of the passing and placed a dollar coin on each of Horace's eyelids to hold them down. The coins had disappeared overnight and the lids had opened slightly from the coins leaving too soon, and Adelene never missed a trick. She had been more worldly-wise than most fifteen year olds, this precocious bairn of his; his other girls had never been that much trouble.

He wondered what the world would bring to Adelene, or more likely, what Adelene would bring to the world. Nothing ordinary, that was for certain. The "fighting Irish" was a term that epitomized this child. He was sure she was going to be a handful for any man. That tirade when he brought home the new bull was completely unreasonable. Ellen had been making supper for all the men coming to see the new acquisition, and Adelene had thrown a fit. She had screamed that no one cared about the cows and the large calves they would bear from the big animal. She lamented that the poor cows would be assaulted by the savage creature and be forced to endure difficult births, and no one cared, and that she would never marry any of the uncouth youths who had cheered the huge animal on in his duty, and that the whole thing was disgusting. He had been unable to reason with her that the enhancement of the herd was his primary consideration, and that she knew nothing about husbandry, but she had refused to listen. She closed her mind to what she considered "the world's undesirable elements."

Daniel thought it best if he found her a husband as soon as possible, before she became any more opinionated and high-strung. Perhaps with a house full of babies she'd be too busy to practice the adventure he could see in her eyes. Their sparkle told him, she too, was seeing more than most, and she was here, alive and vital. This one would fight to move Heaven and earth, sure and she would—she'd be too impatient to wait for the Gates of Heaven, this one. Good Lord, she should have been a boy!

There was only one thing to do, find her a job until he could find her a husband. There were rumors that the upper ridge schoolteacher was leaving; he would talk to the town fathers about considering Adelene for the job. She could teach music as well as the regular studies. Yes, he would bind her to this town, he would not lose his difficult little princess!

Turning back to his work Daniel chopped at the weeds in the garden patch. The herbs meant so much to Ellen he had taken a day's break from his butchering—not much doing this time of year, anyway, and Ellen was a good cook. He was a lucky man, blessed, he was, with wife and children, and he'd never regretted coming to America—but a pub would be fine, indeed!

CHAPTER 12

1882

Although her teachers' salary was meager Adelene had decided to spend a part of it on a portrait. Uriah Dyer lived just under the ridge in his farmhouse. He usually did commission work on ceilings, painting murals around ornate plasterwork. He had done a beautiful ceiling for S. J. Gushee. It was the talk of the town. He always made a pen and ink drawing first and many of his clients had them framed and hung in the rooms with the finished ceiling. It was quite an event when one of his ceilings was finished, prompting a celebratory open house. It was also a good excuse for all the ladies to show off their baking skills and the men to get together and rehash the last town meeting or champion some new cause or discuss the crop production or failure thereof, as in the recent celebration down in the village. The canal was usually included in their important confabs, whether it was being filled in as had been designated by law and who was getting any benefit from parts not yet filled. Of course Mr. Gushee had complied, in fact had been most pleased with the closing of what he considered a bad idea in the first place. Of what use was a canal that froze over in the winter and went dry in the summer?

The S. J. Gushee house had been built on the corner of Main Street and Elm in Appleton Village, near the mills of Archibald and Fergus McLain, just South of Fergus McLain's own large Federal style home. The Gushee house was well planned for the location, the front door facing his general store to the South. The many windows made the house bright in the daytime, and Mr. Gushee was considering adding a porch about the front and side of the house that faced the streets. Inside, ornate oak furnishings glowed in the light of the oil burning ceiling fixtures, and the largest library in town, with its leather bound volumes, held all the classics as well as poetry, reference books and almanacs.

The Gushees welcomed anyone with a thirst for knowledge to partake of their extensive literary fare and many a time sat and discussed new arrivals to the library with interested friends. Mr. Gushee maintained that a good library was the backbone of a town, and with the lack of a public library, his door was always open.

The parlor ceiling was everything anticipated. A cream background was overlaid with green and gold leaves radiating from the candelabra hung from center plasterwork, with intertwining ivy of varying shades of green, darker in the center and lighter on the outer edges. The corners were similarly designed, but in a triangular pattern. Its simple symmetry and balance created an arbor effect that was entrancing, and the intricacy of the leaves and vines so realistic one felt they could be plucked from the mural as from a woodland canopy. The visitors strolled through the house and then gathered in the dining room to congratulate the Gushees on their choice of the artist and his work before sitting down for the refreshments of a social hour.

The dining alcove was flanked on either side with matching mahogany china cabinets. Carved clusters of grapes adorned the upper corners, and the leaded glass doors revealed silver cups and trays, along with fine English chinaware. The table had been set with a fresh flower centerpiece, peonies and foxglove and trails of English ivy creeping out from a crystal bowl, candles lit in Grecian design silver candelabra, and china and crystal dinnerware, arranged buffet style. Embroidered linen napkins with E. J. G. satin stitched in the corners were starched, ironed and folded into small bird shapes, and the tea service was filled and steaming. No element of entertainment finesse had been neglected.

Julia Page had brought her great lemon flavored "Chicago" cake, and Milton Simmons baked his "chocolate cream cake" for the occasion. Geneva Robbins brought her wonderful little potato rusks, which were arranged on a platter with several kinds of cheese, dried venison strips and small bits of salted cod, prepared with horseradish sauce for dipping. There was great fun for the young folk taking turns churning the ice cream, with Lulie Ufford supervising the production and stopping the pilfering of the precious chipped ice. It was quite an evening, but when the children began to fuss and grow sleepy, the guests started leaving.

Adeline had enjoyed the celebration, remembering the many evenings of musicales and theatrical study with the Gushees and other musically inclined citizens of the town, but now she was ready to use all she had learned and practiced. The theatrical productions at Riverside Hall had been enlightening—actors and musicians from New York had been entertaining but she knew she was destined for higher accomplishments than what she had witnessed there.

In having her portrait made for her mother she would feel less guilty about leaving home. Ma was beginning to have some knee problems and Adelene hoped to make life easier for her someday, someday soon. Papa wasn't getting any younger, and although all the other children had long since left home, he was still working full days, and she thought it was time for him to slow down. God knew he deserved it. Yes, she must take steps now to ensure their comfort in their old age. Her dreams must come true, they had always been so real.

Walking north on the Ridge Road, past the four corners where the road to the left led to West Appleton, past fields where the Queen Anne's lace was blossoming white as a new babe's christening gown, their clustered heads nodding in the sun, Adelene crossed the road opposite the Brown's farm. She slipped down through the pasture, stopping to pick a handful of boxberries on the way. When the last of the crimson berries bearing the cross mark and tiny hairs had been popped into her mouth and the checkerberry tingle on her tongue began to diminish, she chewed on the shiny green leaves she had picked with them. Their pungency left her mouth feeling fresh and tangy. Holding up her skirts she made her way through the juniper bushes whose bristly needles scratched and tickled her ankles above her buttoned boots, then as she clambered over the gate that kept the cows in the upper pasture she entered the fringe of woods at the bottom of the hill. Following along the brook edge suddenly she burst into sunlight. Hurrying through the field where the snowy crabapple tree had turned its blooms into small green nubs, she reached the slate bottomed brook again, where it bounced its way from the ridge to the river beyond. Lowering herself to the edge where the clear stream pooled and gurgled over the stone, she sipped the cool moisture, then wet her hands and brushed the loose hair that had tumbled from the ribbon that held it back from her flushed cheeks.

DOWN WHERE THE PULPETS GROW
THEIR STRIPED HOODS SHADING THE SUNLIGHT
AND SLIDING RAINDROPS THAT DRIP BY THE NOSE OF THE
    SILENT PREACHER
HIS QUIET SERMON SAYING MORE THAN WORDS
FAITH—FULFILLED BY THE RETURNING SPRING
PEACE—LIKE THE QUIET OF THE WOODLANDS
LOVE—HURTING NO OTHER LIVING THING
THE SILENT WOODLAND WATCHMAN STANDING
    SOLEMNLY IN HIS MANTLE OF GREEN,
HIDDEN THERE AMONG THE DARK STONES.

Gathering her skirts she slowly made her way though the pale grass of the back yard where a blue jay scolded the world from the bent apple tree, and entered the set of gray shingled buildings though the back door of the shed.

"Mr. Dyer! Mr. Dyer! It's Adelene!"

Looking up from where he was sorting glass negatives, Mr. Dyer exclaimed, "Adelene! What a sight for these sore old eyes you are! Step into the kitchen and we'll talk about the neighbors! Annie! Adelene is here!" To Adelene, "I call you Adelene, as you wish, though Adelaide is a perfectly fine name."

The sweet smell of fresh raspberry pie wafted through the doorway as she hiked her skirts and climbed the two steps to her right and stepped inside. She loved the Dyers, they were her kind of people. The house reflected their artful lifestyle, the odors of fresh baking mingling with the oily smell of their artwork. Mrs. Dyer was an artist in her own right, and she was currently working on pansies to complete a monogram commission for O. R. Butler; a gift for Mrs. Harriet C. Wentworth. It was a delicate work, pen and ink border of the most intricate design, with scenes drawn within circles and squares depicting events in Mrs. Wentworth's life, with her initials entwined in the center, and the pansies, (her favorite flower) gracefully forming a bed for the letters.

Uriah led the way through the large kitchen, feeling the warmth of the big "Dorothy" chrome trimmed black iron stove with its steaming tank, (having just completed its duty baking the aforementioned pies), on past the iron sink overlooking the back yard and into the central room where they did their artwork.

There was a heating stove on the far end, (not burning), sitting close against Adelene's favorite part of the room. The rounded wall extended from the door of a bedroom on the right all the way across to the front of the house where there was a door leading to the parlor. Adelene wondered if the wall had been rounded as a heat reflector or simply as an ornamental feature. Turning back, her eyes fell on the wallpaper, the beautiful hand painted wallpaper that always gave her the feeling she was in an art gallery.

Poor Mr. Dyer, he deserved a real gallery. People didn't seem to appreciate artistic genius until after the artist died, and Mr. Dyer and his battle with crippling arthritis would probably follow that pattern. Even his brother didn't recognize his talent or appreciate it. Probably there would be a wonderful room in a college or museum somewhere, someday, that would herald his genius, someday, but not now. Now, even as he aged he would have to struggle, living the artist's life of few creature comforts.

Though his and Annie's work and artistry was rarely appreciated, the Dyers seemed perfectly happy with their lives; their love of art and each other seemed to be enough.

"It's finished, Adelene, and I hope it's what you wanted." Uriah reached down to a stack of canvases by the window and placed one on an easel where the light filtered through the squared panes. Adelene drew in her breath sharply. There, in a simple gray frock she sat, wisps of chestnut hair tumbling and curling softly about her face, a few wild flowers held gently in her hands resting in her lap, and a steady gaze of dark eyes looking back at her. She could see someone with a future. Something in the eyes held a promise, a yearning beyond the innocence portrayed. She knew she would fulfill what Uriah had painted from the photograph he had taken earlier that year.

"Oh, Mr. Dyer, Mr. Dyer! How can I pay you enough for this? It's everything I wanted, and more! You've made me what I want to be!—What I'm going to be—please keep it for me until—until, well, I'm going to spend some time in Portland with Dennis and then take some music courses in Boston. Will you give it to Mama if I'm not back for Christmas?"

With tears in her eyes Adelene thanked the Dyers, and on the climb back up the ridge her mind raced on ahead of her eager steps. I will. I will be all I see in my portrait. One thing she knew, she'd had enough of teaching school.

It had been an advantage, teaching school. She had access to a lot of books unavailable at home, all the plays of Shakespeare and even some copies of new songs that had been purchased for her music class. Adelene had learned most of them while the children studied with only occasional breaks in her concentration whenever some of the boys felt compelled to break out their pocket knives and whittle on their desks or the girls sneaked notes to one another and giggled behind the upright geography books. Many of them received a quick thump side of the head with the big green books they had attempted to hide behind, but usually she controlled their behavior with harsh words. She didn't believe in corporal punishment, and they usually could be coerced into being proper young men and ladies with a look of utter disappointment from Adelene. They became so contrite when she made believe cry they would behave for several hours. She loved them all, but now it was time for her to get on with her career.

She was sure of one thing, she would not be trapped like Borden. Her wedding had been so exciting; the planning, making the dress with the lovely high collar trimmed in the lace her grandmother had tatted, the satin covered bustle that had given her such a dramatic figure with her full breasts balancing the look. She had been so beautiful in her wedding gown, with Ralph standing so tall and straight by her side. It seemed that all of Borden's dreams had come true, but now, after having a baby every year, her hands were rough and she had a tired look around her eyes. Her teeth had become much worse, and she seemed to be developing lines around her mouth. Probably she had no time to do her lard ritual to help keep the wrinkles away, making her look much older than her twenty-six years. Surely she had some moments of contentment, but who applauded Borden?

Not Ralph, who worked long hours to keep the hungry mouths fed, or the demanding children who had emerged from her fertile body. Children tended to want, not give, at least until they were grown. They opened their mouths and held out their arms to receive comfort for themselves, not give it.

Before going home in the fading light Adelene stopped on her favorite ledge and softly hummed one of her favorite tunes, then started for the house. She paused once again and bowed her head, praying:

"At my rising, I hunger for guidance throughout the day, that I will have strength and wisdom. Strength to do all you ask of me, strength to withstand all the trials put before me; wisdom to help others that might come to me for guidance, and to turn to thee for help. I cherish thy touch in my quiet time, to feel your hand in the warmth of the sun, the beauty of a flower, the movement of the wind. I hunger for Thy comfort that I might sleep at night knowing that all is in Thy hands and know that in my final sleep, You will be there."

CHAPTER 13

1884

WHEN THE BERRY FIELDS TURN FUCHSIA
AND THE BIRCHES TURN TO GOLD,
THE ALDER BUSHES QUIVVER
AS THEY SHIVVER IN THE COLD.
THEN JUST A FEW SOFT FLURRIES
HAIL THE COMING WINTER BLAST,
AND THE FEW REMAINING APPLES
GIVE UP THEIR HOLD AT LAST.
A LONESOME CORNSTALK STANDING
THAT DIDN'T MAKE THE CUT,
IT'S BROWNING SHEAVES HANG SOMBER
IN EARNED DISCOURAGEMENT.
SOON SUMMER WILL BE FADING
THE COLORS GROWING OLD,
WHEN THE BERRY FIELDS TURN FUCHSIA
AND THE BIRCHES TURN TO GOLD

Adelene looked down over the valley, taking it all in, etching it
in her heart, and thought about the town, its people, all that she
planned to leave behind.

Not a lot of trees in the town, but small elms were sprouting
up everywhere, so many that the town had named the road by
the Baptist church and Oddfellow's Hall, "Elm Street." The
trees were small now but promised a canopy for the town in
the future, making a haven for Baltimore Orioles and chickadees.
There were tales of giant firs having grown here in past centuries,
giants that were clear-cut for ship masts throughout Europe,

the trees never again to return to their former glory. But, then, everything changes.

There were summer folk who came to Maine for its even-tempered summers. They were a weird bunch. Either they dressed in summer voiles and party hats, playing croquet on their manicured lawns, hiring "locals" to do their work or slummed in tatters in a misguided attempt to blend in with the native Maine people. (They still used them to serve their needs, evidenced by the change of laundry showing up the following spring—the diapers on the lines attesting to the gullibility of some trusting young girls who believed they had found "true love" in the arms of handsome vacationing college bucks). The young men went on their way, their well-planned lives to fulfill, while the spoiled girls were left to make their way in a world forever changed for them. They were lucky if an older widower could be found to rescue them from a life of despair. But nothing stays the same. The very things one believed could be changed in a twinkling. Maine had been a part of Massachusetts, now it was Maine, a state by itself. It just proved that nothing was definite, and she felt she had to be ready to make her own changes before someone did it for her.

Crossing the field before the house she hesitated again. Standing alone in the soft padding of old grass, Adelene looked to Moody Mountain in the East, the darkness of the evergreens mingling with the lighter tones of oak and maple, their leaf laden limbs making a collage of lacy filigree, muting the darker greens. Reaching down to a small bush at her side she swept her skirt back and gathered a handful of dark berries. Bringing them to her lips, she wished she had brought a basket with her. She could have had pie for supper—but they were a delight fresh from the bush and the regret left her in an instant. As her eyes wandered once again to the village below, the two church spires glistened in the sun. The animosity of some of the loyal churchgoers struck her as humorous. The Baptists considered their church to be the true church of the town, but their strict rules made acceptance of their order difficult.

Her parents were Catholic, but there was no parish for them to practice their faith. The Union Church, although considered a church for all faiths, did not include any semblance to Catholicism. The church itself was more beautiful than the Calvinistic Baptist church, and with its stained glass windows could even be considered a cousin to Catholic style architecture. It entertained a much smaller congregation with sporadic attendance, mostly comprised of those disgruntled with their previous fellow Baptists, but not about to make Catholics welcome lest more rules and attitudes be brought in to complicate their thinking. The Sullivans had attended both churches off and on, and they studied the Bible at home on Sundays, making a trip to St. Dennis church at the parish in Alna on Christmas and Easter. The twice-yearly visits made their confessions very long indeed, so Adelene usually left out the minor sins she felt she might have committed. Why should the priest and God be bothered with her little sins when there were murderers and thieves everywhere, and even girls that stole books and lied about it?

Further across the valley Pine Grove Cemetery stood naked on the opposite ridge. The small pines were hardly a grove, but given time it would be a pleasant place for a final rest, with the whispering in the needled branches a soft song of peace for those who perhaps had not known peace before. And Sennebec. The pond shone like a sapphire in the afternoon light, the wisps of moisture having risen earlier. My jewel, she mused. If she never attained her ambitions, if the theater never accepted her, if success, fame and fortune were never to be hers, she would have this. She would come home to this beloved ridge and stand in the morning sun with the cool breeze on her face blowing her hair back, skirts billowing around her, and the blue jewel of the Sennebec would sparkle in the sunlight and she would be whole. Nothing would ever erase this place from her mind or take its wonder from her soul.

Noticing the first autumnal reddening of sumac and the yellow tinge on a maple leaf as she began to walk back to the house, she thought of her mother peeling potatoes and carrots for a stew. Ellen Sullivan had always been content just being a good Irish wife. She was a wizard in the kitchen and would make a meal from whatever they grew or Daniel had hunted or butchered. There was plenty of game, and rabbit, turkey, venison, bear or moose meat went into her grand Irish stews. Better than most, for her mother raised herbs and dried them, their savory leaves in jars standing in neat rows on a shelf by the wood stove. Ellen was a genius at mixing them to make each stew a culinary delight. She possessed an exceptional talent for using rosemary and sage and thyme for pork and venison, tarragon and summer savory and a bit of juniper berries with fowl and marjoram with fish. She baked hot biscuits and yeast rolls, corn bread, brown bread, berry and apple pie and fruitcakes at Christmas filled with currants and raisins. Raisins that were made from the fox grapes that grew over the rock wall, her cakes made moist with chopped apples and darkened with molasses and spices, served up with whipped cream from their old Guernsey milk cow.

How many times had she watched her mother whip cream or egg whites with her old whisk made of small alder switches tied together, whipping them to froth in minutes, making unbeatable sponge cakes and meringues with ease. "Sauces and gravies, homemade butter, fresh milk."

Adelene would miss this comfortable home, but she felt her destiny was south, the theater, the city lights. She knew where her roots were, their tenacious hold on the rocky ridge overlooking the blue jewel of the Sennebec would be forever calling her home.

PART II

CHAPTER 1

Slowly packing the open carpetbag she had placed on her bed, Adelene paused and looked about the small room where her dreams had repeated themselves year after year since her childhood—dreams of fame and fortune, dreams of gowns and feathered hats and peau de soire slippers, dreams of applause. Sometimes as she lay among the soft quilts of her bed she could feel the warmth of the stage lights, the admiration of the crowd, and now perhaps it would all come true. She had studied all the Gilbert and Sullivan musicals and knew all the words and tunes by heart, learned all her favorite Shakespeare heroines' lines, and she could read music thanks to the piano lessons her mother had made sure she received since childhood. She had practiced all the songs for which she could find the music, over and over again, standing on her favorite slate ledge with her feet in the gray-green moss and the birds echoing the choruses. This trip was what she had been waiting for; the time was right. She would stay at the United States Hotel where her departed sister Sarah's husband was the manager. Boston was the beginning of her journey into the future and Boston wasn't that far from New York, where she believed she would realize her dreams.

Folding her clothes carefully, she placed her two best dresses in the bag, her stockings and extra corset in the side creases. Next, several pair of bloomers, her hairbrush, Vaseline for shiny lids and lips, the gentle complexion soap her mother had made for protecting her fair skin, (with less lye than the soap she made for washing clothes and general use). Next a cotton nightgown and the fluffy slippers her mother had crocheted especially for the trip. Most of her things were already packed in the metal-banded wooden trunk and loaded on the buggy she would ride to meet the stage taking her to Portland.

Mama. How gentle and kind she was. Right now she was busy in the kitchen frying doughnuts to put in her daughter's lunch for the trip. Little did Adelene realize how heart wrenching it was for Ellen to let her youngest child leave home. For her daughter, the thought of it all was almost dizzying. She'd spend some time with Dennis and Annie before taking the train to Boston. There, she'd be staying in the big hotel Alonzo managed. She had never stayed in a hotel before. On all the trips to Augusta to be with Ella and A. H. at parties, she had stayed with friends or relatives. Oh, the Appleton House Hotel in the Mills was always busy, especially if there was a stage show in town performing at Riverside Hall. She had never spent the night there, although she had considered it when the theatrical companies from New York came to perform. She would have enjoyed mingling with the actors as she sometimes missed parts of the performances when the small hall filled up with cigar smoke. Mr. Ingraham did a thriving business selling his "Uncle Job's Cigars" and there was seldom a troupe performing that did not draw him into town to hawk his wares.

Closing the carpetbag and fastening the latch, Adelene went to the kitchen. Ellen was just lifting a string of doughnuts on the curved wooden doughnut stick, having passed it through the holes of four or five doughnuts. After letting the fat drip off into the bubbling pot of golden liquid she carefully placed them in a paper-lined tray on the kitchen shelf. How many times had Adelene watched her patient Mama fry the week's doughnuts, but it never seemed as special as today. Probably because she knew it would be a long time before she would witness the rite again.

CHAPTER 2

As Adelene settled herself into the stage carriage for the bumpy ride to Portland she tried not to look back. She knew she was doing the right thing, right for herself and right for her parents. It was continual heartache for her mother, (who thought every girl ought to marry and be "taken care of"), and her refusal of every suitor had been discouraging for Ellen. She had finally convinced her mother that she was not suitable for raising children because of her distaste for anything messy, and Ellen had become resigned to Adelene's becoming a "career girl." It was a new concept in the world and especially in the little town of McLain's Mills.

"They'll get over it," Adelene told herself as she smoothed her skirts and leaned against the puffed and buttoned horsehair covering of the carriage seat. Resting her hand on the smooth mahogany of the door edge she glanced across the valley that was just beginning to show the early tinges of autumn. "I'll miss winter," she mused. Winter in Maine, with the snow covered fields where taller grasses poked their flaxen tips out of the snow, their frozen casings shining in the sun and the fields sparkling like millions of diamonds.

McLain's Mills, now called Appleton, was a busy little town, and really quite modern. With more than seven dry goods stores included in the seventeen businesses, (besides a watchmaker and millinery shop), one could purchase or have manufactured nearly everything needed for daily living.

It also had its fair share of failures, the biggest being the canal whose sections connected Liberty and Points West to the sea. The old canal was filled in now, except for a small section beyond Gushee's store at the crossroads where the young folks skated in the winter. The canal had worked somewhat for transporting lumber and produce to the coast for a few years, but someone should have figured out the canal would dry up in the summer and freeze over in the winter. If it didn't work for General Knox a hundred years before, what made them think it could ever be profitable for them? She planned to have her life thought out better than that. She would look at all the possibilities before she made any life altering moves. To her mother's regret, finding a man to run her life was not in the picture.

CHAPTER 3

Daniel Sullivan was discouraged, confused. His youngest daughter was on her way to Portland, and after spending some time with her brother, she'd be taking the train to Boston. It seemed dangerous to him, a small girl traveling alone with Heaven knows what kind of heathens and cutthroats taking passage on the same train. Perhaps she could take care of herself. SHE certainly thought so. At supper last week he had mentioned the problem of someone losing their farm from not paying taxes. The town fathers had met to discuss raising revenues to pay for road repair and to support the schools, and how tax penalties would help with the bills. Adelene had set her chin and declared, "I wouldn't give up my home if I couldn't pay! I'd find a way, I'd earn it somehow, even if I had to take care of a sick old man or-or-dig ditches, or shovel the roads if I had to! I'd do whatever it took, but I wouldn't give up."

He had looked at his diminutive daughter, thinking, "If a boy had that fire, what a man he would be!!" Too bad it was wasted on a girl, and such a tiny one, at that. She was going to be one handful for some man. Taming her into a wife would be one unholy job. He hadn't been able to think of a single young man in McLain's Mills, Hope or Union, not even Belmont, that he considered up to a task that challenging. There must be one somewhere, he concluded, that would be willing to attempt it. Daniel hoped if and when that day came, she wouldn't be taken too far away. He'd miss that pretty face and her straightforward attitude, even though he did become exasperated with her at times.

Daniel looked across the room at his wife. Her furrowed brow told him that she, too, had concerns, yet she had agreed to Addie's leaving more easily than he.

Ellen glanced over at her husband and smiled, lest he discern her true thoughts. She was remembering things she wished she could forget, such as the day years ago when Adelene had come to her, announcing, "Borden said," (always that Borden giving her ideas), "My cousin Ralph showed me a book about a far away land. He's been everywhere, he sailed with Captain Pendleton and he drew pictures and wrote down everything he saw. There are people who live on islands where it is warm the whole year 'round, and they don't have roads and carriages or horses and they hardly wear any clothes, so they make skirts out of grass and leaves and they eat with their fingers and they dance like this." Jumping up, Adelene had put her forefingers and thumbs together and waved her hands about while gyrating her hips, her skirts brushing the floor as she swayed from side to side.

"Adelene! You stop that this instant! You don't know what you are doing!" Ellen admonished.

"But Mama, the hands tell a story, the ocean waves, the wind, the mountains. Borden said Ralph showed her how"—

Cutting her off, Ellen declared, "Lord, have mercy! Adelene, that is sinful! The heathens in other lands do a lot of things that are sins against God and you are going to stop right now! Oh, Adelene, can't you be content to just grow into womanhood and be a wife and mother as nature intended? The missionaries have failed in their duty. God help them, they must teach those wild creatures to live Christian lives. Someday, Adelene, you will understand what such actions do to men, but get ye back to your cross-stitch for now and forget these sinful actions if ye ever want to get to Heaven. What would Papa say if he ever saw such behavior? Mother Mary, Adelene, just do your cross-stitch and I'll forget this ever happened."

Ellen had returned to her bread making with a sigh. How could it be that her daughter, her lovely little daughter, was so stage struck she couldn't see the evil in so much of it? She had feared even then that the stage and theater would some day take her daughter away from home, and only God and the Saints in Heaven could protect her in those places. Oh, Adelene!

From the corner of her eye she had watched as Addie sat on her stool by the fireplace, picking up her embroidery and holding it in her lap. She thought for a moment her heard a soft humming over the crackle of the fire, and slight body movement—and perhaps she was holding the needle and floss differently, with a sort of flair, taking stitches while her body moved slowly to an unheard rhythm. What was a mother to do?

This unmanageable child, and now the forbidden island swaying had gotten into her and Ellen would have to decide whether to lecture more or just hope she would forget it if she let the subject drop. The obstinate teen years with Adelene had been difficult, but most things were just passing fancies, so Ellen had kneaded the bread harder and bit her tongue on the matter.

And now it had happened. Addie was a grown woman and had taught schools in Hope and Appleton and Union, and studied all the music and plays available, and with or without their Blessing, she was on her way to her "career."

God Protect her. God Bless her. Please.

CHAPTER 4

Arriving in Portland late in the evening, Adelene glanced around and extended one trim leather-clad foot to the small metal stair below the casing of the carriage door that creaked as it swung open. Ducking her head slightly to keep her feathered hat from being caught on the bulkhead she bent forward and suddenly a large hand reached out and caught hers, then with both hands grasped her firm waist and boosted her down. Wide eyed with surprise she gasped in recognition of the broad face of the man who was assisting her.

"Tug! Tug Edgecomb! How in the world?"—

"Hey, Addie! Yes, It's me all right! I told Dennis I'd come by and get you. I was working late over at the factory and I promised him I'd see you safely to his door. I have to put in extra time now that I'm a super. 'Gotta get those old beans in the can, you know, and now that I thought up putting out brown bread, too, they think I've got more brains than I can lay claim to. Shucks, after eating Saturday night beans and brown bread your Ma cooked up, it just came natural to want to share good eatin'. Poor Dennis stays so busy with that big old store and those twins of his he hardly has time to eat at all. I tried to tell him years ago to come on over to Burnam and Morrill. It's a lot less hassle and I get all the beans I can eat."

"Are you married, Tug?"

"No, Addie-girl. No one as fine as you ever took a liking to me, and how can I take less when I've seen the best? If I was ten years younger I'd be on my knees to you," and he smiled his warm gaping grin at her.

"Oh, Tug, you know just how to make a lady feel special. One of these days some lovely lady is going to snap you up. I would, myself, but I'm on my way to a career, and I can hardly wait! You're just saying those sweet things because you know you are safe from me. But just you wait! One of these days you'll be grabbed, and by someone who can cook, and I want to come to your wedding!"

"If you say so, Addie, I couldn't deny you anything you ask, nor could any man with eyes in his head. Come along, now, show me your luggage so I can load it on my buggy and we'll get on over to your brother's place. They've been waiting for you, and those boys won't go to bed until they see their sweet Aunt Adelene. Annie's been a little poorly lately so we best hurry over there so she will get to bed early and get her rest."

Dear, dear Tug, what a loyal friend he has been to Dennis, Adelene thought. His jolly, lovable roundness drew adoring children to his side, women trusted him, and men accepted him with never a jealous thought. They should be jealous, she reasoned. He had so many fine qualities; hardworking, trustworthy, honest, and yes, lovable. Lovable old Tug. He'd be snapped up one of these days. Perhaps he enjoyed his freedom but he must endure some lonely times. She might have to become a matchmaker if she stayed in Portland long, but it was only a stopover. She had her own agenda. 'Best she concentrate on that.

CHAPTER 5

The weeks with Dennis and Annie whizzed by. Her attitude, her whole way of thinking adjusted to the city bustle, becoming attuned to carriage rides through the busy city streets and evenings at the theater. Every performance she witnessed made her more anxious to get on with her training, and by the first of October she would be on the train to Boston. It was a little frightening. She knew she was prepared for city society, having attended parties and teas with A.H. and Ella at the Blaine house in Augusta, with all the pomp and protocol associated with the governor's mansion. S. J. and Alvina were invited often and they usually made arrangements for her to sing. She hadn't minded "singing for her supper," so to speak. Of course they didn't realize she was practicing for bigger and better things. Boston would be more exotic, a different world, she imagined. She had signed up for a season of voice and theater training, and she hoped for a chance at some small parts. When the opportunity presented itself she would go on to New York! New York, that was the place to be, but she knew the next few months would be crucial. Get the training, become the best she could be before attempting her ultimate goal.

Staying at the United States Hotel while she attended classes would be exciting, as other students would be staying there also. She saw it as a great opportunity to learn from their theater experiences as well as her own schooling, and she'd get a "feel" for the competition she'd face when auditioning. She looked forward to meeting others with the same ambitions as she, and having competition would raise her level of determination and performance.

"Adelene." Dennis' voice brought her out of her thoughts. "Adelene, I need your help. Annie is feeling so poorly, before you leave I would appreciate it if you would help me find a housekeeper. She has always refused help on my suggestion. She prefers to do all the housekeeping and caring for the children herself, but this big old house is too much for her to keep up. I'm sure you could persuade her to accept someone of your choosing."

"Of course, Dennis, I would love to be of help, (laughing). I owe you a lot for all the trouble I caused you when we were children. Remember the bow and arrow incident? Papa was so angry!"

"I didn't realize how little you were, Adelene, I was just a teenaged boy and you were the bratty little sister that always got her way. You were the youngest and I can't blame Ma and Papa for indulging you. I will probably do the same when this new baby comes—I don't believe there will be more after this."

"I don't understand this child, Dennis, I mean, how you could put her through another pregnancy. She's so weak, I don't believe she ever fully recovered from bearing the twins, and now she's carrying another babe struggling to enter the world. It may kill her this time. Of course I'll do all I can to help."

"I know, I know. I can't forgive myself for doing this to her. You have never been married, Adelene, perhaps never even been in love, so its easy for you to look at this from a more sane point of view. When a man and a woman have shared all Annie and I have, we cannot control our expression of love.

When we were young we were so alive. Just the other day Annie and I were talking about how young folks were probably sitting by the river, splashing their feet in the water with the birds singing and the sun shining through the trees and they would be saying, "Remember old Annie and Dennis, those eccentric old folks that still walked hand in hand until the day they left town?" And that's the way it was with Annie and me when we were young, splashing our feet in the water beyond the bend, where no one could see. She was so delicate and beautiful, with her golden hair blowing in the air currents rising from the river. It's just the way of things, Adelene. We held hands and splashed by the riverbank, and probably Ma and Papa did the same, even though it's hard to imagine them ever being lovers like we were. Love always feels so new, like it could never have been the same for anyone else, making love like we did, but it must have been. That's the way life is. And now Annie is so weak I'm afraid I will lose her because I loved her so much. It's hard for a man to bear. I've advertised for a housekeeper and if you will choose one from those who apply, I will be forever grateful."

"I'm honored, Dennis, that you trust my judgment in this and I will certainly do everything I can to help."

Arm in arm they walked to the dining room where the children and Annie were already seated. How fine a family this was, and she felt a kinship with her only brother she had never felt before, and silently vowed to do all in her power to help him keep his Annie.

CHAPTER 6

The train ride to Boston was amazingly short. She had imagined it to take longer than the stage from home to Portland. Arriving at the station fresh and with spirits high, she hailed a buggy and was on her way to the hotel.

She felt confident of her choice of a housekeeper for Annie from the applicants. Georgia Holbrook was lively and cheerful and young enough to handle the children with patience. She was several years younger than Annie but they had chosen her together. Annie had taken an instant liking to the girl, and acted as though she had found a long lost friend, calling Georgia her "dear soul mate."

One afternoon when Annie was especially weak and Georgia was covering her with a knitted robe on the couch, Adelene heard Annie whisper to Georgia, "If anything happens to me, you will take care of my darling Dennis, won't you Georgie?" "Of course, I will," she had replied, "but you must deliver this child and take care of him yourself, you must promise me that, Annie." Adelene had backed away from the doorway, feeling the moment they were sharing was much too personal for any intrusion. Yes, that family was in good hands, and now she was on her way.

Her heart beat faster as the buggy wound through the streets from North Station, then through Chinatown towards the hotel where her sister's husband awaited her arrival.

Adelene was amazed at the smoothness of the ride as the carriage clattered over the cobblestones. There was no bumping over the ruts as when riding over the dirt roads and streets in Maine. The rattle of the iron-banded wheels was steady but the ride was nearly

as smooth as riding on fresh dragged roads. She sighed with
exasperation. Why didn't they make roads like this in Maine? There
certainly was no shortage of rocks. All New England was full of
rocks and plenty of smooth ones. Then she noticed street signs on
every corner. Everyone in the whole busy city knew which way to
go because of the street signs—but why not have the roads
numbered, then it would be really easy, easy to make maps and
with the numbers on the map anyone could find their way
anywhere. Sometimes Adelene scared herself with her own
adventurous thoughts and ideas.

Sarah had redecorated a suite for Addie two years before,
when Adelene first mentioned she might study in Boston. Their
children being grown and in their own homes, they were
delighted when she and Alonzo first heard of her plans. Sarah
had taken great delight in refurbishing the bedroom with a
canopied four-poster, outfitting it with lace trimmed sheets
and counterpanes topped with a blue satin goose down
comforter and crocheted toss pillows. An ivory framed hand
mirror and matching comb rested on the marble topped base
of a tri-mirrored dressing table. There was a small sitting room
and a dressing closet, complete with a private bath where a
deep copper tub awaited her individual use. Remembering the
fastidiousness of her baby sister had made choosing furnishings
and accessories a great adventure for Sarah. Her sudden death
robbed her of the pleasure of seeing Adelene enjoy the room
she had so carefully prepared, but sweet of Alonzo to keep the
room as his wife had planned.

Adelene was indeed pleased with her sister's labor of love, and
after eating a small meal in the dining hall was soon bathed and
snuggled in the soft bed that had awaited her. She felt like a princess
and as she let sleep over take her, her mouth turned up at the
corners into a satisfied smile of contentment. Tomorrow. Tomorrow
her real life would begin.

October 20, 1884

Dear Mama and Papa,

After spending several weeks with Dennis and Annie I have safely arrived in Boston. Alonzo has given me the most delightful lodgings. There are excellent opportunities for new actresses and they say the voice training here is unsurpassed. Please stay well and not worry about me. Alonzo will take good care of me and will advise me on the ways of the city. I will write again in a few weeks when I can give you a report on my progress. I assure you I will spend my time wisely, with much study and practice. I am consumed with happiness because of this opportunity before me, and will do my best to honor you by doing well.

Your loving daughter,

Adelene

December 5, 1884

Dear Mama and Papa,

I am auditioning for an engagement with the Grand Opera Stock Company this week. I did not expect the opportunity to arise in such a short time, but other actresses have encouraged me to audition as soon as possible to enable me to become familiar with the workings of the theatrical circles. If I am fortunate enough to be selected for a small part, the compensation will be more than enough to sustain me. My teacher, Miss Ryan, is pleased with my progress as an actress and my music studies have been most enjoyable and rewarding. There are also many fine theaters in Providence, with excellent opportunities there. I am told that working with a variety of thespians is most educational and advantageous.

My agent, Mr. Haworth, has been exceedingly kind in his assistance with my career. Of course Cousin Louella has assured me the door will always be open if I wish to further my career in New York, should an opportunity present itself. I have no cause to doubt the sincerity of her invitation and will accept her hospitality if an opportunity arises. I look forward to seeing you in the spring when the theater season is over.

Your loving daughter,

Adelene

CHAPTER 7

Acting courses were everything Adelene had imagined. Although the stock company did not select her for their season, they had given her much hope for her future, assuring her that with a few years of study they would be sure to find a place for her in their company. Until then she would be considered for small parts in local theater groups, and she was quite content with her situation. Her respect for the written word was renewed, as all she had studied about the theater had materialized in the classes she was taking. Her music lessons were a great joy and she found her acting classes exceedingly rewarding. Not only was her enthusiasm heightened over her accomplishments toward her chosen profession, she had the comradeship of others with the same ambitions.

Her dearest new friend was Dora, Dora Wimple. Dora had struggled to find funding for her theatrical education, but was managing. Timid and small, her pale skin and slender body starkly accented by thick curling black locks, locks that were so springy it required constant tucking into the hair rat encircling her head to keep tendrils from popping away from the pins straining to hold the coiffure together. It was a constant worry to Dora, who was continually trying to keep the wondrous curls in place. Adelene thought the casual trails of escaping curls gave her an adorably disheveled look that was not unbecoming. The luminous dark eyes with their fringe of black lashes were so large they belied her timid personality. Adelene adored her and worried about her like a mother. Dora was not musically talented and was too delicate for the long hours of practice classes required, but she had worked hard and though her progress was not as fast as Adelene's, she was holding her own.

Soon it would be Christmas and Adelene was spending her first winter holidays away from her family. This time of year the snow would be deepening on the fields, and at night it would be a soft comforter blanketing the town as it slept. From the ridge the sounds of the town stirring at sunrise would softly drift up from the valley, a rooster's crow, puppies waking and calling their mother, a steady livening of the farm animals. It was another world from the one in which she was now living. Sometimes she longed to be home with Ma and Papa, smelling the warm fragrance of spice cakes and pies and herb-roasted venison, but the theaters were bursting with activity and there were seats for Miss Ryan's aspiring actors and actresses in one theater or another every night. It was not the time to be homesick.

Addie decided a trip to the ocean on a Sunday would dissuade homesickness, so she hired a carriage from Alonzo's stable and had the driver take her to the bay. Finding an isolated spot was easy, and she ventured from the carriage and let the cold winter wind from the ocean blow against her body, feeling it through her wool coat until it was as though it was cleansing her soul. It was a cliff-like edge, the water thrashing and fighting with the rocks on the shore. The foam crawled over the top of the surges as though reaching for salvation, not realizing that upon reaching its objective it would be dissolved and lost forever on the jagged stones.

Adelene felt a pull, a pull that made her feel part of that deep, dark swirling abyss. What strange magnetic attraction could it be, this frightening, longing, loving embrace that tugged at her very being—this strange beckoning? Was it her Irish blood? Was this a connection to the ancestors who had found their peace in the sea? Lost ones, some of whom had emerged on the rocks and were saved, while others were dashed on those same rocks at the whim of the pounding surf, waves jealously guarding their briny depths and casting all that trespassed onto beaches. Everyone considered the "finds" on the shores to be finder's treasure, but maybe those finds were only remnants from the sea, cleansing itself of transgressor's belongings.

She wondered if the urging of the sea on her soul was Ireland beckoning to her. Someday she would go there and find out for herself about her heritage, and afterwards perhaps this attraction would subside. Perhaps so, perhaps not, it was all before her to discover.

IF I WERE A STONE UPON THE SHORE
WATCHING THE WAVES IN THEIR ENDLESS DANCE,
WALTZING IN, THEN BACKING AWAY,
RELUCTANT TO MAKE THE FIRST MOVE
TO THAT VAST OCEAN BEYOND,
WHEN FINALLY PULLED BY THE MOON'S DEMAND
THE TINY WAVES GIVE IN,
AND TRAVEL ON WITH THE THRASHING SURF,
ON TO WORLDS AWAY.
MAKING THEIR JOURNEY TO FOREIGN LANDS
THROUGH TROPICAL STORMS TO GOLDEN SANDS,
THEN HOMEWARD THEY SURGE, RETURNING ONCE MORE
TO WASH A STONE UPON THE SHORE.

Feeling strangely exhilarated, Adeline was content on the ride back into town. She was bundled against the frosty December air and arrived at the hotel with a happy heart. Hearing the sounds of a piano as she ascended the staircase she followed the melody to the second floor sitting room where Randolph was sitting at the grand piano running his hands over the keys, as always, searching for a new melody.

Randolph was a light skinned Negro, (commonly called "high yeller" in the South but more accepted in modern Boston). His snug brown curls and gentlemanly manners had endeared him to Addie. His life had been tragic. His mother had hated him from the time of his forced conception by her owner just outside Richmond. It had been so repugnant to her it further complicated the pregnancy. Whether nine months of nausea was physical from the mixed blood or mental from the hate and trauma was uncertain, but the hate had driven her crazy and Randolph was taken from her at birth and smuggled north by Samantha, warm, loving Samantha. Her freckled skin and red tinged hair told the story of her own birth. She had rescued him from his crazed mother and savage father and had given him new life. She would always be his real mother. Her employment at the hotel had given Randolph an opportunity to explore his talent. Addie spent many an evening by his side at the piano, singing the popular songs of the day, old favorites, and learning new melodies that rose from Randolph's deft fingertips. Sometimes as she helped him with words to love songs, they became so sentimental they eventually convulsed into laughter or tears at their folly. It was a good thing.

In January Dennis' Annie succumbed. Adelene had anticipated losing Annie, she and the baby had both proved too weak to live. Annie had lost her struggle to bring a very wanted testimony of love into the world. Remembering that Sarah had suffered only one agonizing moment of pain, clutching her head in both hands and sinking to the floor into merciful unconsciousness made Adelene feel that life could be so unfair. She felt the urgency of reaching for her chosen star lest the opportunity be lost forever. Yes, she would reach for her dreams and catch them before it was too late.

Being in the hotel and using the room Sarah had planned for her brought Sarah close to Addie. Sarah, darling Sarah, who had always been like a second mother to Adelene, always so sweet and kind, always there to give advice and support with never a hint of judgment, only gentle counseling whenever Adelene needed unprejudiced guidance. Alonzo had the running of the hotel to keep his mind occupied by day, but she knew the nights must be agonizing even after two winters had passed. Remembering Dennis' attempt to explain married love helped her to be kind to Alonzo and understand his grief. Adelene decided she would never truly love anyone, because losing a true love seemed to be more than a person should be forced to bear. How could love be worth such pain? She resolved to work even harder on her career. That would be her life and she would be shielded from the anguish of loss. The stage was her destiny and it was a burning desire within her.

CHAPTER 8

1885

Spring arrived, lush and green, the kind of spring that always followed depressing March rains and April torrents, granting only brief interludes of sunshine before the skies would again darken, sometimes showering, sometimes only threatening. When June arrived and the black fly pestilence finally subsided, the sun coaxed the land into thick green foliage and the fields fairly burst into abundance. The roadside shad sprinkled their white Chantilly aprons throughout the woods and spindly wild cherry sprawlings shook their lacy petticoats in the breeze. Patches of velvety cats-paws softened the fields as they struggled to burst through the fresh carpet of the first grass of spring. With the meadow lupine's tropical greenery as a back drop for the blossoming fruit trees, July brought the lupines into full bloom, their towers of pink, blue, white and lavender dancing their joyous ballet in the gentle summer air. Newly hatched blueberry patches huddled together on the hillside, having anchored their spreading roots to the rock-strewn ridge, bracing themselves against the earlier spring winds and torrents. The fresh leaves had erupted as tiny dots of green on the wispy branches and now were full blown waxy green leaves, crowding the rock walls with small white blossoms, promising a fruit harvest in August.

This first visit home to the ridge she loved was as soul renewing as she had dreamed. She would spend the summer here and not think of Boston or classes or the theater for the next two months. She would help her mother and renew herself in the process. Knowing she was ready for auditions in the fall gave her a peaceful calmness, a promise to herself. For now, she would fill her lungs with the sweet air of home, feel the soft moss underfoot, and practice her music a'capella from the ledge. Home. How could she not be called to Maine this time of year? It was a beckoning even stronger than the tides.

The first morning home Adelene awoke early, breakfasted with her mother and father, grabbed her shawl and walked through the fields to the second ridge to the West. Stumbling in the soggy dip before the rise to the next hill, Adelene picked herself up, brushed the grass and dirt from her frock and continued on. She thought of herself as the bear that went over the mountain and began to sing.

"The bear went over the mountain,
The bear went over the mountain,
The bear went over the mountain
To see what she could see," (changing the "he" to "she," of course).

Why was everything a "He"? She was a "She"—bear and "She" was going to see what was on the other side.

Rounding the top, she found herself looking down on the slow moving waters of the Pettingill Stream. It was a magnificent sight that took her breath away, so close to her home, yet seemingly so far from reality. The winding waters meandered through acres of bog, unapproachable bog. From the lofty view from the ridge top she could see the earth and twig dams here and there the beaver had built. She thought about all the bungalows hidden under the water, where the baby beaver were born and hidden until they were old enough to swim and discover what their little flat tails were for. What a miraculous place! How astounded those little furry creatures must be when they surfaced from the den and entered such a wonder-world! They must be filled with awe at the sight of the gray limbs of dead wood rising from the nearly still water, the geese searching for food, diving, shaking their heads free of swamp grass. And how surprised they must be at the sight of herons and shit-pokes balancing on one foot waiting for an unsuspecting fish to swim by. Imagine their astonishment at the sound of the trilling and twittering of finches and chicadees, spring peepers with their evening chorus and the buzzing of dragonflies, bees and locusts.

How good it was, this ridge beyond the Georges. This was the place to feel one with the earth, and on a clear spring night when the stars came down close enough to almost touch the dark hills—this was when she truly felt a part of the universe, and she lost herself in the wonder of it all. She wished she could stay all day and watch the sun go down, but she hurried back towards the house. It was still forenoon and this was her first full day home. She would see the stars tonight.

Approaching the house, Adeline noticed her father stepping through the door onto the open porch, rolling up his shirtsleeves as he always did before beginning his day's work. "Late start" she thought. He carefully turned the cuffs back first, then one more roll so they wouldn't become stained as he worked. When he was younger he rolled them above the elbow in the summertime. She recalled the firm flesh, the bulging biceps. Now, still muscled, the skin somehow seemed looser, the muscles underneath strangely detached from the outer covering, the splotched skin of his wrists wrinkled even when his hand was unbent; his fingers and knuckles were enlarged from a life of heavy labor. He was the same, but different. Age. That strange, creeping affliction.

CHAPTER 9

New York, 1882

Francis J. Oakes was riding high. Business was booming. The Oakes Manufacturing Company on Stone Street in New York City had more orders than it could fill. Woolen factories all over New England clamored for the quality dyes manufactured there. His workers were happy with the management and bragged, (deservedly so), to workers from other factories of the benefits they received. Where else could a workingman enjoy a mid-morning and a mid-afternoon break, as well as an ample lunch hour? What other company took care of medical bills if a man were injured on the job? And blacks, he hired a lot of blacks and gave them equal pay with the whites and would not allow them to be called "niggers." Anyone caught disobeying that rule would lose his cherished job at the Stone Street Dye Works. Production increased continually because of his progressive methods, and soon racial barriers were broken within the domain of the company. The workers realized regular pay raises from their cooperative work ethics. The thriving company improved the standard of living for the dye works employees and Francis Oakes became a millionaire. He was an innovator, and the reputation gained from the testimonies of his workers not only made his business boom, but the satisfaction of those workers made them more productive. Instituting protective work gear did not escape his attention. Isinglass goggles were issued to those working with powders, and gauze masks kept them from inhaling the dust. Clean wash rooms were provided and a stock room was set up where sandwiches and coffee could be purchased, further adding to his workers' satisfaction and his factory's efficiency.

Yes, life for F. J. Oakes was good. The children had come quickly, four in ten years, his beloved little miracles.

Suddenly things went sour. Eliza had taken a fever and was gone. He hadn't been prepared for such a tragedy. He couldn't accept that someone so young, so vibrant, so alive, the mother of his children, could go so quickly. No more could he lie with his head against her soft bosom at night; no more would the roundness of her body comfort him when he was fatigued or satisfy his instincts when he had need. He was devastated. For a year nothing could comfort him, until one night he cried out in anguish, "Merciful God, take this grief from me, I can bear it no longer!"—and mercy was granted.

Francis emerged from his room when morning came, a new man. A widower with four children to support and comfort, he realized he had neglected their needs in selfish indulgence and he set about making it right. He immediately rented a cabin at Lake Wallenpaupack, taught them all to swim and play and laugh. When winter came they shushed over the snowy mountain trails by day and huddled in furry robes by the glowing fireplace at night, telling stories, sharing their feelings and concerns. He loved them deeply and did all he could to ensure pleasant memories of their mother carried over into their lives, making them the kind and loving people she would have wanted them to be. When his manhood stirrings returned, he spurned them. That part of his life was over.

Regular church attendance had been an important part of his life with Eliza, but since she had been gone Francis had become somewhat neglectful in that duty. He had trouble with the thought of attending church where he had last seen Eliza's pale face resting in her satin lined coffin, so he had the nanny prepare the children to attend the Dutch Reformed Church at Steinway for services on Sunday. It would be a life-altering move.

The church was large, with alcoves containing statues of the Saints and stained glass windows of great beauty and intricacy depicting scenes from the life of Christ. How beautiful, how peaceful, he thought. The children were awestruck by the grandeur of the church and its amenities.

As they were seated the pipe organ began playing softly. Then a sweet trilling voice sounded, the voice of an angel, and his eyes rested on a vision in white, a vision with jet-black hair and amazing dark eyes that seemed to harbor some great mystery, some haunting secret that called to him.

Louella Merrifield, he was to discover, was the angel with the sweet melodious voice, Louella Merrifield from Maine. It was as though a plan had been secretly drafted for his life, the arrival of someone from a state he had only heard about from factory orders, a place he hardly thought about as even being an actual "place," and from there this beautiful flower had materialized.

It was only days before he had arranged to meet her, and only weeks before he fell to his knees before her, begging her to marry him. Her dark beauty had completely captivated him; her cool aloofness intrigued him. He was absolutely and hopelessly in love with her.

CHAPTER 10

Francis' ardor was slow to cool. Louella's protests were difficult for him to understand. Eliza had never turned him away, except for a few days each month when she was indisposed, but with Louella it was different. Thinking her distant attitude the result of her New England upbringing, he bought her jewels and gave her free rein to redecorate the house on West 73rd street. He didn't understand why she insisted on her own private rooms, he had wanted the marriage to be as warm and loving as his union with Eliza had been, but he granted her every wish. He even tried to understand her reluctance to accept his children. His hope that she would be a second mother to them was dashed as she sent them to spend time with their grandparents whenever it could be arranged. Francis rationalized it as being good for the children and grandparents alike. Perhaps their being away would increase the possibility of Louella's conceiving, since it gave them privacy he had not been able to enjoy with Eliza. During his first marriage one or the other of the children always seemed to wake up and (1) "feel sick," (2) "had a bad dream," (3) "need a drink of water," or (4) just want to sleep with Mama and Papa. Eliza had conceived easily enough with only their snatched moments together, but Louella had not been a day late with her curse since they had been married. Perhaps with the children away and more time to play their love would combine and create a miracle. At any rate, things were going well at the plant. Yes, Francis Oakes was still riding high.

As the New Year 1886 ushered out the old, things were not exactly the way Francis wished them to be. Louella's reclusive ways were interfering with his plans. He was granted very limited access to Louella's suite, and limited access to Louella herself. She spent more and more time in her rooms. He reasoned she needed time to herself. She was such a rare beauty, her sleek black hair always perfectly coiffured, her make-up impeccable, her elegant clothing perfectly fitted to her tantalizing body. She seldom emerged before eleven and retired shortly after dinner. Francis seemed to be forever trying to find ways to approach her and it was causing him to feel as awkward as a schoolboy. Perhaps she was lonely when he was at work, perhaps if she were happier when he was away she would be more receptive when he came home. His mind reeled at the confusion of his thoughts, the excuses he was making for her, the reasons for his failure or her failure or whatever was happening. One thing was certain, he was becoming a lonely man.

CHAPTER 11

The winter of 1886 proved to be a wonderful one for Adelene. Auditions had been fruitful and her acceptance by her peers had been of great encouragement. Randolph was writing more and more music, and her rendition of his latest compositions gave her considerable confidence. Randolph himself would sometimes wake her in the middle of the night, calling, "Adelene, Adelene," at her door, and she'd grab her robe and they would softly sneak to the music room, close the doors and go over his latest inspiration. Her personal life was comfortable, and her music and acting lessons were promising success. From the intense lessons given by her voice teacher, Kate Ryan, she was learning to control her range and vibrato until her lilting voice commanded attention even beyond her acting ability and stylish carriage, and she had been offered parts in small local performances for which she was very grateful.

Randolph had suggested a change in her career, which she resented at first as interference. She had flounced out of the room in anger and sulked in her quarters. Pacing the room with arms folded across her chest, she paced and thought, paced and thought. Stopping, she pulled the pins from her thick hair and shook the chestnut locks loose in a heavy cascade down her back. Catching her reflection in the cheval mirror standing in the corner of the room she brought herself up short. Randolph had more experience. He had contact with people in theatrical circles, he knew his way around.

Turning, she tore open the door, ran down the hall and flung open the door of the music room where Randolph was sitting calmly at the piano.

Adelene announced, "I'm ready. You are right, Randolph, please help me."

"Adelene, you cannot use your surname if you want an acting career. The Irish are not popular here. There are more Sullivans in New York City than there are in Dublin, and more Gaelic spoken than English. The Protestants hate the Catholics and they fear the influence of the Pope. The poor Irish are honest and hardworking and someday they will rise and make their place in this country. I realize the bitter feelings against the Irish do not extend to your small New England home, but in Boston and New York things are different. The Irish are used as servants and factory workers and are generally looked upon as inferior, a position I well understand. You are beautiful and talented but you must not use Sullivan as your stage name if you wish to succeed. John L. Sullivan is admired and respected for his pugilism, and Arthur Sullivan has teamed with W. S. Gilbert to write great operettas, but they are exceptions to the rule. Being female, the name "Sullivan" will go against you."

Adelene was quiet for a long moment. When she found her voice she spoke softly. "My last name will be, will be—Sylvane. No, no, it is too much like Sullivan. It will be Syloane, Estelle Syloane!"

"Good girl! Some day in this country, backgrounds will no longer matter, prejudice will be a thing of the past and the animosity between the North and the South will disappear. If parents educate their children to accept differences, we may even have a Catholic president someday. When that happens it will no longer matter if your name is O'Houlihan, Kennedy, Sullivan or Flynn, but for now, let your Irish soul and beauty capture all."

"Oh, Rand, I will be forever grateful for your wisdom and concern. I owe so much to you!"

Standing behind him Adelene put her arms about him and rested her cheek against his short, thick locks. Had she seen his closed lids and the deep crease of pain making a groove above the bridge of his nose she would have also seen a glistening droplet at the corner of his eye fighting to escape the tightly curling lashes. Clearing his throat he began running his fingers over the piano keys. "Run along, Addie, I mean Estelle. You need your rest if you are going to become a star."

Watching the small beauty happily tripping from the room Randolph sighed. "Oh, Adelene, if only—

CHAPTER 12

Adelene remembered her sister Sarah and thought back to the time when she was small and her older sister had so indulged her, especially Adelene's love of hats. Finding Adelene's collection of dried flowers and feathers and bits of fur, she encouraged her baby sister's ambition, giving her ribbon and yarn, beads and buttons. Feeling it would be a way to keep Sarah closer to her heart, Adelene decided to make hats again. She approached Alonzo for use of an unoccupied ground floor flat. It had been a small tailor shop but old Lectner had passed away, and leaving no relatives his sewing machine remained as he left it and even some bolts of wool still sat on the shelves. Alonzo had planned to clean it out but with Adelene's pleading he agreed to her use of the shop and even had his handymen clean and paint the rooms at the back for her personal use. He could rent her present suite and come out even. It was difficult to leave the rooms Sarah had decorated, but many of the furnishings were moved to the new quarters.

Withdrawing her savings, she made a trip to the warehouse section of town and purchased buckram and felt, buckles and bows, edge wires and blocking forms. Feeling fortunate to have inherited a stove and steaming equipment from Mr. Lectner, she used the last of the money she had allotted for the project at the sign painter's shop. A sign, "Millinery, A. Sullivan, Proprietor," would swing on its hangers outside, and inside, the raw goods would await transformation.

Adelene felt a fierce surge of independence. She was a business owner, and after all, everyone should have a hobby.

As soon as she was settled and her private rooms filled and decorated she spent every spare minute in the shop, her busy fingers working to create the latest headwear styles. The heavy wools were boiled and blocked into felt frames; ribbons were gathered and pouffed, feathers dyed and trimmed. By March the spring line of organza bonnets and picture hats with silk roses in rainbow pastels were tilted on wire racks and wooden stands. Adelene's business was thriving and paying Dora as her assistant did not prevent her bank account from steady growth. Whenever they had an audition or daytime practice Randolph enjoyed watching the shop and his commission was gratefully given. He had kept the business profitable even when they had a three-month run of a new show in Providence. The confidence she gained from being independently comfortable kept her there throughout the next two summers. Though it was painful not to return to her roots, she felt the need to increase the stock in her shop, continually creating original designs and inventive color combinations. With the Victorian vogue being so popular she felt compelled to add color and style to accent drab, constrictive clothing. There was, of course, such a thing as being too tightly laced.

By the fall of 1890 Dora and Randolph ran the shop with practically no help from Adelene. She drew the designs and made elaborate notations as to color, fabrics and trims and they busily followed her artistic lead. Life was good and she knew it. She auditioned for a part in a play at the Grand Opera House in Boston and she received the note of her acceptance for the part by courier. Her elation was further enhanced when she discovered that Dora had been chosen for a small role, also. Dora had seemed pale lately but had not missed a single lesson or her hours working at the millinery shop. How wonderful that the business had allowed her, and her friends, the financial security to pursue their ambitions!

The performances went well. Adelene thrived on applause. Her only worry was Dora; she did not seem well. She had visited her home in Waltham for three weeks in summer, and instead of having renewed energy she had seemed quieter, distant, subdued.

Finally, Adelene felt the need to discuss whatever might be bothering her, so when evening came she went to Dora's door and knocked softly. "It's Adelene, Dora. Let me in."

The door clicked and even in the dim gaslight she could discern the tear streaks on the pale face.

"What is it, Dora. Has someone you loved died?"

"Yes, Adelene. I have died. I don't know what I am going to do. I'm with child, and I can't go on."

"Oh. Dora, who?"

"It's not a fixable situation, dear friend. I attended a reception while I was home. After the reception I made a poor decision and accepted an invitation from councilman Ryan's son. He will never admit to violating me. I would never have accepted his offer to ride through the city at night if I hadn't trusted him. It was so foolish of me. I knew he had spoiled other girls, and then his friends followed because they felt they weren't hurting anyone by using girls that were already "spoiled." There is no thought beyond physical need with that kind. I believed those other girls didn't really protest. I believed those girls must have led them on. I was just stupid, Addie. My protests and screams went unheeded. Wild young men don't care whose life they ruin because it means nothing to them. I was just beginning to feel good about my career and the successes I've had. I never dreamed I'd be taken advantage of in that way. I don't know what I'm going to do."

"Don't worry, Dora, we'll think of something. Meet me in the dressing room after the performance tomorrow and we will think this through."

After hugging her injured friend, Adelene left the sobbing girl and softly crept back to her room.

Drat. Drat the world. Dora didn't deserve such misfortune. Poor weak Dora, and now this. Adelene knew she would not have let this happen to herself. She knew just where to kick if such an attempt was made on her body. No, she would not have let anyone do this to her. She would not allow her career to crumble. She was going to New York as soon as she got Dora settled, and no one or no thing was going to stop her.

CHAPTER 13

Dora entered Adelene's dressing room after concluding her part and looked at Adelene's dressing table—the neatly placed powders and combs, the carefully hung clothes on the silk covered screen. The pale pongee gathered within the frame of the privacy screen was so elegant and soft. She walked over to the screen and ran her hand over the soft folds, and then her eyes fell on a woven straw basket. Adelene had knitted a small rose, a rose for one of the new line of hats for fall. Her slim hand touched one of the long knitting needles protruding from a ball of lavender wool yarn. With a fixed stare Dora thought, "Adelene, I knew you would help me. Thank you, Adelene."

Inserting the needle to destroy the unwanted embryo within, Dora felt a sharp pain, followed by consciousness slowly leaving her being.

"Dora! My God, my God! Someone get a doctor. Hurry!"

Adelene grabbed a towel from the rack by the washstand and falling to her knees tried to staunch the flow. Finding her efforts useless, she lifted Dora's head to her lap and stroked the ashen forehead. "Oh, Dora, I would have found a way. You are my dearest friend. I mustn't lose you. Please don't die. I'll take you to Maine. You will get strong in the clear air and from the good food my mother will cook for you. You can walk the cliffs in the sunlight, you can dance under the stars, you can sing in the moonlight! Oh, Dora, you mustn't die!"

As life ebbed from the still figure she held close to her bosom, Adelene cursed a world that could do this to one as sweet and defenseless as Dora, and she vowed, "Never! Never! Never will I allow this to happen to me! Whatever may come I will find a way out. I will not be defeated in this way no matter what life brings!"

As the room filled with shocked performers and the doctor leaned over Dora searching for a pulse, Adelene sat motionless. Soon the lifeless body was placed on a stretcher and someone reached down and lifted Addie to her feet.

Stunned as she was, she began straightening her dress, walked to the dressing table and with one hand on the tabletop she leaned forward and looked at her reflection in the oval mirror. With her free hand she gently moved an errant curl from her line of vision and sharply commanded, "Someone fetch me a bucket of water! I must be ready for Act 3!!!"

CHAPTER 14

Under the watchful eye of her manager, Adelene's parts became more frequent and of more importance as the season developed. Until this season her performances had been low paying, the salary of a struggling would-be actress, but now she was being groomed for a professional role with the Grand Opera Company. She was becoming one of the more popular new actresses, though her style and beauty brought as much acclaim as her ability. The company was doing a six-week run in New York and she could hardly wait. Having contacted her cousin Louella in Manhattan with the news of her performance there, to her great delight, the cordial invitation to stay at the Oakes residence at 242 West 73rd Street had arrived the previous day.

He was tall and dark, with silver streaks shining through wavy black hair, a full curling moustache beneath an aquiline nose flanked by snapping black eyes. His straight back, squared shoulders and elegant head carriage presented an impression of authority, all combining to confirm an image of command. Adelene drew in her breath sharply and hoped Louella had not noticed the sound of her soft gasp. She wouldn't want to begin her visit with Louella badly. How fortunate her cousin was to have a man like that! Adelene knew Louella must be accustomed to envious glances, for he would electrify any room with his presence, but then, Louella, also, was confident and secure. This was the man whose memories of Eliza, Louella had erased, and now she was his queen. Adelene had to hand it to her. To capture the heart of a man like that couldn't have been easy. She knew Francis had children, and Louella was not the motherly type. Serenely beautiful, she had always enjoyed long hours at her toilette, every hair had to be in its place and her complexion moisturized and powdered to perfection, and she certainly was beautiful this evening in a cream velvet gown with sable trim on the sleeves and hem. She carefully hugged Adelene and then turned to present her husband.

Adelene bowed and nodded as she was introduced to her cousin by marriage, holding forward her hand. The surprising gentleness with which he held it for a moment sent chills up her arm and she felt her hair stand as though she had been touched with a static charge.

"Ah, Adelene, we welcome you to our home. Please feel that it is your home as long as you are here. We in New York are always glad to have family visit, and we certainly have plenty of room for so charming a young lady."

Adelene noticed a slight southern accent in the greeting and certainly his demeanor was that of a southern gentleman. She knew him to be a Bostonian, but his years in Virginia serving his country had left its mark in his speech. Living in New York, and being a shrewd businessman dealing with folks from all over had not erased his experiences from his voice nor tempered his noble manners.

"I'm so grateful, Mr. Oakes, for this opportunity to stay with you and Cousin Louella while I attempt to fulfill my ambitions for a stage career. I hope I will never be a disappointment after your kind hospitality."

Adelene hoped her voice had not wavered. She was keenly aware that he was a male and she was a female. It was a feeling of great intensity she had never before been called upon to wrestle. With all the concentration she could muster she managed to hold back the blush she felt rising toward her face.

"I'm sure you will be a great success, Adelene." As she nodded her thanks, he continued, "You must be exhausted. Alice! Please take Miss Sullivan to the room you prepared for her earlier." Turning again to Adelene, his dark eyes caught hers for a mere instant, sending vibrations throughout her entire body.

"Are you hungry, Adelene? Even though the hour is late I will have Alice bring you up something. Our kitchen is always open."

"No, thank you. I had dinner on the train and I am quite satisfied.

I bid you goodnight, Dear Cousins. It's true the trip was quite tiring. I look forward to visiting with you tomorrow."

Grasping her skirts she followed Alice up the curved staircase. Swiftly behind them came the soft footsteps of Nathan, the butler, with Adelene's satchel in his stout hands.

"Miss Sullivan, your trunk will be brought up later, will your satchel of belongings be enough for now? A warm bath awaits you."

"You are most kind. I have plenty and you may wait until morning to bring up my trunk. I am much too tired to unpack tonight."

Entering the room, Adelene was amazed at the opulence of the furnishings. Leaning against the mantle, she placed her hand on the cool marble slab that topped the carved mahogany side panels, brushing her hand against a porcelain figurine. Slowly she slid her hand around the piece and gently lifted it from its resting-place on the mantle. It was a finely worked piece of unglazed porcelain, not rough to the touch as in cheaper quality ware, but sanded and polished to such smoothness as to feel almost alive, warming to her touch. Louella really knew quality when she saw it and had settled for nothing less than the best. In all the furnishings and accessories she had seen so far, quality obviously was a priority—even in her choice of men, but Adelene decided not to let herself think about that.

The bed was so high she needed the step stool provided to clamber onto the elegant embroidered coverlet. She started to sit, but the softness upended her and she sank into the luxurious feather bed. She began to giggle. How could this be? She felt she should pinch herself. New York. NEW YORK! New York, at last! And she wouldn't be starving and struggling in some garret, suffering with the want of a slice of bread! She was in a mansion in the middle of New York City and it was exciting and exhilarating and wonderful! Like a dream, a dream that was coming true!

Struggling, she pulled herself to the edge of the bed, then after unpacking her bag she bathed—she slept—she dreamed, and the dreams and reality were so intermingled she could not tell when one ended and the other began.

Adelene would soon learn that all was not well with her cousin's marriage. Louella seemed oblivious to any form of affection; she did not demonstrate any love for Francis, nor did he, her. In the meantime, she had a career to manage and their marriage was not her problem. She decided to keep to herself as much as possible, and not interfere in what was clearly not her business. What a shame for a man like that to seem neglected. If he were hers, she would not neglect him, but he was not hers.

As time passed in the Oakes household, Adelene would also learn that Louella's demands caused many an hour of sweat trickling down in front of poor Alice's ears as she stood by the hot stove heating the sad irons. Steam rose from the petticoats as she pressed as carefully as she could, knowing that she would be chastised loudly if one small wrinkle were to be left undone. Her mistress was fastidious to a fault, demanding that every item of undergarment be pressed to wrinkle-free smoothness. When Louella was satisfied with her clothing, coiffure and make-up it was usually ten-thirty or eleven, at which time she would make her way gracefully down the staircase, a vision of royal loveliness. How could any man resist the perfection of a beauty like Louella? Adelene did not know what the problem in the Oakes household was, but there was definitely a problem.

CHAPTER 15

The six-week run had been such a success that Adelene decided not to return to Boston. She would study in New York and take any small part in any small production that would accept her talents, hoping for the big break and the stardom for which she yearned. Being so comfortable at Louella's played a large part in her decision to remain in New York. Life with the Oakes was perfect. Although she rarely saw her cousin Louella, the household staff was friendly and caring and as hard working as any in New England. Many of the servants were foreign born and were so grateful to Mr. Oakes for their employment they bent over backwards to ensure he and his family received all the care they could give.

And she loved Alice. Alice was especially thoughtful and seemed to warm to any kind word from Adelene. Adelene wondered why Alice was less happy when Louella kept her in her quarters for hours at a time. It was almost as though she were relieved when she completed her duties in that section of the house. It was no concern of Adelene's, so she put it out of her mind. It was best not to pay attention or pry into affairs that didn't concern one. Addie was happy, things were going her way and she was smart enough to know when not to rock a boat, especially when there was a hint of an impending storm.

Looking down Broadway, Adelene watched the twinkling lights and was reminded of the starry nights on Appleton Ridge, and she knew what Clement C. Moore meant by the "luster of mid-day." Those nights when the stars seemed so close she could almost reach up and grab them, so bright even the quarter moon became a sailboat drifting across the sky. Yes, those lights were in her heart and soul, and would forever be, but now it was these lights that held her heart. She would have her stars in Maine later, but this was now.

Knowing the Dermot sisters from Rockland had made successful debuts in New York encouraged Adelene. She made arrangements to study under Mr. Dion Bocicicault, as the Dermot girls had accomplished their goals from their studies with Dion. With days of study and evenings of performances, the winter season was flying by.

New York in winter. The yellow glow of the city lights gave one a friendly feeling. How could anyone say a city was cold and heartless. It had not been so for Adelene. The busy streets with the prancing horses drawing the many carriages to and fro, their steamy breath bursting from damp nostrils clouding their proud heads in the frosty air, the fur-bedecked Yorkers bustling about doing their Holiday shopping; shop bells ringing, trolleys clanging.

Francis said they were building horseless carriages in Germany and he was going to get one as soon as they were made available this side of the Atlantic. She imagined such an invention would cause a big ruckus. Dogs would bark and skitter and horses would panic and the strange vehicles would be a general nuisance. After all, wouldn't they get stuck in the mud and slush? Without a horse to pull them out the drivers would have to get out themselves and push, getting all splattered and their nerves all tattered. She could see the advantage of not having to feed and water a horse, and it might be nice not to be required to use caution when walking because of the droppings, but of what advantage would it be if one had to find a horse whenever trouble came along? No, that was one invention they'd have to improve a lot before she'd put money into it!

But the excitement of the city and the opportunities if offered stimulated Adelene. Her voice lessons were enjoyable. She loved pushing her vocals to the limit and she was learning breathing control, which seemed to inflect a more mellow tone. Sometimes she even impressed herself. She never imagined herself to be in the same class as Jenny Lind, but she was pleased and surprised with her progress, and her teacher seemed to think her voice was developing well. Her voice coach was very strict and demanding, but seemed to take extra time with Adelene's training. She even smiled once, (a rare occasion), when Adelene was in particularly good voice, racing up the scale and holding the last note with a very resonant vibrato.

Adelene felt good about herself, good about the auditions she had attended, and good about New York in general. What a wonderful town! Sometimes she missed her home on Appleton Ridge, but that was worlds away. By this time of year the wind would be starting its steady howl and the snow would be whirling and biting and stinging. The roads would be clogged with snow and the horses would be pulling the rollers to pack it down. The struggling animals would be snorting vapor that would rise and fall on their thick winter—furred hides where it would freeze in frosty crystals as they labored to make the roads passable for lighter carriages.

Summer, that was the time to go north, just as soon as the black flies bit their last bite in mid-June. Broadway plays would be over by then, and she would pack her bags and go home for the summer. Louella had been acting strangely lately, so perhaps her welcome was wearing thin. Her mother had told her that company was like fish; that after a time it started to smell. Although Francis had assured her she was always welcome to stay as long as she pleased, and it was such a large house she did not have constant association with them, it would probably be a good idea to leave when summer came. It would be hot in the city, and wonderfully cool in Appleton.

Francis was so gracious. It was as though he could not do enough to make her stay comfortable—a carriage at her beck and call—anything she desired, anything at all. She enjoyed their occasional evening games of Flinch, although Louella never cared to join in, begging off to get to bed early for her "beauty rest," which worked, of course, as there was no denying Louella's exotic looks. Adelene and Francis often played cards until eleven on nights she had no lessons or performance, then after a glass of wine they retired to their respective quarters.

One evening during a particularly spirited game that brought forth laughter from both Adelene and Francis, their hands had both reached for a card simultaneously, and she was surprised by the jolt of electricity she felt as their hands met. Pulling back, she wondered if he had felt it, also. Looking up into his eyes she felt a pang deep within her bosom, and knew she must be more careful in the future. Her heart fluttered so violently she feared he would notice, and she hoped the burning sensation rushing through her body toward her face was not visible.

Francis only smiled and commented that the hour was late, so she decided her secret was safe. She must hide this wild desire within her body and direct all her energy toward her career. How glad she was that the object of her wildest passion was married. If it had not been so, she would have flung herself at his feet and destroyed her chance to fulfill her lifelong ambitions! God, in his mercy, had chosen this method to give her heart love, but to prevent the consummation of it from being physically attainable.

Sometimes it was all too much. If only she could spend an hour or two sitting on her favorite ledge looking across the valley to the glacier smoothed mountains to the East. The East, where the rounded mountain crests had a flowing rhythm to their form, up and down as a melody on a sheet of music, with the green treetops marking the notes. The fluid transition of the hills to the valleys, beginnings and endings blending into a heart-song that always eased any ache of mind or body that she was forced to endure. This love for Francis was unreasonable. He belongd to Louella, and though he filled her every waking thought, she refused to allow herself any ambition to fulfill her fantasies. He was far beyond her reach for a myriad of reasons. Rich, handsome, intelligent, married, a father—how could she be so enthralled by someone she could never have? Why couldn't she push him from her heart? Perhaps this was part of her destiny, to love the unattainable so that she could concentrate on the career she had always dreamed of having. God had found a way to stir her heart to better enable her to understand the parts she was to play, and if true love was never to be hers she could accept it. She would love Francis from afar and never let her feelings show to anyone, except on the stage, of course. There, her emotions could erupt with all the passion and heartache she held within her body. This would be her gift to her profession! Every note of every song would speak of her all-consuming love and overwhelming heartache. With this gift from the Almighty, how could she fail?

The busy season and constant study left little time for pleasure outside the thrill she received from her performances. The winter was rushing by and Addie's life was quite separate from that of her hosts, but the occasional dinners and parties did not escape her notice. She was a guest in the Oakes' household, but a working guest, usually arriving home from the theater as the last visitors were leaving.

In March following a late performance, Francis met her in the hall and grasped her hand in his. The unexpected contact so surprised her she flinched and pulled back as her face flushed from the touch of his hand.

"Adelene, my dear, I didn't mean to alarm you. I just need to discuss something with you. Please come into the study. I wish to make some plans that involve you."

Nervously, Adelene followed him into the study and he motioned her to sit. Her mind raced. Had she done something wrong? Was she about to be asked to leave? Was Louella ill? She had seen less and less of her cousin who spent most of her time in her suite. Perhaps she was expecting a child and Adelene was about to be informed. All these things ran through her mind as she lowered herself into the leather chair that he had nodded to by his desk. Fingering the brass tack heads that decorated the leather on the arms of the chair she braced herself for whatever was to come.

"Adelene, you work and study too much. It's time for you to have an evening of relaxation. I am planning a party, a celebration of spring, actually, and having watched your comings and goings I see you spend Thursday evenings in your room. I assume that is your one free evening so I have planned it for the Thursday after Easter. Everyone will be in a party mood, Lent being past, and there are some people I feel you should meet before you make plans for your return to Maine in late June. I trust this date will agree with you?"

"Why, yes, Francis, it will be quite lovely. I will be honored to attend."

"Then you will give me a list of some of your friends in the theatrical field, won't you? I know some business people, who would, I'm sure, enjoy meeting you, and you, them. If you give your list to Alice I will take care of the arrangements. It would be good for your career to socialize with friends and business people alike as a preparation for next year's season. I assume you will return to us next fall after spending some time with your family."

As she rose to leave, Francis followed her to the door and as she left he gave her shoulder a squeeze. "You are part of this family, Adelene, and I fear we have neglected you."

Barely able to speak for the trembling the touch of his hand had initiated, Adelene protested, "Oh, no, Francis, you have given me the opportunity of a lifetime, and my gratitude is undying. May God Bless you, and good-night."

Climbing the staircase took a concentrated effort. Her mind was confused, thrilled, but yet she felt ashamed that her cousin's husband could evoke such emotion. She hoped it was a condition she could keep under control.

CHAPTER 16

"Mr. Keenan, may I introduce Miss Adelene Sullivan? Although a very distant relative of Sir Arthur Sullivan, she prefers not to use her given name to advantage in theatrical circles, but instead uses her stage name of Estelle Syloane, quite courageous, I think. She is obviously talented and certainly not lacking in looks, and her voice is quite compelling. I'm sure she will be well received by both producers and audiences alike whenever she performs, (then with a chuckle), but of course we must consider that she is also related to our John L., so be cautious lest we rile the lady!"

"Thank you, Mr.Lermond. I'm pleased to meet you Mr. Keenan. Mr. Lermond has certainly given me a pre-review that will require considerable effort on my part to do justice. I only hope my ability will meet the challenge."

"Gracious Lady, we look forward to the next season of theater with great anticipation. We will be sure to attend your performances. We understand you are auditioning for the season very soon, and that you will be journeying to Maine to study for any parts you are selected for. Having met you, we see the only problem you will be forced to endure is that of choosing, which, of all the parts you will surely be offered, you will select."

"You are so kind. I am glad you were able to attend our party tonight, and I very much hope to see you in the future."

Mr. Lermond and Mr. Keenan both placed their drinks on the tray resting on the marble-topped table, then turned to their host.

Mr. Lermond grasped Francis by the arm and smilingly joked, "Mr. Oakes, you are indeed a fortunate man to have two such beautiful women under your roof. You are undoubtedly one of the most envied men in this city!"

"If I am envied it is well deserved," Francis bantered, "especially since the envy concerns the women in my household. I regret my wife was indisposed this evening, preventing me from flagrantly displaying all the beauty I must bear in this life. But, then, you have met Louella and you know I am truthful. Now you have met our Adelene and I trust you will be content resting your gaze on her alone. I must brag further by telling you not only is she beautiful but quite an able adversary at cards. I understand she is also a demon at croquet, but since she spends her summers in Maine, I have yet to challenge her at that game. She sings, she dances, she ice skates."

"Francis, I implore you to cease," Mr. Keenan interrupted. "I'm sure Mr. Lermond considers you to be a master of exaggeration. I must tell you, however, I look forward to the day I might share the stage with that lovely creature. I'm sure it will not be in the too distant future."

Turning to Adelene, Mr. Lermond spoke directly to her, "Miss Sullivan, I hear you are very interested in women's position in life and that you feel they should receive equal treatment with men. Surely, as attractive a woman as you must realize your place is to be lovely and admired. We men are better equipped to handle business affairs; it is our natural bent. Our minds are endowed with logic and understanding. You should be satisfied with your station, that of attracting we who would preserve that station. We gladly provide for and protect our females, willingly go to war and lay down our lives to defend our women and homes and do all we can to ensure their safety. Surely you will agree that women should not fight or bear arms, so why should they have any part in determining their use?"

"I beg your pardon, Sir, many women prefer the status imposed on them and are quite content to remain in the shadow of their spouses, but I believe all men and women should have the privilege of making that choice for themselves. Many women have been thrust into the position of protector of their children when their men are away, and find themselves ill prepared, and forced to use firearms they are not familiar with operating to protect their children and homes from marauders. Don't you agree that it would be much better if they had practiced warfare rather than being initiated into it unprepared?—And if forced of necessity to fight, perhaps having some say in the matter would be fair. Women feel no challenge in fighting, no glory, and we do not seek out controversy. You speak of our nature as being weak and in need of protection. Perhaps if we were allowed to enter the political arena there would be fewer wars, as our so-called fragile nature might seek out alternatives to combat. Certainly you are familiar with mother bears who fight for their cubs when necessary, but peacefully roam the forests when undisturbed."

Silently observing this exchange, Francis thought, "What a corker she is! What a genuine Irish corker! No easy conquest, this one."

Snapping back to reality, Francis dismissed his thoughts as just so much fantasy as Mr. Lermond continued, "I see some truth in your statements, but, (laughing), warriors in skirts would be something to behold!"

"Perhaps you have not heard of the Scots, Sir. Greater warriors have not lived. Their skirts did not prevent them from winning their battle for freedom. If Robert the Bruce's skirts did not offend and his legs did not appall, why should a woman's? Again we are looking at different standards being imposed. I assure you, if I were to wear a kilt into battle, there would be plenty of protection underneath, so please don't let your imagination overtake you."

"My God, Francis. This woman practically preaches insurrection. You had better control her or we will have another civil war on our hands."

Adelene instinctively picked up on the new subject broached. She felt she was not being taken seriously and her dander was up. "At least, Sir," she retorted, (with all thought of her career set aside). "If I had fought in the Civil War, I would not have been so vain as to dress in my most elaborate uniform with a flowing scarf and then ride before my troops that they might shoot me as with the flamboyant Mr. Jackson!"

She immediately felt guilty, having never spoken badly about the South before, and in her heart she had no ill will toward those now suffering so from their loss, but she had felt challenged. Well, let that be a lesson. Men were too concerned with glory and sometimes didn't have good sense. Francis did not fall into that category, he was always so fair and charitable. She liked his quiet manliness, his self-control, and only the twinkle in his eye spoke of his sense of humor.

"Well, Francis, if there are many more out there like Adelene, we might lose more than our hearts. We may have to agree that she would be a formidable foe on the field of battle, as she certainly has a fire within that any soldier would envy!"

"I meant no harm, sir, and I am afraid my emotions are too easily inflamed. I apologize if I have offended anyone," a red-faced Adelene confessed.

"Dear lady, we appreciate a female view, and look forward to our meeting again, socially or occupationally. And now, we must bid adieu, as we really must be getting on."

With that, Francis gently took her by the arm and guided her to the punch bowl. His heart was pounding strangely. "She doesn't need to fight to conquer men," he thought, "her beauty and spirit alone could conquer," and he felt the magnetism of her charm pulling him under her spell.

It was getting late and the guests slowly drifted toward the foyer. As the last were helped into their wraps by their host and the door softly closed behind them, Francis approached Adelene and took her hand and placed it on his arm, escorting her to the stairs. Turning to face him, she looked into his eyes and said, "Francis, how can I ever thank you for this evening? Not only was it a delightful party, you gave me the opportunity to meet so many important people. You have given me such hope for advancement in my career!"

"No more than you deserve, Adelene. Don't you know that I would do anything I could to make you happy?"

"Thank you again, Francis. I only wish Louella had been able to attend!"

With that, she removed her hand from his arm and slowly ascended the stairs. His overly generous compliments had made her heart race, and when she had her hand on his arm she had felt the muscles tighten, and the glint in his eyes had again awakened feelings she knew she must suppress.

March 22, 1891.

Dear Mama,

   Louella and Francis held a most delightful party that I might meet many of their friends as well as financiers in the theatrical business. I hope I behaved in a manner that would give you and Papa much pride. I will soon be auditioning for a new musical that will be performed here in New York next fall. I am so excited sleep escapes me, but writing to you will help me relax. I miss you so very much but my dreams may yet come true here. Louella and Francis are very kind, though Louella spends most of her time in her private rooms. Sometimes I fear that she is not well. I have every necessity, and more, so please don't worry about me. If I fail I will return home for good and marry a cooper and be content watching his barrels fill with apples and potatoes to be freighted to the ships docked at Thomaston, but for now, this is what I must do. I do so miss seeing the chestnut trees blooming in the spring, with their little clustered flowers looking for all the world like miniature Christmas trees, with their bright decorations hidden in tiny blossoms, trying to out-do the birches as their newly sprung coin-like leaves flutter in the breeze. Soon, all the birds will be heralding spring, and even the brooks will be jumping like playful kittens.—But I will be home soon and we will have a wonderful summer together.

   Know that I love you, and my affection for you and Papa will never fade.

Your loving daughter,

Adelene

CHAPTER 17

Ellen folded the letter and tucked it in her apron pocket. She couldn't help worrying. Her daughter would come home for a few months, but she would not stay, she would return to New York. She would have to continue to share her, whether she liked it or not.

Ellen remembered her own childhood; the harsh winters, the cold board wall of the farmhouse, with only a thin straw mattress beneath her and too few covers over her cold body. She couldn't remember a winter night when she did not have cold feet. She would try to pull her worn nightgown down as far as she could to cover them, and then fold the thin blankets double to huddle under for warmth, but when she folded them there was none to tuck around her cold shoulders. The frigid air seemed to come up through the mattress, making sound sleep impossible. She remembered the sound scolding she had received from taking a glass of water to her chamber room, and the water had frozen solid, bursting the glass, a costly transgression in such a poor household. She felt rich in her warm home with Daniel.

She decided to make Adelene a quilt. She knew Adelene was not cold, but in her mind, (probably because of her childhood experiences), a warm quilt was a mantle of comfort. Knowing Adelene was under a warm quilt Ellen, herself, had made, would give comfort to both, so she set to work. Busily, she went through her bag of scraps, then through the closets, finding any bits of velvet or silk or items of outgrown or partially worn out clothing of elegant materials. Every spare minute was spent piecing the small irregular sections together, then carefully adding herringbone embroidery and hemstitching with colored silk thread to all the seams, adding bits of lace to the curves and corners. Her Adelene would love such a quilt, nothing plain or ordinary for that girl! Ellen felt closer to Adelene as her fingers worked on the elaborate coverlet. Each square, strip and triangle brought back a memory to Ellen as she lovingly sewed each piece in its place.

The blue ribbons from the bonnet Adelene wore when she was three; squares of brown velvet from the coat she had made her for the Harvest Home celebration in '59; and here, the brocade from the time Addie had decided she wanted to be a Geisha. Fingering the many colors and textures calmed Ellen.

What a joy her youngest daughter had been. Smiling, she set aside a length of suede fringe as unusable in the quilt. It had been left over from the jacket Ellen had made for Adelene to wear to the "Wild West Show" in West Appleton. William "Buffalo Bill" Cody was such a famous entertainer it was not a show to be missed, especially by Adelene. Of course she had insisted on dressing "appropriately" for the occasion. Ellen had carefully cut the tanned deerskin into a delicate fringe and sewn it to her wine colored velvet jacket, with a "V" design on the back, across the top of her shoulders and down to another "V" in front. The more difficult task was sewing the fringe to the tops of her leather shoes. Her fingers had become sore from the effort, but the effect of the outfit had been rather rewarding; delicate and ladylike, but distinctively western. Together, they had blocked a felt hat, giggling in the kitchen where they had soaked it in a pan of warm water, wrung it carefully, then patted it into shape over an upturned bowl, pressing the brim flat all around. When it dried they added a ribbon band and a cockade of bobwhite feathers.

Yes, Adelene's worrisome ways had really been wonderful adventures, and her theatrical leanings had brought joy to those around her. The town busybodies had been entertained, (being always anxious to see what she would come up with next), and usually she gave them something over which to cluck their tongues. She hadn't failed to cause a stir at the Wild West Show, either, as the entertaining troupe had cast an eye her way, with even an envious glance from Annie Oakley herself. The Sullivans had arrived late because several buggies had become stuck in the waterlogged earth where the West Appleton Road crossed the Pettingill Stream. The earth-covered rock the townspeople had placed over the stream had not been sufficient to handle the onslaught of the heavy spring rains. They had been forced to wait while horses were unhitched and doubled up to pull the carriages through. Adelene had fretted about being late, but by the time they turned left towards the McLain farm she had settled down, thinking about the opportunity of making a grand entrance having been afforded her.

There was something about Adelene that turned people's heads; something beyond her pretty face and elegant carriage—an ember, a fire, an aura. Adelene was special and Appleton was not the same without her. Ellen felt that some spark had gone out, something was missing, and even the farmhouse on Appleton Ridge did not feel as warm.

With a sigh, Ellen continued her quilt piecing until Daniel came in from the evening chores. Striding softly to her side he put his hand tenderly on her shoulder.

"She'll be back home soon, Ellen. She will always come back in the spring. She loves the theater, but her true heart is here, and she will return with the song birds."

May 4, 1891

My Dearest Mother,

    I will cherish forever the beautiful quilt that arrived this morning. It is folded at the foot of my bed, and the last thing I do at night before sleep is to unfold it and pull it close to my heart. How I love each patch of remembrance and each precious stitch from your loving hands. I can envision your many evenings by the fireside working on this wondrous gift, with Papa close by drawing on his pipe, (I can almost smell the familiar tobacco smoke). You have made me feel so close to you through this warm quilt, its firm weight reminding me of your love for your family. It will be only a month until I will see you again, and until then I can feel your touch as I hug this comforter. I love you. Kiss Papa for me.

Your loving daughter,

Adelene

    By the way, Louella has been feeling poorly and has been hospitalized. We are looking forward to her returning to us soon. I have been assured her ailment is not serious and no cause for worry. Francis feels she is merely exhausted and will be home as soon as she is recovered.

Adelene

February, 1892

Louella returned home, rested and in good spirits. Francis was elated. He knew Louella had injured her health with drinking, but he felt sure her hospitalization had performed a cure. His hopes were that at last they would have the happy married life he had longed for. It was not to be. Every advance he made since her return had been spurned and in his rejection he began to notice the difference in the two cousins from Maine within his household.

His mind reeled. This stunning girl from Appleton Ridge had shaken him. Not just that she was beautiful. He knew many beautiful women. It was an air about her, as though she moved in a field of light, an aura that emanated from her. She was like the warmth of a candle in the dark. Certainly Eliza never failed to arouse him, but she was gone, and Louella's dark beauty was tantalizing, but her coldness after their infrequent relations was discouraging. She lacked response and the warmth that he craved. She was also devoid of maternal instincts, still sending his children to visit their grandparents whenever possible. He had tried to tell her it wasn't fair to Eliza's parents to send them so often, but his words fell on deaf ears.

"It's good for the children," she would always answer. Perhaps she was right, they certainly received a lot more love, as well as cookies and special treats; certainly more hugs and smiles. Since young Francis had married he seemed bent of giving him grandchildren, and they spent more time at 73rd Street than in their own home. It was a great delight to Francis, bouncing them on his knees with their pale curls bobbing and squeals of laughter echoing through the house, letting them play with his watch fob and pulling his moustache. He had never seen Louella hug any of his children or grandchildren. He had hired one of those plump, sweet voiced widows needing a place to live since the war as a nanny, and that seemed to work well. Whenever he planned an out of town adventure or vacation, Nanny Rose and all the children and grandchildren were invited and usually attended. Louella did not care to leave her home in the city, so Francis went without her.

He saw no reason to deprive himself just because she opted to stay home.

As for the sex part, Louella had been trained from the cradle that sex was sinful, so what could one expect? When he met her he was still at the height of his hormonal activity and he had perhaps imagined himself wildly in love, but now his ardor had cooled and he could look at her a little more objectively. With her thick jet hair and pale skin she was a striking woman, and since she'd had no children she could lace her waist to eighteen inches. He could fit his hands thumb to thumb around her waist and her lovely face had held his gaze.

Now he could see meanness in her dark eyes. Even during lovemaking and after, when he was weak and spent, she never lost her tension. She would hop out of bed and pin back her "messed up" hair, then smooth her skirts so "no one would know," (as though the world would not realize they ever had sex, or even care). The quick gratification he was allowed hardly seemed adequate to produce children, and it hadn't. He began to hope she would tire of him and find someone less sensuous than he and want out of the marriage, but she seemed perfectly content with her private rooms and reclusive ways. He'd heard of worse marriages, and he was sure Louella was faithful. She was much too proper to ever have an illicit affair. He kept hoping the marriage would improve. What the hell, at least he was getting some satisfaction, and what he had was better than no satisfaction at all.

What bothered him most was the odor of bourbon that always hung in the air of her quarters. When they were first married he had thought she drank to relax herself when she anticipated his nocturnal visits, but more and more he suspected it had become a nightly routine. When it got out of control he had sent her to the health home and he had assumed she had been cured, but now he knew she was drifting back to her old ways. He was bitterly disappointed. Now, fine lines were forming around her eyes that no makeup could cover, and her eyes, even as late as noon, were still streaked with small red threads. The drinking was more than just for medicinal purposes and it was becoming a habit he worried about. She never cared to attend theater or the exciting day trips he planned. Adelene, though, was always willing to accompany him on any adventure.

Francis paced the floor of his bedroom, feeling angry and bewildered. Louella avoided any closeness, even in passing when she emerged from her rooms pristine and coiffured. He had been close enough to notice that her once minty breath was becoming more fruit scented as time advanced. This morning he was especially dejected. He had knocked on her door and received no answer, even after repeated tapping. Questioning Alice as to Louella's health, Alice had responded in her quaint drawl, "Oh, she's foine, Mr. Oakes, she's only tired."

As Alice turned and walked towards the kitchen, Francis thought, "Tired? Tired from what? The servants did all the cooking and cleaning, the children were all grown, and his grandchildren had their tutors who kept them busy all day. How could she be tired?" Then from the window he saw a rental carriage pull up to the side door and Alice talking to the driver. It had been a quick trip, as she had been in the hall only a short time before. Noticing a package clutched tightly to her bosom as she paid the driver, he wondered why she had hired a carriage when there was one at her disposal if she had only asked. Glancing about, Alice stepped quickly inside. What could it be about, he wondered. Why the stealth when he considered his house open and all his servants trustworthy? Without putting on his jacket, he pulled his suspenders over his shoulders and ran down the back stairs, meeting Alice once again in the hall. Her face blanched as he greeted her.

"Hello, Alice. What have you there so early in the morning?'

"Nothing, Sir, nothing a'tall."

"Well, it must be something, Alice, to warrant your leaving your work here so early. Let me see what you have."

With frightened eyes she reluctantly handed the package to Francis.

Opening the sack he pulled out a bottle of bourbon and a bottle of wine.

"Oh, Mr. Oakes. Please let me have it. She'll hit me if I don't take it to her right now. You don't understand, Mr. Oakes. I must take it to the Missus or she'll beat me again."

Alice crumpled onto a chair with tears streaming down her soft pink cheeks. Shaking and sobbing, she cried, "Oh, please, Mr. Oakes, I must take it to her now."

"Alice, stop your blubbering. How long has this been going on?"

"Ever since she came back from the hospital, Mr. Oakes, but she wasn't mean at first. Now I have to be quick or she will hit me. She said she'd tell you I stole money if I didn't do it. I'm so sorry, Mr. Oakes, I'm so sorry. Am I to be fired?"

"No, Alice, it's not your fault. Go and wash your face and continue as usual. I'll pretend I never discovered her little secret. And he turned on his heel and returned to his room and readied himself to go to the dye works. Now he, too, was crying. Damn. Why hadn't he realized her refusal of him was because of a greater love? He felt confused and guilty. Guilty because he hadn't figured it out more quickly. He had been more concerned with his own desires to make a reasonable analysis of his wife's needs; guilty of letting love blind him to the fact that one so beautiful and with the voice of an angel could be so addicted to drink.

Sinking slowly to the chair by the window he held his face in his hands and sat motionless for a long time, then he arose slowly and gazed out at the street below. He would talk to Dr. Harrison today. This was a problem he couldn't handle by himself.

September 8, 1892

Darling Mother,

Summer at home with you was a wonderful rest. I hold
the moments spent with you and Papa next to my heart.
You are always with me. I have to again become accustomed
to the fast pace of New York. New folks arrive from across
the sea every day, and I think all their many languages have
become all mixed up and melted together. It's almost a new
language with a different dialect from nearly everyone. Life
moves so very quickly here in the city, it seems that what
should take an hour, takes only a minute. I guess one could
call it a "New York Minute." The streets are all numbered
and one can go anywhere without becoming lost. It would
be wonderful if the roads in Maine were numbered like it is
here. I know they have been pushing the rock walls into the
roads there and covering the rocks with gravel to give better
drainage in mud season, making them much more passable,
but if the new horseless carriages they are making in
Europe are brought over here, they will have to make
the roads a bit wider. Following directions in Maine
wouldn't be too difficult up there, but how a New Yorker
or Bostonian would get about is a mystery. They wouldn't
understand instructions like, "Turn left at Newbert's
corner, and such directions as we are accustomed, but
they could travel fine with "North on road #5, then
turn left on Road # 8. Mama, if I wasn't an actress I
would become a politician and run for office. I could
straighten things out in Augusta! I guess the world isn't
ready for women politicians, we have to get the vote
first. Someday women will be able to vote and run for
office, then things will run more smoothly. We would
see that the old towpaths and trails were fixed up right,
and numbered properly. Perhaps when my acting career
is over I will turn to politics. Women need to be able to

vote, Mama. Men try, but they need us to organize things. It's a thought, isn't it?

Your loving daughter,

Adelene

Ellen shook her head as she read the letter. That girl is heading for trouble.

Head-long into it.

CHAPTER 19

1893

Torn between two worlds, Adelene pondered her situation. Even her restless dreams were filled with endless confusion. Sometimes they seemed prophetic, sometimes a tracing of her life or an outlet for her emotions. She had kept her heart from reaching for the love she craved, but being near Francis was becoming a torture. She thought she could control herself as long as he made no move, (which she certainly didn't expect, not with his being married to her beautiful cousin). She felt her path was becoming a tangled one, so she tried to disassociate herself from the reality of her life's path, and think only of a walk along the Georges, her haven from the tangled web into which she felt herself being pulled.

COME WALK MY PATH, WHERE COLUMBINE AND PULPETS
   GROW,
WHERE VALLEY LILLIES SHAKE THEIR BELLS AND TENDER
   GRASSES BLOW.
THERE BESIDE THE LICHENED STONES A TRILLIUM MAY
   PEEK
AT FAIRY SLIPPERS NODDING THERE, WHERE VIOLETS
   MIGHT SLEEP.

THE DOGWOODS SPREAD THEIR FRAGILE BOUGHS OF
   DAINTY LEAVES AND BLOOMS,
A CANOPY OF LACE THAT MAKES A QUIET GARDEN
   ROOM.
THEN AS THE PATH MEANDERS ALONG THE RIVER SIDE,

THE MOSSY SECRET GARDEN PATH, ITS ENTRANCE
    OPENS WIDE TO SUNLIGHT, WHERE THE BREEZES
    PUSH THE COTTON CLOUDS ALONG,
AND DANCING WATER SPLASHES ITS ENDLESS SEAWARD
    SONG.

But New York had the same attraction, not just her feelings
for the theater, not just her feelings for Francis, but for the city
itself. She marveled at the hold it had over her, the way it stimulated
her senses and captured her imagination.

THE LIGHTED CITY AT NIGHT
    ITS SPARKLING BRIGHTNESS
    AGAINST MIGHTY PILLARS
    FLARED LIGHTS
    PLAYING IN A BLACK SKY
    CREATING AWSOME WONDER
    OF MANS' ABILITY
    TO CHANGE STONE AND METAL
    FROM GOBS OF CONGEALED MATTER
    INTO A STARTLING COLLECTION
    OF ARRANGED BUILDINGS
    IN BALANCED PROPORTIONS
    AND FUNCTIONAL DESIGN
    STIMULATING THE MIND AND EYE
    A CELEBRATION OF INGENUITY
    OF MANY COLLABORATORS
    TO CREATE
    A CITY OF WONDER.

Yes, New York would always be her second home, no, her
other home. If only God would grant her secret desires as well as
her admitted ones, her life would be perfect. Adelene wondered if
perfection in life were possible, or would there always be doubts,
worries, trials,—yearnings? Perhaps.

CHAPTER 20

In deep remorse over the situation with Louella, Francis spent more and more hours and longer and longer days at the dye works. If he could not have a normal family life, he was determined to have, at the very least, the most efficient, well-managed manufacturing company in New York. He spent days roaming his factory, his melancholy apparent to his loyal workers who felt helpless to aid him in his undisclosed sorrow. Out of respect for his privacy they refrained from prying into his personal affairs. His visible sadness did not affect his kindness and concern for his employees. Their continuing enthusiasm and pride in their work was of some comfort to him.

Arriving home exhausted, he sank into his favorite chair in the drawing room each night, and only the attentiveness of Alice, urging him to take the nourishment of the hot soup and corn bread she brought kept him in reasonable health.

On a dark and rainy night in late September, the gaslights glowed in the hallway as a gaunt and rain soaked Francis dragged himself in from the chilling weather, and there he found Adelene, waiting by his chair. His robe rested in her small hands, the blue brocade reflecting shadows from the flickering lights, the gold tassels of the cord sash dangling and swaying. His eyes followed their movement, mesmerizing him for a few seconds. Slowly he raised his eyes to hers and held—"Francis," (breaking the spell with her voice), "you must remove that wet shirt and let me help you with this robe."

Francis, fatigued into obedience, silently followed the bidding of her commanding voice and slowly unbuttoned his shirt and slipped it from his shoulders. How warm is her touch, he thought, a woman's touch. He had not realized until this moment how much he had missed such a caress.

The comfort Francis was feeling from the touch of her fingertips did not escape Adelene. As she gently massaged his tight shoulders she felt the gradual relaxation of the firm muscles lying beneath the warming flesh. Slowly and gently she kneaded the tiredness away, felt the slackening in his body and then his head rolled and the soft dark curls rested against her bosom. A few tendrils fell to the bare breast rising above her bodice. It was as though a branding iron had touched her skin, not with pain, but nevertheless, with searing heat. She closed her eyes, placing her hands atop his shoulders, thrilling in the nearness of him,—squeezing out all thought of Louella, of his being her cousin's husband, reveling only in the moment, knowing her feelings were piracy, but unwilling and unable to relinquish them.

Finally Adelene drew away, placed the robe on his warm and reddened frame and said, "I hope you can relax, now, Francis. Take a hot bath and get some rest. Alice has made a wonderful chowder and I'll have her bring some to your room."

Adelene hoped he hadn't noticed how shaken she was. The experience had rocked her and she wondered if she looked as flushed as she felt. With great dignity she held her head high and left the room, walking quickly down the hall and up the stairs to her room where she turned and latched the door, then sat quietly on her bed while her mind reeled. Oh, Francis!

It was a new day. The experience the night before had been so exhausting Adelene had slept soundly. She tried to put the whole episode behind her, but nothing ever really goes away. Things stay in the mind and pop out in strange ways. For Adelene it was in the form of her lost friend, Dora. Dear, sweet, Dora, how tragic that her dreams were never fulfilled. Doctors and apothecaries were constantly finding new cures, but too late for Dora. Had there been any available help for her plight, a safe choice with clean conditions, Adelene would still have her friend.

On the other hand, if every ailment were cured, the world would soon be filled with weak creatures and they would in turn breed more weak progeny, and the world would eventually be filled with inferior creatures. There might be a problem someday with someone deciding they should determine who should be saved and who should be exterminated. That would be a real mess. No, too much medicine might not be a good idea, unless they could make everyone with a problem really whole again. That would work!

Of course, Adelene knew she would never be able to breed with a weak male. She would need someone strong, handsome and intelligent so she would bring only bright and beautiful children into the world; she wouldn't take the risk of causing the creation of anything less. But, that was not a likely event. At thirty-seven she didn't plan to marry and breed at all. Her career was her life. She felt fulfilled just being near Francis, and thrilled as she was by his touch or just his glance, she would never consider overstepping his and Louella's bonds of matrimony.

She sensed trouble in their marriage. Louella spent more and more time in her rooms and she'd seen her treating Alice badly. Alice was so dedicated to her service to Louella, it saddened Adelene to see her mistreated, and even Francis seemed increasingly troubled and thought-consumed. Several times she had been awakened in the night by shouting, then the scurrying of footsteps in the hallway. Once she even arose from her pillows and opened her door a crack to see Francis storming from Louella's rooms, and then Alice emerged at the end of the hall and went to be with Louella who was screaming and crying. Alice failed to close the door and Adelene overheard Alice speaking softly to Louella. "Now, now, Pet, you just calm down. You don't have to do anything you don't want to. Have a little nip, dear, and get some rest. Everything will be all right."

Addie had softly closed her door, wondering what Alice had meant by, "You don't have to do anything." Didn't she love Francis? Didn't she want him in her bed? She knew if Francis were hers, she would never be able to turn him away, never! Only his vow before God as Louella's husband kept Adelene from completely dissolving in his presence. Her will and her resolve comprised her chastity belt, and it would hold as long as Francis was bound in marriage to her cousin.

CHAPTER 21

Francis knew he had turned a page in his life. Liquor was a demon in a bottle that never let anyone go once he had a victim in his grasp, and Louella was a willing, no, eager bride of that demon. Dr. Harrison had tried to talk to Louella but she was so in love with the devil she saw no wrong, saw no reason for giving up her liquid lover. Dr. Harrison had given Francis no hope of her recovery. "Too much for too long, Francis," he had said. "We can put her in a sanitarium and we can wean her off it for a time, but she will not be recovered. She will go back to it at the first opportunity. She will declare her healing, but it will only be a guise. She could escape confinement and even believe she is cured, but she will return to this condition in just a few months, or even weeks. She is lost to you, my boy, and she will never be yours again, of that I am sure. You are the means by which she can keep her true love, and her condition now is so serious she will die if she is not confined. If you do not commit her within the month you will be conferring a death sentence on her. A good facility will save her life for now, although I'm sure her liver is surely as severely damaged as her mind. You may take her home and provide a nurse and the liquor she craves, but I must warn you, she may become a danger to herself and others. I assume she has a personal maid that looks after her needs?" It is a difficult choice you must make, Francis, but I implore you to make it as soon as possible."

Saddened, Francis decided to make one more attempt to save Louella and his marriage. Arranging a mountain vacation, he gathered his children and their families for two weeks at a mountain retreat in the Fishkills. The mountain air had soothed him when he lost Eliza. Perhaps the clear streams and small lakes would be the healing balm for his ailing family situation. Alice packed and planned and organized the vacation along with keeping Louella calm and satisfied. At the last minute things went sour. Louella became unhappy with the arrangements and expressed her desire to remain in the city, and that Alice must stay with her. With obvious disappointment, Alice remained loyal to her mistress and a disgruntled Francis refused to cancel plans that would have affected his children's happiness. They would rent a carriage and team at the rail station when they arrived in the mountains so only the cook, Nanny Rose, and one driver took the train to the resort with the Oakes family. Oh, yes, and Adelene.

In the quiet of the mountain chalet Adelene's thoughts roamed. Boys were allowed to swim and splash in the ponds and rivers, always with their nakedness hidden from the delicate view of the female sex. She wondered what it would be like. Here in New York there were bathing clothes for women which were fine for dipping white feet in the edges of the water along the shoreline, but if one ever attempted to swim they would probably drown from the weight of the water-absorbing wool puffs and pantaloons. She had sneaked enough peeks to know how real swimming was done, and she was sure it could be done as easily by a girl as it was by a boy. Here at the lake in the Fishkills she would have her chance. She would sneak out in the night when everyone was asleep. If Louella had come she would have tried to convince her to try it with her, but since her cousin had declined the two week retreat in the mountains she probably wouldn't have agreed to the adventure of night-swimming, either.

The moon was bright and the trees cast their shadows across the path to the shore. Pulling her white voile nightdress over her head, Adelene stepped cautiously to the water's edge, dipping one foot carefully into the calm liquid. Warmer than she expected! Warmer than the cool early autumn air! She felt a chill now, as a breeze stirred the leaves on the nearby trees. Slowly she advanced into deeper water. Now the sun warmed water was up to her waist, and she felt the cooler current against her feet. Leaning forward she flattened her body and kicked off with her sturdy legs, keeping them under the surface to prevent telltale splashing. Now moving her arms outward from her breast she felt herself glide almost effortlessly through the moonlit water, sensing the coolness when her feet dipped too deeply below the surface. Completely exhilarated, she continued moving back and forth, keeping her eyes on the shore lest she wander too far from safety. What freedom she felt! What joy!

Finally she swam back to the shallow water and waded to the pebbled beach, slipped to the bush, pulled her nightgown over her head and made her way back to the cottage. After quietly tiptoeing past Francis' bedroom door and carefully drawing the latch, she entered her room and closed the door behind her. She hung the damp nightgown by the window where it would dry by morning. Feeling utterly refreshed she pulled back the covers and crawled into bed. How delicious was her life, and here she was, naked in bed, with Francis sleeping just next door! She wished—but, no, he was not hers. As she closed her eyes she thought she heard a door close. She wondered if someone else was stirring, but sleep overtook her before she could think more on it.

Adelene was not the only one to take a nighttime excursion. Francis had been unable to sleep and had decided a walk would help him relax. Strolling the path by the edge of the lake in the late hours helped him sort out his thoughts. What was he going to do about Louella? She was killing herself with liquor and had become totally unreasonable. There was no companionship, no romance of any kind between them, and the time she spent in her rooms had become nearly total. Meals were sent in, but they remained untouched. Business was booming at the dye works, but what good was it with no one to share his successes with? His children would always live comfortable lives, but for himself, he saw no real happiness in his future. Louella would have to be institutionalized to keep her from killing herself. She would not take a doctor's advice and give up drinking, and the last time he had entered her room unannounced she had screamed and thrown a vase at him, and accused him of all kinds of wild transgressions he had never even thought of until then. Yes, the time had come to do something about Louella.

Sitting on a large rock by some bushes on the beach he contemplated his options. He could let her die with a bottle in her hand or he could do the deed—have her declared insane and that would be it. The first option would mean a quicker death, but he could not hurry a sentence she had already imposed upon herself. He would have to choose the latter. She had become so irrational there was no talking to her. Alice knew. She tried to care for her and seemed willing to accept the constant abuse. Just last week he had found her in the kitchen holding a bloody cloth to her head. She had been reluctant to reveal it was a wound Louella had inflicted when enraged because Alice had not returned with more bourbon as quickly as her mistress had desired. "What a fool I am to have left Alice at home with her," he thought. He hoped Alice would call on Nathan to help if Louella became uncontrollable, and decided to cut the vacation short and hurry back to the city to prevent any mishaps. Yes, the time had come when he must protect his staff and Louella herself. Dr. Harrison had diagnosed it as "incurable inebriation," and he must take action for the sake of all in his household.

A great sadness weighed on Francis. He had obviously made a very big mistake. Louella had been so beautiful and her voice so enthralling that his emotions had been completely carried away by her. But it hadn't lasted. She had no spirit, and now he suspected that his money had perhaps swayed her in her acceptance of his proposal, affording her endless access to her true love. She had already been married, to her wineglass.

Francis picked up a pebble and was about to throw it in the water when he heard a rustle on the path. A sylph-like form in white brushed past, stood on the beach and then pulled her gown over her head. The white flesh shone in the moonlight. The perfect roundness of her hips, the curve of her breasts, he couldn't move. It was as though an angel had appeared in his moment of agony,—Adelene.

He watched as she slipped into the water and swam about like a mermaid. Breathless, he sat completely motionless lest he be discovered. This accidental event, (or was it some preordained plan?), settled his mind. As one door closed, another had opened. He hardly dared to breathe as she left the water, walked up the short beach, donned her nightgown that clung to her wet body, then made her way towards the chalet. He sat a few more minutes to be sure she had time to reach her room, then with a calm mind he, too, made his way to the house and to his own room where he slept peacefully for the first time in months.

Adelene Sullivan Oakes

Francis Oakes

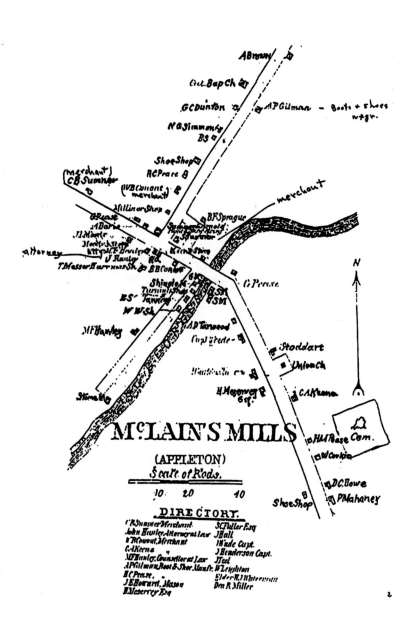

A Brown

Cal. Bap Ch

G C Dunton   A P Gilman — Boots + shoes
                                          mfgr.
N G Simmonds
        BS

ShoeShop
(merchant)   R C Pease 8
C B Sumner   (W B Conant,) 8
                    merchant   merchant
        Milliner Shop
G Pease   B F Sprague
A Davis   Saml Arnold
J J Moore   A P Gilman
Howe & Co.   A Shoe Store
J Hanley   A.P.B. Conant Co. Brick Store
T Messer Harness Sh B B Conant
                                    G Pease
        Shingle &
        Turning Shop G SM
E S Tanning   G SM
W W Sh
M F Hawley   A P Towood
            Carp't Shade
                    H Meservey
                    6 sf
            Stone Mill

        McLAIN'S MILLS

        (APPLETON)
        Scale of Rods.
        10   20   40

        DIRECTORY.

attorney

N

Stoddart

Union Ch

C A Keene

H M Pease Cem.
W Conkea
D C Howe
ShoeShop   P Mahaney

C B Sumner Merchant   S C Fuller Esq
John Hunter Attorney at Law   J Hall
N R Conant, Merchant   Wade Capt.
C A Keene   "   J Henderson Capt.
M F Hanley Counsellor at Law   J Teel
A P Gilman Boot & Shoe Manfr. W Leighton
H C Pease,   "   Elder W J Waterman
J E Howard, Mason   Den R Miller
H Meservey Esq

2

St. Dennis Church, circa 1840
(Now called St. Denis Church)

S.J. Gushee House

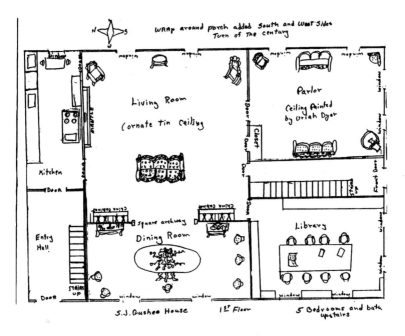

S.J. Gushee House Floor Plan

S.J. Gushee House ceiling motif

Uriah Dyer Painting

Baptist Church

Union Church

S.J. Gushee Store

Riverside Hall

Lottie Young's Millinery shop

Valley House

Norumbega

Mount Battie Hotel

Evolution of the Sullivan-Oakes Mansion

Parlor-Sullivan-Oakes Mansion

Ellen Sullivan

Paul Oakes

Recipes Used at S.J. Gushee Party

Chicago Cake . . . Mrs. Julia Page

Ingredients:
4 egg whites
½ cup butter
2 cups sugar
1 cup milk
3 cups flour
1 teaspoon cream of tarter
½ teaspoon soda
1 teaspoon lemon extract

Cream butter and sugar, add milk alternately with sifted dry ingredients and extract. Fold in beaten egg whites. Bake in moderate oven.

Chocolate Cream Cake . . . Milton Simmons

Ingredients:
3 egg whites
½ cup corn starch
(Beat ingredients to a froth)

½ cup butter
½ cup milk
½ teaspoon cream of tarter
¼ teaspoon soda
1 cup sugar
1 cup flour

Cream sugar and butter, stir in dry ingredients alternately with milk, add flavoring, bake in moderate oven. Flavor cake batter with lemon, frost with chocolate icing.

Recipes, continued:

Potato Rusks . . . . Geneva Robbins

Ingredients:
6 medium boiled potatoes, mashed fine
½ cup sugar
A little salt and a little flour
1 cake of compressed yeast
Mix with the above and let rise (sometimes overnight)
2 eggs
1 cup milk
Enough flour to make a stiff dough
Mix with the above and let rise
Roll out thin, spread with butter, lap one half over the other half
Cut out with a biscuit cutter
(Cut out the remaining or have a loaf, mix in a few raisins)
Let rise and bake in a moderate oven.

Lulie's Ice Cream . . . . Lulie Ufford

1 cup sweet cream
2 cups sugar
3 cups scalded milk
4 eggs
Vanilla

PART III

CHAPTER 1

1893

It began with just a slight tingling in her fingertips, as though they had fallen asleep and were having a difficult time awakening. Then came the exhaustion. "The heavy schedule of voice and dance lessons have caught up with me," Adelene thought, "but I'm a corn-fed farm girl and a few night's rest will put me straight and I will be good as new."

Francis noticed her malaise. She was not her usual buoyant self. "Probably her time of the month," he reasoned, but by the end of the second week he was sure there was something seriously wrong. His mind was so heavy with his problems with Louella he had difficulty concentrating on his suspicions about Adelene's health. His wife had become increasingly distant and her accelerated drinking had made her disagreeable during the short periods she ventured from her rooms. The lines had deepened in her beautiful face until she could no longer hide the illness overtaking her body. The odor of liquor oozed from her pores and her breath. Francis knew he was losing his wife, actually, already lost her. She no longer accepted his visits and became abusive if he even attempted any sign of affection. He had tried everything he could think of to stem the progress of her disease but all to no avail. He would do anything to help her but Louella did not want help. She was married to the spirits, not him. How could such a beautiful and talented woman like Louella succumb to the lure of the bottle? And poor Alice, he had caught her sneaking past the study again with a bundle under her shawl, having made her daily pilgrimage to purchase more spirits for Louella.

"Alice," he said, "You don't have to sneak liquor for Louella. We both know she orders drink and that there is no hope that she will ever be cured of her obsession. You may give her what she wants from my stock. I know you are a loyal servant and I appreciate that loyalty, but there is no need for secrecy."

His understanding and the relief it offered had brought forth streams of tears as pretense need no longer be a part of her service to the family.

Placing his arm about her slim shoulders he further consoled her with, "I am in constant contact with Dr. Harrison and Louella's health is being closely monitored. Together we will do whatever is best for Louella." He ushered the now quieted girl down the carpeted hall to Louella's quarters, left her to care for his wife and then returned to his study. There was nothing he could do for Louella, but he must have his physician attend Adelene.

Dr. Harrison was baffled. Francis had called him because of his trust in his care of Louella, and the doctor had called in several other physicians for consultation after seeing the seriousness of the malady. Adelene had developed a fever, an unrelenting fever. Her heart was beating at the alarming rate of one hundred five beats a minute and she was having increasing difficulty breathing as she lay motionless day and night.

Francis hardly left her side and spent hours placing cool cloths on her forehead, patiently dipping the cloths in the pan of ice water he had ordered to be kept filled by the bedside. He held her still hands and fed her broth whenever she roused enough to receive nourishment.

The physicians agreed that they would treat the disease symptomatically, and at the end of three weeks they informed Francis that there was little hope of recovery. Her limbs were not responding to any stimuli. It was as though the nerves in her body were sleeping and there was a steady worsening as the disease advanced.

Francis decided it was time someone of Adelene's family should be called. It was too far for her mother to journey from Maine in the winter weather but her sister Celestia lived just across the river. It was with a broken heart he sent word of the seriousness of her condition and her sister arrived with much haste. Being brought immediately to her side, Celestia held her limp hand, and softly whispered, "It's Celestia, Dear. I'm here with you. Don't worry, everything will be all right."

Adelene suddenly rose to a sitting position, and blankly stared straight ahead, surprising both Francis and Celestia.

"Celestia, the ship. I see the ship."

"What ship, Adelene? What are you talking about?"

"Your ship, Celestia. The Mary Celeste. I see it, but they are gone."

"I know, Adelene. Don't worry about the past. It's all right, Dear."

"All gone. They are gone."

Sinking back against the pillows, her pale face wet with sweat, she quietly slid back into her dreams.

Celestia did not understand. Adelene was confused and was obviously of a muddled mind. She had probably heard the news that the shops at home in Camden had burned, the center of town destroyed by fire and the whole block was gone. Surely that was what Adelene was piecing together in her dreams and confused thoughts. Fever was like that. Camden's center was all gone. Yes, that was it. The Mary Celeste had disappeared years before and whatever Adelene was experiencing could have nothing to do with its mystery.

Celestia stayed the afternoon, and after assuring Francis she would return daily to visit her gravely ill sister, she took her leave. It was a lot to worry about. If Adelene was indeed dying, she should inform her mother, but she did not want to worry her unnecessarily. After all, Mother was getting on in years and although she had been told Addie was ill, the seriousness of her condition had not been reported. And what could she tell her? No diagnosis had been made. It was a baffling condition. Celestia decided to wait a few more days. Surely by the end of the week Adelene would be improved. She had to believe that.

Francis was beside himself with grief. He paced the floor in his study, crossing and re-crossing in front of the burning fireplace, hands clasped behind his back and his head tipped forward in concentration. It couldn't be, it mustn't be. He felt threatened and confused. Must he lose all the women he loved? Women he loved? No, the woman he loved! Oh, Adelene, I cannot lose you, too. I will not lose you, Adelene. He sank to his knees and pounded the floor with his fists as tears splattered down his cheeks and onto his extended hands.

"My God, my God. I didn't ask you to bring her here. I didn't ask to love her, but now I couldn't live if she doesn't. Don't leave me alone without her, I beg of you. I beg of you, my God, my God!"

Rocking back and forth on his hands and knees in anguish, he prayed, while in the room across the hall the evening sun cast shadows across the sheets where Adelene lay. The room turned gray as dusk fell, and a broken man remained on his knees before his God.

It was midnight when a soft knock at the door brought Francis back to the physical world. Without opening the door Francis answered the knock with, "Yes?"

"Mr. Oakes, I must rest. I have brought a fresh basin of ice water for Adelene and I have tended to Louella's needs. She is asleep. May I retire?"

Rising from his knees Francis opened the door and took the porcelain washbowl from Alice and answered stiffly, "Of course, Alice. I will sit by Adelene tonight. Rest well. I will see you in the morning."

Stepping from the study Francis crossed the hallway and entered the room where Adelene lay sleeping, her shallow breathing barely moving her still form. Placing the bowl of ice water on the commode Francis lifted one of the towels from the rack above, leaned over and splashed some water on his tired eyes, rubbed his face briskly with the "O" initialed towel, then folded and placed it back on the rack. Taking a deep breath, he strode to the bedside and sat on the edge and looked tenderly down at the quiet form beneath the soft covers.

Taking her hand in his, feeling the softness of the palm, gently touching each small finger and tracing the line of her nails at her finger tips, he gazed at the still, pale face before him.

"Oh, Addie, Addie. You must live. I need you so. This house will be a mortuary again without you. I love you. I love you. You must recover and be my love."

He thought he saw the quiver of an eyelash, but then decided he must have been mistaken. Bowing his head as he continued holding her hand in his, fatigue overtook him as he sat leaning over the bed. Try as he might to fight off his exhaustion, he could not, and in his failure his head sank forward and rested on the figure before him.

Adelene felt she was in a deep, deep pit from which she was trying desperately to escape. Reaching, reaching, trying to pull herself up and out of the darkness that held her captive. But she was so alone—so alone. If only someone would help. And she was so cold, so very cold. Mama. Where was Mama? If only someone would give her strength she could emerge from this dark pit.

She felt a hand on hers, a warm hand, and then a head resting on her bosom. With her other hand she reached up and her fingers rested on the thick dark curls of the exhausted sleeping man.

Softly she murmured, "Francis."

CHAPTER 2

Adelene slowly returned to an awareness of her surroundings. There was a new atmosphere in the house since Louella had left. She was not sure what had happened as she had only heard a commotion one night with heavy footsteps on the stairs and muffled sounds coming from Louella's quarters, followed by silence after a carriage had rattled its way down the street. She thought she heard sobs coming from Francis' study but in her weakness she fell back into oblivion, unable to concentrate on the affairs of the household.

It was Alice who came to her and quietly told her that Louella had been taken away again, that it was for her own good and that her condition was so serious that she was beyond help. "She is gone from our lives and there is nothing anyone can do. Francis has endured every kind of abuse from her and he is devastated that he can do nothing to save her. So, do not worry your head about Louella. She is being cared for in the only way possible to save her life. Let us not speak of her, but go on with our lives, and right now, you must rest and try to recover your own health."

The weakness in her limbs would have discouraged almost anyone, but she had been bred in the arduous hills of Maine and didn't know the meaning of the word "quit." Celestia had visited again, this time a more comfortable meeting, as she felt her baby sister, though still weak, was on the road to recovery.

"Why don't you come and stay with Richard and me? We will care for you and we are family. You can't be sure you will walk again, and in your condition I think it would be better if you were with us. You will be much more comfortable. Please do."

"Celestia, I know you speak with love, and I deeply appreciate the invitation, but I am not in a "condition." I am recovering and I am nearer my career right here. Besides, I am being very well taken care of."

"But Adelene, there will be talk. You must consider your reputation. You just can't stay here under the roof of a married man with his wife away!"

"Celestia, I am not a child. I realize your desire to protect me is valid but I am not as naïve as you think. Let me worry about my reputation, and just let me cherish you for your most loving concern. You know I care deeply for all my family, but I am not married, nor have I children to consider. All I have is the theater, and I must regain my health and return to acting before I am forgotten. That is the reputation I must preserve."

"Very well, Adelene. I understand, although I am not sure Mother will."

With that she leaned over Adelene and held her sister tightly, then donned her wrap and left after calling for her carriage.

"That girl," she muttered as she placed herself into the waiting vehicle. She had done all she could, but Adelene was determined to do things her way. And Celestia was sure Adelene's way was not the way she had been raised.

The following months were both a joy and an agony. She had left the darkness and entered the world of light. Francis spent every minute he could by her bedside, and soon she was making plans.

"Alice! Bring me my books and my building notes! I want to work on my plans for my dream house. I have some new ideas and I want to get them written down before I forget."

"Now, Miss Adelene, you must rest. You should use all your energy to recover, Dearie."

"Alice, I may have crippled legs and I may need to use my strength to regain their use, but there is nothing wrong with my mind. Bring me my book, I say. Now!"

With a beaten look on her face a resigned Alice retreated to the study and gathered Adelene's notes and books, some extra paper and pen and ink. Hurrying back to the sick room she placed the items carefully on the bed, putting the ink on a side table to prevent its spilling on Adelene's favorite velvet and silk quilt, then began to back out of the room.

"I'm sorry, Alice, I truly am. You are so good and kind to me. I am just so exasperated with the slowness of my recovery. Come, come here and let me hold your hand."

A quiet Alice did as she was told. "Alice, it is so very difficult for me. One day I was a vibrant, ambitious person and then the next I was struck down with this terrible disorder. The awful days I was in and out of consciousness were terrifying. Whenever I closed my eyes I saw horrible creatures. Alligators and crocodiles were winking their heavy-lidded eyes at me, ready to devour me at any minute and I was unable to escape, and I was too exhausted to keep my eyes open to keep them at bay. I assume now that it was the laudanum giving me the wild visions, but at the time I was too tired to figure it out. When I couldn't move it was all the more painful. My legs cramped with such agony, and I had no control over them, and wondered if I ever would. Everyone treated me as though I were also deaf and mindless, discussing my condition by my bed as though I were not even there. I felt like a non-existent person. But now, dear, I am getting better, and I must get completely well. Will you help me?"

"Of course, Adelene. All I can do, I will."

"Then Alice, put these things to the side and help me up."

"But Miss Adelene, you mustn't!"

"Oh, yes, Alice, yes I must!"

With Alice's help, Adelene turned to sit at the side of the bed,
dangling her white feet over the edge.
"Now, Alice, help me to my feet."

The strong arms of Alice helped her to her feet and held her
tightly as Addie stood for the first time since she had been stricken.
Sweat popped across her brow, but she was smiling. Hesitantly
she put one small foot forward, then tentatively, the other. Feeling
the body she was holding start to sag, Alice guided the exhausted
girl back to the bed and tucked her in, moving the papers and
books to the side table for another time.

"Sleep, Miss Adelene. You will be stronger tomorrow."
The two smiled at each other, each realizing that recovery was
not far away.

Soon strength began to return and it was the strong arms of
Francis supporting her as her hesitant steps were accomplished.
Gaining strength daily she was soon walking on her own and the
bloom returned to her cheeks, (more bloom whenever Francis
entered the room). He ordered a huge bathtub built especially for
her and demanded it be filled with hot water twice daily. There
was a paddle on one end that Alice operated with a crank that
stirred and whirled the steaming water. Generous amounts of
Epsom salts were added and Adelene was assisted in and out of the
tub by a large Norwegian woman trained in massage whose kneading
and pounding of Adelene's tired body made her sleep soundly and
awake refreshed.

The physical recovery was nearly complete—but the health of
her love-heart was another matter. There was a delicious awakening

in her body, but it remained unfulfilled. Feelings that had never before surfaced now made her very aware of her womanliness, and she felt an urgency she still did not understand.

Days went by in a blur. Soon she was able to resume a nearly normal life and she spent every free minute she could manage at Francis' side. Just touching him sent waves of delight surging through her very soul. All her life she had thought of men as, well, men. She knew there was a big difference between men and boys, a big difference. Of course, men's apparatus was quite odd-looking, while a woman's, being hidden, was a mystery. If it was God's will or nature or both, she didn't know, but men seemed to know what to do with theirs.

Her longings were to be held, to be kissed—to be loved, tenderly. Men seemed willing, no, driven, to cast their seed indiscriminately, the act being more important than any feelings of love. That was it. For men it was desire. It seemed to dominate their thoughts and influence their decisions, while women, (except for those who played upon men's desire to further selfish ends), felt that love was the all-important factor in their relationships with the opposite sex. There would always be propagation by the will of men, and intuitive love for the resulting offspring by women, but a world with no true love between men and women? Unthinkable! Perhaps some day she would get it figured out. Maybe not today, maybe not this week, but it would come to her. Perhaps in the middle of the night, but she would get it settled in her mind sometime, sometime soon.

For now, her love for Francis consumed her and she had a different view. There were men, and there was Francis. It was as though the rest of the males in the world were nothings. Francis was all that counted. Not men. Just Francis. It couldn't go on this way, this having him but not having him. Even in their most intimate moments the shadow was there—the shadow of Louella.

Adelene had always thought that if she ever loved a man, really loved him, it would be from the very depths of her soul, with her heart completely open to receive his love in return. That's the way it was in all the books she had read, that was how true love was supposed to be, but now it was too late for that kind of completeness in the love she could give. She'd seen too much disappointment. Dennis had lost his love, and Alonzo had lost her sister, Sarah. Only her mother and father had held on to the kind of love she had dreamed of having—and lightening didn't often strike in the same place twice. Now she was in her late thirties and perhaps seeing a lot of unloving relationships had made her cynical. She vowed to save a small corner of her heart, hold back a secret place that would always remain hers and hers alone. She might forget about it, but it would always be there.

Adelene paced her room. She was so thankful for her returning health. It had been a long winter, and she had missed nearly a whole season at the theater. She was anxious to begin her career again. Francis had encouraged it, and she had contacted Mr. Dexter, her manager, and Miss Ryan who allayed her fears that she might have been forgotten and suggested she study several parts. She chose that of "Gertrude", and plunged into study with a passion.

She had studied until she was sure she knew every line and every nuance, and suddenly she threw the scrip and music across the room and flung herself across her bed, clutching the comforting quilt her mother had made for her to her breast. Why hadn't Louella just dropped dead. Why wasn't she just DEAD, DEAD, DEAD! Why hadn't she choked on her drunken vomit or something! It wasn't as if Louella had wanted Francis, all she wanted was the bottle! Adelene felt sick and torn. She desperately wanted Francis, and he wanted her, and Louella was still in their way. Louella had been taken away to the hospital during Adelene's illness and away from her bottle, but for how long? What if she got out of the sanitarium? Francis said if she did he had a plan—Please, God, don't let him kill her. Desperate situations called for desperate measures, but not that. Too many men had killed for love, and then killing had not only sent them away to rot in prison forever or put a noose about their necks, but the love they killed for was lost too. No, not that. Tears spilled on the comforter until suddenly she arose, washed her face, straightened her hair and stormed out of her room and down the stairs to the study where she confronted a surprised Francis.

"Will you become a Mormon, Francis, so that you can have Louella and me at the same time? If you are friend to Brother Joseph you will feel no pain or guilt, but if you let us consummate our love, it will be my pain to bear. Francis, I cannot and will not give in to lust. I have loved you from the moment our eyes first met, and you have given me the means to fulfill my dreams of a stage career, but something must be done before I can give in to my desires. I implore you, Francis, do not push me beyond my control or we will both suffer. I will suffer the pain of my conscience, and you dearest, will feel the pain of my suffering. If we are to love as our hearts dictate, you must first be free."

"Adelene, Louella is not here. When I had her committed I knew it was the only help I could give her. I cannot help her, and I am free. Perhaps you will not accept me on these terms, but I implore you, understand. The hospital she is in will take good care of her. If I kept her here she would soon die, and I have done the only humane thing I can for her. I no longer love her, I have only pity and I am as free of her as if she were dead."

She ran to him and with his arms about her she looked into his eyes, searching for his honesty, and her tears again flowed down her cheeks and pooled in the indentation at the hollow of her neck. "Oh, Francis, I love you, but I can't bear to think of being cast aside and then looked upon with pity or shame."

"My Darling Adelene, no one could ever look down on you. You are all that is precious and pure to me. They can release Louella when she is sober, that is possible. She could become sober and sane, but only because she is locked away from the evil demon she craves. She was released before and her first words were, "Bring on the bourbon, the drought is over." The love of her life is at the bottom of a bottle, not me. She can scream and cry and obtain her freedom from incarceration, but she will never be free from her true lover. There is no way she will ever be allowed in this house again. I tried for years to be first in her heart to no avail. You are my true love, my life, my everything, and I will not let her or anyone else change that. She is determined to drink herself to death and she will accomplish it as soon as she is released. Our feelings have not caused her downfall, and nothing we do will change the destiny she has promised herself. I will always make sure she is well cared for, and if she ever is released I promise you a legal settlement will ensue. Do not worry yourself, I am free and I love you. Come sit with me and dry your tears, and let our love comfort us."

Francis had much to bear. He had visited Louella and it was a disaster. She had read the newspaper account of Adelene's performance and the descriptions of her elaborate clothing and jewels. She had demanded to know if Francis had bought them for Adelene and his hesitancy in answering had brought on such a rage the orderlies had been forced to subdue her. He stopped by the office and completed papers transferring her to permanent placement Connecticut. Her screams of "I'll kill her! I'll Kill her! Just you wait, Francis. I'll get out of here and I'll kill her! I promise you that!" resounded through the halls as he left the building.

CHAPTER 3

The cross of white light that shone through the center of the pale moon glowed outside the window, streaming in ever widening pathways, casting its light on the lovers as Adelene lay with her head against his bare chest. He spoke softly of his love for her, how he had loved her from the first moment he saw her, of his loneliness because of Louella's drinking, and of the long nights when she was in a drugged stupor that no one could undo or prevent. How he had needed someone to share his thoughts and dreams, someone to make his life worth living again. The deep resonance of his voice reverberated through his chest against her ear in soft rumbling murmurs. The magic of it all filled her with love and peace and promise. As her body was left shimmering with delight her heart told her this was truly the only great love she would ever have or want.

March 16, 1893

My Darling Papa,

Tonight the air was so clear I went out to see the stars. They are not as close to the earth as there at home, but I put my hand up and spread my fingers like you taught me, and watched as they tumbled between my fingertips. If I were there I would be outside with you tonight counting stars that I can almost grasp in my hand from the ridge.

I remember being outside in the early morning when the fog was smoking over the river making a soft cloud covering that turbulent stream with a blanket of gossamer, the waking birds chirping cheerfully with happiness that dawn had arrived. I can still hear the whip o wills, calling out their wondrous song. Although I miss those mornings, still, the stars are my favorite things to clutch to my heart. You took the time to show me the dippers and Orion and the amazing shooting stars that burned so briefly but so wonderfully. I loved them so much I wanted to be a star myself, so I hope you understand why I must be here to fulfill my destiny. Perhaps I am just a shooting star and I will burn out before I shed all the light I desire, but, dear Papa, I hope when you look to the heavens and see a shooting star in the midnight sky, you will think of me and know that I love you and will always return to you.

Your loving daughter,

Adelene

CHAPTER 4

Whatever Francis J. Oakes had to endure, he would. Adelene was all that mattered and he would keep his promise that Louella would never come between them. Adelene, too, was enduring her share of criticism. To be living in the home of a married man, albeit estranged, was bad enough, but his being her cousin's husband further complicated the situation. They had managed to hide their feelings from the general public, as New York was not exactly a close-knit community. The theatrical world was rather liberal compared to other areas as well, but in Maine there was no containing the gossip. As word came to the Merrifield family of Louella's incarceration there was a "wondering" about Adelene's stay at the Oakes' home on 73rd Street. The Merrifields were not shocked at the hospitalization of Louella as the imbibing of spirits was not unusual in their family. Inebriation seemed to be some irresistible illness easily contracted in the family line. They were, however, unhappy with the remaining presence of Adelene in the Oakes' household. Pleas from Ellen and Daniel were answered with loving letters and assurances that all was well with her life and that they should not worry, that her career was blossoming and that she would see them in the summer.

Life for Francis and Adelene was nearly perfect. For every minute they enjoyed no more than a second of doubt plagued them. This was tolerable. Their beings were consumed with the enchantment of their love.

CHAPTER 5

Louella Oakes was sober, sober and angry. She had expressed her anger violently and certainly her keepers were aware of her discontent. Windows had been broken, dishes had been thrown and meals flung to the floor until she had spent many nights in a dark room with soft walls and floors where she thrashed and gnashed her teeth and screamed. First it was for the drink she so desired— the craving, the vomiting, the pain rushing through every vein in her body. Her eyes burned and she pulled her hair out by the fistfuls. Shaking followed, shaking for days on end as though chilled by winter's blast, and then finally, exhaustion. Sleep. Sleep to ease the cravings, sleep to ease the pain of her ruined life. Merciful sleep.

And now the sober and weakened Louella was finally allowed to join the other patients at meals. As her behavior improved, so improved her situation. Her hair regenerated, her health seemed to have returned. A somewhat jaundiced but determined inebriate returned to the world, and Louella Merrifield Oakes made plans. First she would become a model patient, then she would seek and find her revenge.

CHAPTER 6

1894

What a wonderful, glorious winter! Every dream Adelene had ever entertained had come true. What more could any woman wish than to have a career on the stage, wearing elegant gowns and magnificent jewels and then return home into the arms of her true love. Weekends offered either a party or art gallery opening or some entertaining soiree of one kind or another. Trips to the cabin in the mountains were worth the long train rides as a warm fire in the fireplace burned brightly and toddies and delicacies always awaited their arrival. Francis left no small comfort she might enjoy to chance, and soon thoughts of Louella faded from her mind. She knew he visited her on occasion but they did not discuss her condition. Since she was confined for her own good it seemed unnecessary to mention such an unhappy subject. No, it was far better to continue as they were, completely engrossed in their love for each other.

That is, until the papers were served. Francis was to appear in court in June. He quickly arranged for Adelene to return to Maine for her annual pilgrimage to her home. A little earlier that usual, but he wanted to spare her any agony over the events he foresaw in the near future. It looked as though things were going to become nasty, and the further away she was, the safer she would be from scandal.

Adelene's bags were hastily packed and she was soon seated in her carriage and on her way to the train station. She was ashamed of the tears she had shed in front of Francis. Usually she had better self-control, and letting her emotions show was not to her liking, especially since it streaked her face powder and took the shine off her lashes. Disgusted with herself, she embarked from the carriage. Not waiting for assistance, she pointed the porter towards her bags, stepped onto the platform and after checking her ticket in the station house she entered the car that had been reserved for her. It was pleasant to have a space all her own. Francis had made sure that every luxury had been afforded her, and she was grateful. He had given her only sketchy information on the court action that was to ensue, but she valued his judgment and was not anxious to create problems for him by her presence.

In the past, traveling in the regular passenger car, the trip was not all that pleasant. The problem with traveling, she decided, was the traveling itself. For the most part it was boring, boring, boring. The packing part was all right, as the work was masked by anticipation, making it not an unpleasant chore, but the actual traveling was not so pleasant. The rattling and jouncing of the carriage made one feel somewhat scattered even before reaching the train platform. Then there was only time for a quick touch-up of hair and powder, straightening of jabots and a quick checking of boots for dust before emerging as gracefully as possible from the vehicle lest some acquaintance by happenstance be at the same station. (Of course, her public must always see her at her best).

Then came the long train ride, the sideways motion of the train as its wheels edged against the tracks always tired her. She felt bounced and shattered by the end of a long trip, and the scenery was never so outstanding as to hold her attention for long. She found some entertainment in the other passengers. Usually present was some portly gent squat in his seat, his heavy body seemingly unshaken by the train's constant motion. Obviously a salesman of some sort, sometimes wearing a striped waistcoat with a gold chain attached to a hidden pocket watch swaying on a rotund stomach and his narrow shoulders making him look as though he had been plopped in his seat like a sack of salt, (with most of the contents settled to the bottom). Almost always these men sat with their ankles crossed as their poor crowded legs were squeezed aside by their round bellies. A smelly cigar in the corner of the mouth, a small round hat precariously tilted at what was assumed to be a rakish angle and trousers a bit too short covering spindly legs completing the picture. Their advances disgusted her, as she imagined they had families at home, but she remained polite in discouraging their familiarity.

The women were different. They at least had the decency to corset themselves into some kind of more human shape. Even those of noticeably more meager means held their heads high and had taken care that their clothing for the journey was clean and pressed, with the required hankie and purse held tightly and primly. She wondered how many had unkempt, cigar—smoking portly men in their lives. She had seen many longsuffering wives doomed to bear children by overweight, tobacco smelling husbands. The act couldn't have been pretty, but by the families she had seen, obviously conception had been possible.

Then there were the newlyweds. Always at least one set on every trip, rolling mooning eyes that spoke of their desire while making believe that night things were the furthest from their minds.

It never took Adelene more than an hour or two to have inventoried all the passengers and return to boredom. This time she would not be bored. The comfortable compartment with sleeping arrangements would save her from the misery of a monotonous ride. The anticipation of being with Mama and Papa made the trip worthwhile, but, oh, she would miss Francis. Her trips home always refreshed her and gave her strength for the next theatrical season, but her heart ached to be near him and as soon as whatever trouble he was attending was settled she planned to return to his arms.

She was anxious to see the additional rooms to her parent's house on the ridge. They had been a gift to her parents that she had paid for herself with money from the millinery shop, and she hoped they were enjoying them. She would be comfortable sleeping in her little room under the eaves, but the added space would make things easier for her aging parents. If rumors were flying about her personal life, at least the addition was proof of her love and success.

A lot had changed in Maine besides the Sullivan's house. Since Mclain's Mills became more popularly known as "Appleton," there seemed to be a change in the atmosphere of the town. It bustled with activity, with seventeen businesses as well as Lottie Young's millinery shop, a corset shop and a watchmaker, the population being well over a thousand. The outlying stores in Burkettville and North Appleton never lacked trade, and Vandellyn Keller's blacksmith shop under the hill by the river did a flourishing business. Sparks from his forge could be seen late at night as he took on all the work he could muster, declaring he was sending his son to medical school as soon as he was old enough.

The changes in town prompted mixed feelings. The building that housed Mr. Page's carriage shop and the blacksmith shop (with the town office on the floor above) was once the lower ridge school she had attended as a child. Schools had been consolidated and her old school moved to the village. Perhaps the changes seemed gradual to the year-round residents, but to Adelene, shockingly pronounced.

She had heard that automobiles were being made and she wondered how they would affect the little town. The dirt roads didn't seem adequate for horseless carriages, and what if trips to Camden or Rockland became so easy that the little shops in Appleton were ignored? If the population fell below a thousand it would affect the tax revenues, and what of Riverside Hall? What if the New York and Boston theatrical companies no longer came to perform there? What if it all fell to ruin? And if the church bell no longer rang its call to worship on Sunday mornings, or was not there to ring in the twentieth century or the millennium, how sad that would be. Well, she would just have to wait for the one and hope for the other. One thing for certain, she would do all she could to preserve the town. She could not imagine Appleton without a Post Office or the stage running every day. She could not allow herself to think that some day the soul of the town might be ripped out.

CHAPTER 7

Francis knew it was going to be bad, but not just how bad. At least he had gotten Adelene out of town. She could contend with the gossipmongers and certainly handle the Merrifields when she arrived home, that is, unless they were all too drunk to listen to reason. He had come to know of the family reputation, the hard cider and elderberry wine consumption in that family was an accepted fact. But he couldn't stand to have her suffer through the court proceedings, even from a few blocks away. The newspapers would be filled with the scandal of it all, and eventually find their way North, but it was his experience that a distance of eight hundred miles from any trouble usually softened even the worst reports. Distance was an ally. By Autumn, things would be calmed down and they could resume their lives. Perhaps it was better that the situation with Louella had come to a head. He had done all he could to save her, but a drowning person has to cooperate or the rescuer will also perish. His last visit was so ugly he was sure she should remain incarcerated, and the ugly threats against him, Adelene and his children convinced him she should remain confined. Now it seemed possible that she could win her release and he would be forced to take protective measures for the safety of his family.

After bathing and shaving he donned a gray menswear suit and was struggling with his collar pin when he heard a tap on his bedroom door.

"Enter."

"Mr. Oakes, I'm so sorry things have come to this. Is there anything I can do?"

"Yes, Alice. You can help me with this damn collar pin."

As she reached up to push the bar in place and cap the end he noticed the redness in his housekeepers eyes.

"Don't worry, Alice. Everything will be all right. I know you loved Louella and that you also love Adelene, as do I. It was I who was abandoned by Louella, and I thank God every day that Adelene came into my life, and I will do whatever I feel best for both of them."

"I know, Sir. I thought you were going to die of heartache until Miss Adelene came. I'm just worried about how this will all turn out. I'm just worried, that's all."

"I know, Alice. I'm worried, too. I understand Louella feels betrayed, but only because she wants to be free and does not understand that she will be giving herself a death sentence if she obtains that freedom. Now we must let the courts decide, but I will not allow her to harm you or my family, that, I promise you."

It hadn't been easy. Having Louella transferred to Connecticut seemed to be his only option after her wild accusations and threats. True, he wished to be free of her, but he could not bring himself to allow her to return to the inebriate state she was sure to seek if she gained her freedom. With the promise of violence against his household while she was sober weighing heavily on his mind, he knew she would be even more agitated when under the influence. He had seen the abuse she had perpetrated on poor loving Alice when she was drunk. That, coupled with Dr. Harrison's admonition that she would not live a year if she returned to drinking, had convinced him that his only option was the course he had taken. Surely the courts would understand his predicament and the ruling would uphold her continued placement in Darien.

Justice Gaynor's plan to investigate the situation did not worry Francis. It was the publicity the whole affair had generated that troubled him. He understood his wife's wish to be freed. She could reach no liquor as long as she was confined. There had been no problem as long as she was in the private sanitarium in Whitestone until the threats began, and having observed that the security there was not as good as it could have been, he had decided to place her with Dr. Kindred in a more secure facility. He felt like it was a reenactment of Sumter. He had been bombarded as long as he could stand, but in this case he was not going to surrender.

There were always lawyers looking for the moneyed cases and they had really taken a jump onto this one. Knowing he was a millionaire had made him an attractive target for their unscrupulous greed, and Louella was the perfect client. She would swear to anything to punish him for not supporting her habit, and Mr. Rooney and Mr. Heymann were eager to believe in her innocence. He couldn't blame them. Lawsuits were their business and defending clients such as Louella was their bread and butter. They were obviously hoping to stock their pantries for a long, cold winter with this one.

The newsmen at the courthouse were waiting for his carriage as Francis arrived. It was like a circus; shoving, shouting, and jeering. They seemed to enjoy his discomfort, as many less moneyed enjoy the downfall of the wealthy, whether deserved or not. It was as though the rich somehow must have achieved their wealth by some unseemly means, therefore making those in lower financial status, more honest, more upright. It was a way to mask their own inability to become wealthy, to exonerate themselves from any hint of failure.

Pushing his way up the steps he entered the building and by the time he was seated and had composed himself, the swearing in and charges were being presented. All the events of the last few years were twisted and embellished with a viciousness he had not been prepared to hear.

"Your honor, Mrs. Oakes was taken from Whitestone to Darien June 7 of this year against her protest. There, she was shut up in a grated cell with a nurse. There were raving maniacs in the adjoining cells. The transfer was made on the authority of a letter from Mrs. Oakes' husband, and without the knowledge or consent of the Lunacy Commission or any judge."

Francis looked about the courtroom. The doctors, lawyers, asylum officials and all concerned were there under order of Judge Gaynor. Francis hoped fairness would prevail. His twelve years of being married to Louella had not been happy. His plans for their life at Steinway had been a complete failure. He had envisioned pleasant evenings, with Louella at the piano singing and his children about him. He thought there would be flirtatious glances between him and his wife and loving rendezvous at evenings end.

None of it had transpired, and he had been slowly dragged into depression until Adelene had come to live with them. Louella had already spent time hospitalized at Sanford Hall in Flushing and each time she was released she began her binges anew. Three times she had become impossible to care for at home until he finally succumbed to Dr. Harrison's advice and placed her in his sanitarium at Whitestone. Since Dr. Harrison was superintendent of the Kings County Insane Asylum in Flatbush, Francis had felt his advice to be sound. He was shocked when Dr. Harrison reversed his decision on the stand and declared Louella sane and recommended her release.

Someone must have threatened him, Francis reasoned, though he could agree that Louella's sanity, when sober, was readily demonstrated to all contacts except Francis himself. Her ravings and threats were all made in the privacy of their visits, and only the orderlies who restrained her knew her true nature. Probably bought off, or afraid of losing their jobs, as none were present at the hearing. Francis could understand that. They were not wealthy as he was, and had families to feed. No one seemed to understand that he had been forced to take action, to call Dr. Kindred to bring a carriage and nurses to transfer his wife to Connecticut. At least there, if she escaped, he would receive word in time to prevent any harm befalling his family. He readily admitted he had indeed written the letter as read:

New York, June 6, 1894

Dr. D. A. Harrison, Breesehurst Terrace
Whitestone, L.I. New York

Dear Sirs:

I have authorized Dr. J. J. Kindred to take charge of my wife. You will therefore please transfer her to his car and permit him to remove her at his convenience in accordance with my instructions to him, and much oblige.

Yours truly,

Francis J. Oakes

Dr. Kindred had told Francis that the transfer had indeed been ugly, with Louella declaring she was entirely sane and had never been otherwise, that they had managed, (with difficulty), to get her to Darien. She had been so violent they had been forced to place her in solitary confinement for the protection of the other patients. He didn't know how she had been able to contact a lawyer; he assumed she had made the contact while still at Dr. Harrison's hospital.

As Francis listened to the incredulous twisting of events and suppositions of Louella's lawyers, devoid of any recognition of his true motives, he quietly thanked God that Adelene was in Maine away from the fray. Much of what was presented was true. Yes, he had transferred Louella to Connecticut when he received word she was to be released, and that a writ of habeas corpus had been presented, and although she was sober at the trial he knew the show would not last beyond the last day of the court proceedings.

"We make a defense," said George Hill, representing Mr. Oakes. "We do not contend that Mrs. Oakes is insane."

"Where is Dr. Harrison?" asked Justice Gaynor with some show of feeling. "How could he release Mrs. Oakes on a mere letter from her husband, in spite of the fact that she was committed by a Supreme Court Justice?"

"Dr. Harrison is not here," said Lawyer Hill. "I requested him to come but I do not see him."

"These statements are all very well," said Justice Gaynor," but I want to know more about this case. I want to see the doctor. I will make a full investigation."

"Will Your Honor remand Mrs. Oakes to the custody of her council?" asked Assemblyman S. F. Kneeland who appeared with Mr. Heymann.

"Oh, she may go where she likes. We admit she is sane," said Lawyer Hill hastily.

The courtroom was cleared, the case to be continued the following day. It was a wonderful opportunity for Louella, as reporters had discovered a very interesting object of their attention, which was no small pleasure for Francis. He was relieved to be rid of them even though he knew they would be obtaining tainted half-truths and outright lies from his wife. As he would learn by morning, the newspapers would not be stingy with space for the Oakes trial. Louella's cooperation was greatly appreciated, and she enjoyed her moment of fame. The New York Times reporter was granted an interview at the office of her lawyer, where she cheerfully reiterated the exciting details of one of New York's greatest scandals of the wealthy, which was published as follows:

"I do not know why my husband has sought to get rid of me," she said. "I always loved him passionately, and we got along happily together until he placed me in an inebriety asylum in 1891. I was put there on a false charge. I was never inebriated. I have not seen my husband since last Thanksgiving Day, when he called on me at Whitestone. He parted from me with every show of affection. I begged him to take me out. His last words were, "Good-bye, Darling. You'll come home on New Years Day."

When the doctor came to take me to Darien I said I would not go. The man said he had two nurses to take me by force, and he threatened to call a policeman. I appealed to Dr. Harrison. He said he was sorry for me but could not help me. I saw it was no use to struggle and so I submitted. When I reached Darien I was put in a mad house, in a small cell with a nurse, and there were raving maniacs. Oh, I will never forget my experiences there."

"Dr. Kindred told me he had been told I was stark crazy. He said he had been offered any sum he might name to hold me in his place. I was allowed to write to no one but my husband."

Lawyer Heymann intimated excitedly that there was another woman at the bottom of the affair. "I cannot say more about this," he declared. "When I went to Darien," he continued, "Dr. Kindred begged me not to get him into any trouble. When I went to see Dr. Harrison he told me that Mrs. Oakes had been taken to Darien."

"Thank God," said Dr. Harrison to me, "That someone has taken Mrs. Oakes case in hand. You can save her. Someone is trying to get rid of her."

Francis Oakes read the account in the paper with great disgust. How could there be any fair dispensation of the case when it had already been tried in the Times? He had denied any interview and made no statement to the press, not caring to make the situation more notorious, and he was certainly willing for Louella to save her dignity. If she gained her freedom she would also be gaining her freedom from him. He would have paid any sum to save her life, but after this, he would pay any sum to keep his family safe. Yes, the best thing for him to do was to keep quiet and let his lawyers manage his defense. His own council, Lawyer George Hill, did give a statement to the press.

"This is an unfortunate domestic trouble. The record is all straight. Nothing illegal has been done. Under the law of the State, a man can take his wife from a sanitarium without the knowledge or consent of the judge who committed her there. He can place her in whatever sanitarium he pleases. All that was done in this case was done for the best interest of Mrs. Oakes. No one wanted to be rid of her. She is an inebriate, and her husband has had trouble with her for several years. He has done all he could to save her. Justice Gaynor labors under a misunderstanding. If anyone can do more for Mrs. Oakes than her husband, all well and good. We are satisfied to let them make the attempt."

In a separate article on June 17 appeared:

MRS. OAKES WANTS FREEDOM

HER HUSBAND ORDERED TO BRING
HER FROM INSANE ASYLUM

Dr. D. A. Harrison of the Asylum for the Insane at Breezehurst Terrace, Whitestone, L.I., was directed by Judge Gaynor to produce in the Kings County Supreme Court, Mrs. Louella Oakes. Mrs. Oakes is the wife of Francis J. Oakes of the Oakes Chemical Manufacturing Company. Dr. Harrison and Mr. Oakes were in court. It was ascertained that Mrs. Oakes was committed to an asylum while her counsel was preparing to obtain a writ of habeas corpus. She was taken from Whitestone asylum to Connecticut. It is claimed against her will. Counsel for Mrs. Oakes said Mrs. Oakes was taken to Darien, Connecticut on the certificate of two reputable physicians, who found she was a habitual drunkard. She was first committed by Justice Garrison in Long Island City in 1891, then by Justice Cullen in 1892 and again in 1893 by Justice Garrison. Counsel said that Mrs. Oakes had threatened her husband's children by a former marriage, and that he had borne with her for many years, and that he was not willing to set his wife at liberty. He claimed that the proper place to apply for her release was in Connecticut.

"The court has jurisdiction here," said Judge Gaynor. "The husband is here. His domicile is here and she is under his control. She must be brought before me in the court of Oyer and Terminer by next Tuesday."

Counsel for Mrs. Oakes said she was perfectly sane and was detained against her will.

Another article stated:

"Whitestone, L.I., June 19.

Dr. D. A. Harrison, proprietor of Breezehurst Terrace, the private sanitarium here where Mrs. Louella Oakes was a patient said tonight that in view of the case coming up tomorrow morning he did not care to discuss the matter. He stated, however, that his actions in connection with the transfer of Mrs. Oakes to a sanitarium in Darien, Connecticut, was not contrary to custom. He had placed Mrs. Oakes in the care of a doctor from the other institution on an order from Mr. Oakes. He did not discharge patients, but cared for them until their relatives or lawful guardians took them away.

By the twenty first of June it was over.—Over in the courts, but not in the New York Times. The paper of June 21, 1894 burst forth with all the juicy details of Louella's victory.

MRS. OAKES ENJOYS LIBERTY
RELEASED FROM ASYLUM BY JUSTICE GAYNOR

Lawyers admit that they are in the dark respecting the law authorizing the transfer of patients. The judge dwells upon the previous commitments of the Plaintiff. No charge against the Doctor of the Whitestone Asylum.

Mrs. Louella Oakes, the wife of Francis J. Oakes, the millionaire chemical manufacturer, who for three years has been in an asylum, was formally liberated by Judge Gaynor yesterday.

She had first been placed in an asylum on the charge that the excessive use of liquor had rendered her insane. She was committed by Judge Garretson, of Queens County and placed in the Breezehurst Asylum at Whitestone, L.I. of which institution Dr. D. A. Harrison is the superintendant.

Her friends engaged lawyer Stillman F. Kneeland that she might be released, as she was perfectly sane and was being restrained of her liberty against her will. Mr. Kneeland began procedures in habeas corpus.

He charged that when he was making the application for her release, her husband had her removed from the Whitestone institution and taken to a similar asylum in Darien, Connecticut. This, Mr. Kneeland claimed, was done without authority of the court, and he intends to go even further in the case and prove that Mrs. Oakes was never insane.

Dr. D. A. Harrison, the superintendent of the Whitestone asylum was in the Kings County Supreme Court yesterday when Justice Gaynor called the case up. Mr. Kneeland, who appeared for Mrs. Oakes, said in behalf of Dr. Harrison that Mrs. Oakes desired the statement made that she had been treated in the very best manner by Dr. Harrison, considering the restraint she was under.

"We have no charge to make against Dr. Harrison," said Mr. Kneeland. We only object to the removal of Mrs. Oakes to Darien, Connecticut. Dr. Harrison said that the custom prevails in private institutions of this kind to remove patients on the application of the persons at whose instance they were incarcerated, and who are able to secure their discharge at any time, just as they could the removal.

Justice Gaynor, who had taken an interest in the case, was not contented with this statement, and he asked Mr. Kneeland if he had looked up the law in the matter. Mr. Kneeland acknowledged that he had been unable to find anything as to the manner in which a person may be released. He said that it was his belief that it should be on an order of the court.

Lawyer George Hill, who represented Mr. Oakes said, "This case has already reached a stage which we never anticipated."

"Can you refer me to the law on the question?" asked Judge Gaynor.

"I cannot," bluntly replied Mr. Hill, "but persons have always been released from such private institutions, I know, just as Dr. Harrison says."

"There may be no decisive law," Justice Gaynor said, "but I think it is my duty, however, to look at the law as I often commit insane people. I am passing no censure on anyone, but I simply want to see whether you have the power to discharge a patient at will."

"For years, to my personal knowledge," said Mr. Hill, "everything possible has been done to prevent publicity in this sad affair and I want to say here that we knew nothing of this writ until it was served upon us."

"It cannot be doubted," said judge Gaynor, "that this woman is suffering under an infirmity, because she was committed three times by judges who saw her."

"I insist," said Mr. Kneeland, "that this woman be exonerated. Why Dr. Kindred himself told me that she was perfectly sane. We won't let this matter rest in this form. We want a direct admission from the other side that Mrs. Oakes is sane or I will demand a Sheriff's jury. Why, the State Commission reported that she is sane. Then Dr. Harrison went to Mr. Oakes and told him so, and Mr. Oakes ran her on to an asylum in Connecticut, and unless these proceedings had been brought she would never have gained her liberty."

"Yes, that is all wrong," said Justice Gaynor, "but I must take notice of the fact that she was this time committed by judges."

"Well, your honor might send me up if two physicians swore that I was insane," said Mr. Kneeland.

"Oh, but I would have to know the physicians," said Justice Gaynor, "and I would have to see you first and that would convince me that you are sane."

Mr. Hill has said enough to justify me in discharging Mrs. Oakes, and she is so discharged."

Mr. Kneeland then took Mrs. Oakes out of the courtroom, and she was taken to her friends, who will care for her.

CHAPTER 8

Francis could only imagine the celebration Louella was enjoying. The newspaper reports sickened him nearly as much as the wavering of Dr. Harrison. Of course the doctor had his business to protect, and he couldn't blame him for that. Certainly the publicity had not helped him in that respect. Well, she had gotten her way, and now he feared she would live to regret it, rather, "die" would be more like it, but he didn't wish to continue the mess any longer. It would not be long before her lawyers discovered the real Louella. She was going to be in a rage as soon as she realized the amount of money they would be demanding for their services. But on the other hand, he would pay it and be done with the thing. He felt some twinge of pain for her, knowing she had shortened her own life. Perhaps he had been wrong, had failed in some way, but the events of June' 94 could not be reversed. He had confirmed an account for her and if she managed it with any discretion it would care for her more than her lifetime. He imagined she would live high and fast to a quick end, but it was beyond his control.

How he longed for Adelene. By the first of August the whole mess would be quieted. By then the press would have found new victims they could converge upon to destroy their privacy and exploit their pain.

Francis sat in his armchair in the study, dropping the newspapers on the floor. Drained and exhausted, he contemplated his situation. Now he could relax a few weeks, catch up on some reading, perhaps take in a few ball games in Brooklyn. Pittsburgh and Milwaukee were both coming to town soon and it would be a good break from work and his recent plagues.

And so, things did smooth out, that is, until the end of June. He had worked late to be sure all was in order at the plant to allow his taking a day for baseball and returned to find Louella attempting to remove the picture covering the wall safe in the study.

"Louella, what do you think you are doing?" he demanded.

"This is my house," she declared, "and I will do as I please!"

"No, Louella, this is no longer your house. You must leave at once."

"You can't make me, this is my house—and where is the bitch that has taken my place?" With that, she dropped the painting with a crash, then looked about and ran her hand across the mantel, knocking a porcelain figurine to the floor. "I've always hated those idiotic statues," she screamed, "and I hate you and I hate Adelene and"—

During her tirade Alice entered the room and Louella reached down, picked up the broken figurine and flung it at Alice. "And you,—you,—you stupid, fickle witch! I always hated you!"

The figurine narrowly missed Alice as she backed towards the door.

"Call the police, Alice," Francis shouted. "Now!"

It was not an easy ejection, but as soon as the fracas was over Francis sank again into his chair as a tearful Alice attempted to clean up the broken glass and regain order in the room.

"Let it go for tonight, Alice. We can take care of it in the morning."

"But, Sir, how could she say such awful things. I always cared for her and did my best to follow her every bidding."

"She is not responsible for her actions, Alice. Do not grieve for your own feelings, but for her, as she is destroying herself. Get some sleep, we will need rest as I am sure this is not the end of this affair."

And it wasn't. Louella had gone directly to the Second Police Precinct Station and asked Sergeant Roulette, the duty officer, to give her police protection. She told him arrangements had been made following her release from an asylum in which she had been mistakenly incarcerated, to return home, but that she had been staying at a New York hotel to recover from the nervous shock caused by court proceedings. Now she wished to return to her home but was put out of the house. She immediately called Mr. Heymann who promised to secure an indictment against the policeman for the use of undue violence in ejecting her from the Oakes residence.

Mr. Heymann was beginning to understand Louella, and he was slowly being forced to accept enlightenment. She no longer seemed to be the cool mistreated beauty he had mistaken her for; she seemed to be slightly disheveled, but then, she had been through a lot. On, the other hand, it seemed that there would probably be future litigation in the form of a divorce, and the sooner, the better. She was beginning to strike him as someone who had a talent for going through money like Grant through Richmond, and perhaps she should get litigation on the docket before the finances became tight. It crossed his mind that perhaps Mr. Oakes would pay handsomely for his freedom if Louella couldn't. Mr. Heymann tilted back in his chair, lit a cigar, and smiled.

It was July first, and Francis had read the accounts of the trial over and over again. It was a relief to have it done with. He no longer cared if anyone connected with the trial had been bribed, coerced or threatened. He came to the conclusion that none of his suspected or imagined injustices had occurred. It had simply, or not so simply, been a nasty situation but now it was over. Locks were changed on the doors and the servants had been instructed to be wary of anyone unfamiliar—or Louella, attempting admittance, and to call him if there were any doubt about identity.

He would hear no more from Louella for several months. By then the divorce papers would be filed, the settlements decided and he would be a free man.

CHAPTER 9

Arriving in Maine in the first week of June was a lot different than a visit in March. Adelene had avoided the howling winds moaning over the death of winter and the way the earth changed in early April. At first it would be just a peek, a brown eye opening and widening on a hilltop where the morning sun shined on the ice crusted snow. Then it would become a great yawning mouth stretching across the hill. Finally the sleeping field would emerge as the remaining white patches slowly melted and soaked slowly into the dormant ground until the earth awakened to another spring sky. Another year, and everything became a year older—and for everyone, it was a new start.

Yes, she had missed the first greening of the hills, the first mayflowers. The windows no longer frosted on the inside with their cornfield patterns that melted and puddled on the sills when the morning fires were built. Instead, she awoke to the sounds of chirping birds happily flying to and fro gathering food for their new hatchlings.

Being with Mama and Papa was such a comfort. Stretching and wiggling her toes under the fresh smelling sheets that had billowed just yesterday on the clothesline was such a joy she nearly laughed out loud. Sheets just didn't smell this sweet when dried in the city air. She thought about her mother, how she had always made sure the bedding was fresh and clean, washing and hanging the sheets in the sun, then at the end of the day folding them into the wicker basket after checking to be sure a bird dropping hadn't spoiled the white expanse, sprinkling and rolling them. While the stew boiled on the woodstove the sadirons were heated until they sizzled when tested with her whetted fingertip. Adelene could envision the sweat running down her mother's plump cheeks, and the way she occasionally wiped it away with the edge of her apron lest a drop stain the sheet as she pressed it to a glistening smoothness. No wonder Papa bathed every night after a day in the fields or the butcher shop. The sweetness of the bedding made sleeping such a delicious event she vowed she would always remember these housekeeping ways her mother had taught her by example. Someday she would have a whole room full of ironed sheets that someone else had starched and ironed that her mother could choose from, and even a servant to make beds so Ma could enjoy the same luxury she had always afforded others.

Reaching up to the familiar headboard she had slept next to for so many years she stretched and gave it a tug, waking her body to alertness. Jumping out of the warm bed she stood on the braided wool rug by her bedside. Not as soft as the Chinese and Persians of the Oakes residence in New York, but thick and sturdy and comforting.

She could hear her mother in the kitchen, the clunking sound of the iron spider being set on the stove, "bacon and biscuits and eggs"—she could hardly wait. So what if her corset had to slip a notch. Perhaps she didn't have an eleven-inch waist like Camille Clifford, but then, what did an inch or two matter? Camille always looked a little choked, in her opinion, and although she was a good actress her voice lacked volume. Perhaps if she let out a stay or two she could project more. But anyway, bacon and eggs it would be, and honey on the biscuits. Chuckling, she pulled on her robe, stepped into her seal fur slippers and hurried down to the kitchen.

Everything was as she remembered, except again, her parents were a little older. Time seemed to be advancing on them more quickly every year. The small addition to the house had made the home more comfortable but she wished she could do more.

Downing a small tumbler of fresh milk as she finished her

meal, she rose and helped her mother clear the table until Ellen said, "Shoo, shoo—let me finish this Darlin'. You get yourself dressed and get some air. You can take the carriage to the village. Papa and I have some things to do and the fresh air will do you good. You've been in that dirty city too long and yer lungs could take a good cleaning out!"

"Perhaps I will, Mama. It will be good to ride to the river and get my bearings again."

The small open carriage was more cart than carriage. After the closed windowed and curtained carriages of New York, with their leather and velvet upholstery, it was a bit awkward. The seat was high and if it weren't for the iron step fastened to the side she would have had difficulty getting in by herself. Pulling up her skirt she stepped gingerly with her right foot and pulled on the ironwork of the seat until she popped up into the seat and took the reins from her father. Slapping the reins against the horse's back she headed for the village, watching the opposing ridge seemingly rise higher as she rode north, then turned east down through the dark alley of evergreens, bursting back into the sunlight again before the last downgrade as the Union Church steeple across the river pointed the way. She slowed the winded animal before she reached the mills, patted her hair to be sure it had not blown awry and assumed a sedate position in the seat.

It was with mixed emotions she crossed Elm Street and drove on down Main to the river. She was flushed and exhilarated from the ride, (she knew she shouldn't have driven so fast but had been carried away by the moment), but, also, she felt guilty about her feelings concerning the buggy. It was shame and embarrassment with which she struggled. The image she wished to project to the townspeople was that of a great successful actress, not a farm girl. Oh, well. Perhaps they would be saying, "Oh, look! There is Adelene Sullivan, the actress. She is still a home town girl and not above driving herself in an open buggy!" She had heard a remark in the past about the Sullivan girls being "a handsome lot but too uppity and taken with themselves, (but Lordy, good looking, I say)." Even in her discomfort she could see possible salvation in the situation.

Adelene pulled into the space by Keller's smithy and Mr. Page's carriage shop on Canal Street, and looping the reins tightly around the front handrail of the buggy she turned to the side to disembark from the rough chaise when a hand appeared, that of Mr. Page. "Let me help you, Miss Adelene," and as he helped her to the ground, "and how are you today?"

"I'm fine and dandy, Mr. Page."

"Is there anything I can do for you this morning?"

"Yes, may I leave my carriage here for a short time? I was just homesick for the Georges and thought I'd river gaze for awhile."

"Of course, Miss Addie. Take your time. I'm glad to see you back from that old city. Folks here have missed you. The literary club just isn't the same without your acting out the stories and not an event goes by someone doesn't say they wish you were here to sing for us. Take your time, Addie. Take your time."

Glancing up the hill to watch for traffic she made her way to the bridge crossing the St. George. Standing on the raised wooden edge that held the rail she flattened herself against one of the sections that made the pointed bracing and held on tightly with both hands. The river rushed over the falls, dropping twelve feet except for the controlled stream that rushed down the sluice to the gristmill. Off to the right the section of the old canal that hadn't been filled was growing cattails. She wondered if the young people still skated there in the winter. Looking on down river from the bridge she blocked from her mind the noisy grinding of the grist mill, the clanging of the smithy at his forge, the sawing and pounding of the coopers working in the stave mill—all the hustle and bustle of the town—the squeaking wagon wheels and plunking of sawed lumber being loaded on carts drawn by impatient horses on the East side of the river, blocking out even the shouts and whip cracking of anxious men urging reluctant oxen to move their heavy loads of barrels and buckets of whitewash amid sounds of happy children splashing in the shallows upstream.

Adelene looked beyond the town and its confusion to the fullness of the rushing water beyond the bridge. The restless river bounced exuberantly towards the sea twenty miles beyond, searching for the incoming tide where it would finally copulate with the ocean, mingling fluids in joyous ecstasy as lovers meeting in the night. She could hardly wait to be with Francis again!

Suddenly she felt a black fly at the corner of her eye and she quickly did away with it, bringing her back from her reverie to the working world. She stepped back and ran her hand along the rail, then remembered she would get splinters so she smoothed her dress, patted the loose hair that had blown from the pins while she had been caught in the moist updraft from the falls and returned to her carriage. Mr. Page helped her gain her seat and she turned the horse and headed home. Turning up Elm Street she reined in at Lottie Young's millinery shop across the street from S. J. Gushee's home and tied Old Jim to the small elm by the road.

Knocking and calling at the same time she opened the door with its tinkling bell that announced to Lottie that a customer had arrived. Stepping inside she could smell fresh bread baking in the kitchen but she waited in the front room that housed the shop. Momentarily, Lottie herself appeared in the doorway.

"Land sakes, alive! It's you, Adelene, back from New York City! Here, you are, the famous Estelle Syloane, right here in my shop! Take a seat and tell me all you've been up to!"

(Well, Adelene wouldn't tell it all, they'd know soon enough).

"Lottie, I thought I'd catch you up on a few things I've noticed.

Styles seem to be changing. The bustles are giving way to flared skirts, but of course, corsets are still in vogue. The important change, which I thought you might be interested in, is in the bonnets. Hats are beginning to be fashioned with large brims that hold flowers and ornamental feathers. The use of hatpins is quite popular, rods with permanent bobs on one end and a screw bob on the other for fastening it through the hat and the pinned hair underneath. The hairstyles are quite puffy so the pins are long. I believe that in spite of the pins one will be forced to be constantly on guard to hold to the hat in any stir of air."

"And the dresses, Adelene, are they still to the floor in New York?"

"Oh, yes, of course, Lottie, though for evening low necklines are becoming the rage. With the hair puffed and pinned and the low open bodice, more attention is being paid to jewelry."

"My land, Adelene. Don't the men get wild when they see shoulders and bosoms exposed?"

"No, Lottie. They may feel wild inside but most are able to respect a lady when they see one. When we were all covered from head to toe they were intrigued by the show of an ankle. It's all in their heads. I aim to dress as I please and they can just control themselves or take any punishment I care to mete. Women must learn to stand up for their rights, we've been pushed around for too long. We should be able to vote, to plan our own actions and not yield to just any rule men care to impose on us. Someday it will happen, Lottie, someday."

"Oh, Adelene, I hope so, but remember, not all women are as brave as you. If you lead many will follow, but do not blame the faint of heart. They fear for their keeping and that of their children."

"I know, Lottie, but even if we never see equality, it will come someday, and talking about it is the beginning. When that day comes, there will be punishment for men who abuse women and take advantage of them. Now I must go or Mama will worry. When I am far away she has me out of her mind but when I am home I become her child again."

Giving Lottie a hug she hurried down the steps and returned to continue her journey home, up Elm Street, past the Baptist church with its bell tower, left at Belfast Turn and left again at the crossroads. It was easier on Old Jim than the road straight up to the ridge from town. This way she could view the whole valley; the farms, the fields where she roamed throughout her childhood, the church spires and the glistening Sennebec.

Clucking her tongue she hurried Jim over the top of the ledge based rise where the blueberries were crowding the road, their milky blooms just beginning to bud, waxy bells shaking in the hilltop breeze; down the dip in the road, the pathway lined with spruce trees and birches that had fought off the winter cold without snapping their tender trunks, past the "hunting acres" on the right where the multiple springs overflowed. She remembered how she wished years ago that they had been dug out and combined and made into a large pool. She had imagined dipping in it at night naked. She was going to call it "Naked Lady Pool." Throwing her head back she laughed loudly, partly from remembering the folly of her youth and partly from the sheer happiness that the day had brought.

June 26, 1894

My Darling,

Sometimes in the secret darkness of the night I feel your touch, tracing the curve of my cheek with your fingertip, the tender way you stroke my hair and the familiar way you caress my body, teasing my skin and thrilling my

heart. Then as I slip softly into a comforting sleep I no longer
feel lonely. The stillness in my soul follows me to my waking
hours and the smile with which I greet each new day is born
from the love we share.

'Til then, I send my love,

"A"

Adelene couldn't write to Francis as often as she wished. The
news of the court proceedings in June reached Appleton and so she
remained cloistered on the ridge to avoid controversy. She was not
afraid of confrontation but avoiding it was not only easier for her, but
the less said, the better, for her parents' sake. The Merrifields had
sputtered for awhile, but the presence of Adelene on Appleton ridge
for her usual extended summer visit seemed to bear witness to her
innocence, or at least a suspicion of the possibility of her innocence.
She did not have any intention of giving credence to any suggestion of
wrongdoing by being defensive. The only time she contacted Francis
through July was when she rode the stage to Camden to spend a few
days with friends at Norembega. While in Camden she posted her
letter with no return address. Lonely as she was, she refused to
jeopardize her reputation or his by doing anything to confirm gossip.

Camden's new block was a great improvement. Sad as it was when
a town had a serious fire, the rebuilding was usually more attractive
and functional than before. The new brick buildings were charming
and modern, with well-crafted masonry, and the shops and businesses
establishing themselves had quickly become comfortable with a settled
look as though they had always been there. Yes, Camden was
modernized, and the summer crowd was fully utilizing the new
shopping opportunities, to the delight of the townspeople.

The trip to Camden and the luxury afforded at Norembega
made Adelene miss the similar comforts she enjoyed in New York.

She loved the farmhouse on the ridge, but how she would love to have a carefully designed mansion reminiscent of Norembega, perhaps not as large, but on the same order.

She and her friends had taken the ride to the Mt. Battie Hotel for lunch. It was quite pleasant with the windows facing East and a marvelous view of the ocean and Negro Island, which gave thought as to whether the best attributes of both buildings could be combined. She decided to give it more thought when she had time, perhaps on her trip back to New York. Oh, would August never come?

It was the second week of August when the letter came. Ellen handed it to her with a look of some consternation. Adelene turned it over in her hand. It was not Francis' seal and the letter looked as though it had been opened, sort of frayed around the wax seal, and a moment of panic passed through her. She slid it in her pocket and casually left the room, climbed the stairs and sat on the edge of her bed. Taking the letter from her pocket she slipped her thumbnail under the seal and opened it.

August 10, 1894

Dear Adelene,

Manager George H. Brennan wishes you to return to New York as soon as possible. The competition for the part you wished to play has been eliminated from the company. Although her contract will not be legally terminated until December, it is desired that you fill the position from this date forward. Your lodging here is secured until that time you might wish to make other arrangements.

Yours truly,

Francis J. Oakes

She didn't know if she was laughing or crying. How clever of Francis. It no longer mattered if someone had tampered with her mail. She should have known that he would protect her reputation and dignity with a letter of secret meaning.

Rushing downstairs she flung the letter on the table. "Mama! Mama! I have the part! I must pack and leave as soon as possible. I love you, I love you, but I must return to New York immediately! You may read this, but I must pack my things. I'll take the mail stage to Union and catch the train from Rockland. Oh, I hate the new horseless carriages, but there are times I wish one were available! Oh, Mama, I'm so happy!

She left the letter on the table, although she would rather have clutched it to her heart until she was in his arms again, but if any of the Merrifields questioned her mother the seemingly innocent letter would offer an explanation, and Ellen deserved some protection from gossip. If things could remain quiet until they were married, well, postdated criticism would just be old news.

Adelene could hardly pack with any organization. She and Francis would be able to marry in December. "Merry Christmas to Adelene, Merry Christmas."

Ellen was amazed that a part in a play could mean so much to her daughter but she had resigned herself to Adelene's choice of a career. One raised children to be strong enough to leave the nest, but in Adelene's case perhaps they had overdone the effort.

CHAPTER 10

It wasn't exactly the fulfillment of any dream she had ever had of the perfect wedding. Actually, she had never contemplated herself having any wedding at all, that is, not until she met Francis. He had seemed so out of reach that fantasizing about a wedding would have been a waste of time, or so she thought. No white silk gown, no demure veil, not even a bouquet of flowers, but Adelene was not disappointed. She could do without the crepe de Chene, the veil of tulle and the beaming bridesmaids. She had seen too many brides wearing the white gown of purity making a farce of the ritual. She had married the man she loved and it would hit the New York papers by morning and in Maine by the following weekend. She would write her mother and put the matter as simply as she could. There would be no details, only that she and Francis had fallen in love and were married. The Camden Herald was sure to reprint whatever the Times reported, and perhaps add some homilies of its own, but a reassurance from Adelene along with a promise that she and Francis would visit in the early summer should have a calming effect on the family. After the initial shock her mother would be pleased that she had been married at the Church of Holy Innocents and that Adelene had fulfilled her mother's wish that she be married and "taken care of." As for the gossipmongers, they could just go to Hell!

CHAPTER 11

1895

The winter season at the theater proved to be Adelene's best. She was no longer an understudy for the part of Lady Adele Grey in Rosedale, but Lady Adele herself. Following that run she was selected to play Queen Gertrude in "Hamlet." Her stage career was blossoming and her life with Francis was all she could have dreamed. The anticipation of the trip to Maine in the spring kept her heart light and her spirits high. She was sure any doubts her parents held over her marriage would be dispelled when they came to know her husband. As sure as she was that the events of the past as reported in the news had tainted their feelings toward him, she was equally sure they would accept him when they knew him better. After all, hadn't he charmed her, a tough-minded, career bound Yankee with no thoughts of letting any man into her life? Until they were actually on their way to Maine she would bask in the glow of his love and her success on the stage. She had read some reports that her looks, clothes and jewels far outweighed her talent, but she brushed it all aside. They could put her clothes and jewels on a horse and just see if it could play her part!

Adelene was undaunted. Life could not be better than it was at this time and she planned to enjoy every minute of it. And now Francis had planned a Valentine party. His teasing that he had invited a special guest pleased and intrigued her. He vowed that he would not reveal the name of the special guest; that she would have to wait until the party on February fourteenth. She loved every minute of the mystery, begging and plaguing him, loving and cajoling him, but he was not to be bribed in any way, making it even more exciting for Adelene. Perhaps it was some congressman, or even a princess. No, Francis would not invite a female that might compete for attention with Adelene. It must be a man! Perhaps Mr. McKinley! He was running for the presidency and it would be a great opportunity for him to meet many of New York's elite—it was a possibility.

"Alice! Alice! We must polish all the silver and be sure everything is perfect for the Valentine's party. Come, Dear, help me with the menu. Francis will order the drink so we have only the buffet to plan."

Sitting at the drawing room table Adelene worked intently on a design for the menu, entertwining an "A" and an "F". Making an inkblot, she crumpled the paper and threw it in the trash basket and started over, this time with the food items themselves.

Ginger cookies with New York white cheddar slices—

"Alice, what should we serve to an unknown guest? I don't want to offend anyone and I don't want to embarrass Francis. It would be terrible if I gave the wrongful impression that I came from ill breeding."

"I don't know, Miss Adelene, but I think I would serve something safe, nothing too fancy that could cause an objection. I think I would serve home style cooking."

"What a wonderful idea! I think venison stew as close to my mother's as we can make it. I have her recipe.—And many small corn muffins, dainty, not farm style, with plenty of fresh churned butter to go with them. I think shredded cabbage and carrots with raisins in oil and egg dressing spiced with vinegar,—and dill pickles, the smallest we can find, along with sweet gherkins, too. Yes, Alice, we will serve a Maine menu, so everyone will know we Northerners know how to serve a tasty meal. For dessert we will bake a huge chocolate cake in the shape of a heart, iced with fluffy egg white icing and decorated with brandied cherries on top. I would also like a hundred small chocolate hearts baked and iced the same, one for each guest to take home. It always makes a good impression if visitors can take some of the party with them. Oh, Alice, it is going to be a great success, I can just feel it in my bones! And don't forget, vanilla ice cream must be churned early in the afternoon so it can be packed to ripen until it is served. Find Lulie Ufford's recipe and use that. It is the best ever made. I can hardly wait. It will be the best party ever and I do hope Francis will be pleased!"

Adelene placed the list in Alice's capable hands knowing she would see that all was carried out and ran up the stairs to her closet. St. Valentine's Day was three weeks away so she had plenty of time—

Opening the wardrobe door she ran her hands over the shoulders of the gowns hanging inside. She stopped at a green velvet gown with fox fur trim,-no-the style was right but not the color. She would call her dressmaker to bring samples and pay for a rush on an outfit for this special occasion. She had forsaken any party following their wedding to keep the gossip under control, but this was a new year, she was the mistress of the house, and this would be her debut as hostess of the Oakes household.

CHAPTER 12

With great anticipation Adelene donned the new gown her dressmaker had finished only the previous day. She had chosen a deep sapphire blue velvet from the samples she had been shown, and the gown was a perfect backdrop for the diamond and sapphire necklace and earring set Francis had given her at Christmas, diamonds and sapphires that sparkled under the lights and reflected in her eyes.

Adelene had been completely surprised upon meeting their special guest, Mr. William Cody. Curtseying deeply upon the introduction, she wondered if he would remember her from his trip to Maine years ago.

"Mrs. Oakes, you look very familiar to me. I rarely forget such a lovely face as yours. Haven't we met?"

"Well, yes. Mr. Cody. I attended your show in West Appleton some years ago. I am deeply flattered that you remember me."

Francis, entering the conversation, chided, "I assume you found some differences in the language of the Northeasterners compared to the western part of the country."

"Yes, Mr. Oakes, but I am becoming more familiar with it. I try to make a trip north every few years to visit my good friend William McLain. We were army buddies in the war and he is very hospitable to my troupe on our visits there. The lodgings at the stage station are very comfortable and we enjoy performing for the local townspeople. Of course drinking from a "tumbler" and having our bacon fried in a "spider" gave us some concern until we sorted out the meaning. Whatever the language, we were rather surprised that we did not find Maine backward in any way. The men seem schooled in the latest farming and cattle raising methods available, and the women dress in the most stylish manner, especially Miss Sullivan, ah, Mrs. Oakes, today, as when we first met in McLain's Mills. By the way, I hope you don't mind. A few Westerners from my troupe tagged along with me tonight. I am never sure if Easterners hold the same customs as we from the West. I didn't wish to impose, but they were anxious to see what the elite in New York have to offer. This is not the hoedown, chow-down affair to which we are accustomed. I sincerely hope we have not overstepped our welcome."

"Not at all, not at all, Francis declared, but Adelene detected a slight stiffness in the response as he glanced toward the hallway where several rough looking men were giving their coats to a flustered Alice. Adelene knew there would be plenty of food, so she remained calm. Mr. Cody introduced them and they seemed a friendly bunch, but Francis was still not as comfortable a host as he might have been.

They all drifted toward the dining room where she smilingly accepted the well-earned complements on the food, the wine, and especially the cream filled chocolate cake.

Soon the orchestra began playing familiar waltzes and the host and hostess took the floor to begin the dancing.

"Francis, tell me again the name of the blond man over there smiling at all the women."

"Adelene, just keep your eyes to yourself and ignore him. He is one of the ruffians that invited themselves. I can't stand to have you looking at him. He's just some cowhand from out West named Cassidy and he's probably a robber having a fling and looking to seduce unsuspecting ladies such as yourself."

"He doesn't look like a robber, more like a gentleman gambler, and you should speak for yourself, Francis. I saw your eyes unlacing the corsets of that woman "Hedda" that he and his friends brought with them."

Ignoring the dig, Francis countered with, "They may be a handsome bunch, but trying to mix with cultured folk is quite disgusting. They'll be back out West robbing trains within the month and we'll never see them again, and I say, good riddance. It wouldn't surprise me if they went all the way to South America."

"Oh, Francis, forget I mentioned them. I know having uninvited guests has upset you and my curiosity has added to the stress. Please hold me close. I want everyone to know how much you love me. Forgive me if I sometimes feel you have a roving eye."

"Adelene, looking is not doing."

"But the Holy Bible says, "if you've thought it, you've done it.""

"For pity sake, Adelene, stop badgering me with your religious talk. You weren't completely innocent when I was still married to Louella, so let's not speak of innocence or guilt. Just drop it."

Adelene noticed the tightness in his body as they continued their whirl about the floor. She knew they were a handsome couple, with his military bearing, and her own firmly laced waist that his hand easily spanned at the small of her back. Her thick auburn hair was piled in a smooth hive with a braided bun at the top. Yes, they were a fashionable pair, but she felt somehow insecure, a feeling to which she was unaccustomed, and it did not feel good.

As the music ended they gently applauded the other dancers that had joined in the waltz and she reached for his hand as they walked from the floor, but somehow didn't connect. Had he purposely withheld his hand or was it just that he hadn't noticed her movement to place her hand in his?

A strange foreboding crept upon her. Imagination, it must be imagination. She had spoken to him in an accusatory manner and she was very sorry. She had forgotten how easily careless words can hurt. She was determined not to become one of those suspicious wives who eventually destroyed their marriages with accusations and wild imaginings. Besides, she had always kept or left whatever she wanted by her own strong will.

Adelene smiled serenely and stepped into the hall and wandered down to the bathroom. She and Francis had never had words before and she had not been prepared. She had forgotten for a few moments that he was, after all, a man and he would "look," but would not understand her doing the same. She would be more careful in the future. At least, he hadn't thrown her friendship with Randolph, or his fellow musician, Albert Soler, in her face. Albert was much better looking than any of the evening's guests, and far more charming, but she had not been tempted to stray. Her love for Francis was too complete, but yes, she would be more careful from now on.

CHAPTER 13

At breakfast the following morning Adelene was determined to relieve the tension between them that she had felt the night before. The coffee was aromatic, the blueberry muffins crusty and sweet, almost as tasty as those her mother made from fresh berries from the field. Canned blueberries were second best but this morning the muffins were especially delicious.

"Francis, Mama and Papa love the addition to the house on the ridge, but I feel a summer home with more space and comfort would be most enjoyable.

"Whatever you want, Adelene."

"Oh, Francis, you don't mean that!"

"Whatever you want, Adelene."

"Really, Francis?"

She rose and walked about the table. Standing behind his chair she placed her arms around his neck in a fond embrace, resting her cheek against his dark head.

"That's what I said. Adelene, whatever you want."

She flushed with excitement. Knowing all the tension of the previous evening had disappeared by the grin on his face, she had never loved him more. Not just because he was giving her whatever she desired, but because she knew they both understood that their love was so precious that they should never let anyone or anything come between them. "Oh, Francis, may I call an architect today and discuss my ideas? Oh, please may I?"

"Adelene, put on paper what you have in mind and let me look at it, then we will call someone and have the plans drawn up. Of course, we could build a house in the valley and paint the roof with big letters in red "Oakes Dye Works," and it might bring in enough business to pay for everything you want."

"Francis, you are teasing me. You know what I want and where I want it. I just have to take care of Mama and Papa. I want them comfortable in their old age. Papa has worked so hard and he's so honest and good. I've always dreamed of a lovely home for Mama. Dr. Gushee says Papa's heart is getting tired. They'll be fine for now with the new rooms, but I do want to get the plans ready soon."

"Adelene, you know I can't deny you anything. I'll call Mr. Fisher today and set up a meeting to discuss plans. Mind you, nothing will be definite until we go to Maine this summer and discuss this with your parents.—But, Adelene, try to keep it under twenty rooms."

In a small voice with a tease in her eye she answered, "Twenty-one?"

"Very well, my love, but try to be reasonable. You are inclined to extravagance, you know. Just try to incorporate the addition already in place. Let's not go completely crazy."

"Oh, Francis! A water tower! Mama will have running water, inside toilets, many bedrooms like Norumbega, porticos like the Mt. Battie Hotel, and a Gothic design like Mr. Clemmons new house in Hartford! Oh, I can hardly wait!"

"Francis began to laugh. All right, Adelene, you can have your summer home, but let's see what Mr. Fisher has to say. There may be a problem building a large house on a rocky ridge like Appleton's. Just write it all up and we will look over your plans."

Adelene was excited. Her apprehension of the night before melted away in the warmth of the moment. "Her plans! She would be allowed to make HER plans!" She beamed with excitement as Francis turned to her, suddenly rose and picked her up and carried her to the bedroom. He was very late for work that day.

CHAPTER 14

Dew sparkled on the grass, glistening in the rising sun. No wonder Adelene loved this place. The crisp, clean air breezed through the bedroom window, gently fluttering the ruffled curtains throughout the night, making sleep the renewing balm it should always be. Somehow the breakfast cooking smelled more tantalizing as the aroma drifted from the kitchen to their sleeping quarters.

Francis gazed down at Adelene's serene countenance and watched her gentle breathing as she slept. He was amazed that she had accomplished all she had in her life. It was no small feat to leave a tiny village in these hills and make a mark, as she well had, in the New York theatrical world. Yes, his lady was some lady indeed!

Quietly he slipped from the covers and silently dressed, carried his shoes in his hand and descended the stairs to where Ellen was preparing the morning meal in the kitchen. She had just retrieved hot biscuits from the oven and placed them on the back of the black iron kitchen range when she spied him in the doorway standing on one foot putting on his shoe.

"Come in, come in, take a seat before you fall and bust yerself," Ellen admonished him. Obediently, he sat himself at the table and she poured him a cup of coffee, plunked a small pitcher of cream beside the sugar bowl, then returned to the stove where she turned some fresh sausage over in the iron spider, the fat making a hiss as the uncooked side splattered down in the pan.

Francis kept eyeing the biscuits, and Ellen, watching from the corner of her eye, reached over, cut the crusty corner one from the lot, placed it on a saucer with a knife on the side, sat it before him and shoved the butter plate across the table, then returned to the sausage business. Francis paused a moment, poured cream in his coffee, then opened the biscuit and put a lump of butter on each half. Taking a bite, he closed his eyes, tilted back his head, chewed a couple of times, savored it, and then swallowed. To Ellen's delight he repeated the action until the biscuit was gone, then took a few sips of the coffee and sat silently. By then she had finished the sausage and had eggs ready, put a healthy serving on a plate with another biscuit and put it before him. Francis dove in and finished off the breakfast while Ellen busied around the kitchen. "Well," she thought, "At least he has a healthy appetite." Perhaps she would accept this man as a son-in-law after all. Anyone that appreciated her cooking couldn't be all bad.

Francis had not spoken until now and he felt more relaxed on a full stomach. "Mrs. Sullivan, that is by far the best breakfast I have ever eaten. It will be difficult for you to get rid of me if you continue feeding me like this. New York food is never this fresh or this well prepared. My cook does her best, but she would blush with shame in the presence of your cooking."

Ellen blushed under the unexpected praise and decided that perhaps she could tolerate her daughter's husband in time. Surely all the gossip she had heard could not be true. One had to make up one's own mind on the facts presented, and although she had known Francis was wealthy, she hadn't expected him to be as youthful and charming. Yes, perhaps Adelene had made a good choice after all.

"If you will excuse me, I would like to take a short stroll and stretch my legs a little. Trains and buggy rides can cramp one in several days journey. The comfort of your guest quarters went a long way to rest these bones, but a short walk would settle the excellent breakfast as well."

"By all means," Ellen replied. "Adelene will soon be down and we will be chatting away and catching up on the news of the past winter. I'm sure the morning air and the birds singing will be more to yer liking, but here, take yer cup of coffee with ye."

Francis rose and walked to the front porch. Dew sparkled on the grass across the road, glistening in the rising sun. Not only was the quiet of the ridge relaxing after the hustle and bustle of the city, there was something new and intriguing peaking his interest every minute.

He thought he saw movement in the bushes that crowded the rock wall, then nothing. Taking a sip of his coffee he spied movement again in the grasses and weeds by the road bank. He stood perfectly still, not even breathing for a moment, and soon a dark nose appeared, then the full body of a large red fox. The tracings on its face were perfectly symmetrical, the full sleek coat on a slender body told him it was a female, and her gaunt sides that she had only recently emptied her womb of kits. Tentatively she crouched, gazing quickly back and forth, then began a fast lope down the road to the North, her full, darkly furred tail trailing just off the ground. Obviously, she was hunting rodents, or perhaps she smelled the chickens in the coop behind the house. But she was a hunter, needing sustenance to feed her family, and so she would not venture to a coop as long as she could find prey in the wild. She was so beautiful she almost took his breath away. Was this place magical? He had heard a strange cry in the night and wondered what the musical eerie bark had been, and now he knew—hungry kits. Were creatures of more extraordinary beauty bred here than elsewhere? He could see a comparison between Adelene and the feline fox. Both of them were beautiful, but more than looks, wily and wild, and completely in control of their own separate destinies.

Francis set his empty cup on the wooden porch rail and walked south and looked across the land to the Sennebec. He could see another small lake in the distance. This was the perfect place for Adelene's summer house to be built. He would purchase more acreage, and contact Mr. Fisher. The Sullivan farmhouse could be turned and added to the main building, keeping the Sullivans in familiar surroundings in their later years, and since Adelene was planning such a spacious house, there could be rooms at their disposal should they desire them. Yes, Adelene could have her mansion, and selfishly, he was pleased with the thought of spending more time in Maine than he had anticipated.

CHAPTER 15

Francis Oakes remained at the Sullivan home for three weeks. He needed to attend his concerns at the Oakes Manufacturing Company and also have a serious meeting with Adam Fisher, preventing him from a longer stay. The transfer of property ownership in Maine had gone well and Adelene was elated. As they embraced upon his leaving, Francis promised to return in late August for a few days and escort her back home to New York. She didn't feel an escort was necessary but Francis insisted that he return to accompany her. The stony mountain called "Appleton Ridge" presented some problems, not insurmountable, but possibly expensive. After meeting Adelene's family and with the fondness he now held for them, (especially for Ellen), he felt enlarging the Sullivan home a project well worthwhile. He planned to meet with the architect as soon as possible to discuss the problems to be considered, as well as Adelene's wishes.

Taking the stage to Union and then boarding the train heading south, he was able to secure a "Pioneer" out of Boston, the sleeping car bringing him into New York rested and ready to tackle work at his chemical company. It was several days before he had an opportunity to call Mr. Fisher, and the earliest available appointment he could obtain was the first of September.

Francis was somewhat relieved. The scheduling of the conference a month away gave him time to make the promised return trip to Maine. It also gave him time to give the project more thought which might prevent any mistakes made from quick decisions, and the wait would allow Adelene to attend the conference. She might be a handful with her exuberance over the prospective building, but it would prevent any chance of making plans to which she might object. Aside from all that, the trip from Maine to New York had not been unpleasant, and he couldn't think of anything more delightful than fetching his wife and spending the night with her in the privacy of the Pioneer sleeping car. The small house of the Sullivans hardly allowed them the privacy they enjoyed at home, and the clanging and banging of the train on its tracks would beat out a rhythm he could accept. The time could not pass quickly enough for Francis, so he buried himself in the business of running his company.

CHAPTER 16

Daniel Sullivan arose early the morning of Francis Oakes return to Appleton Ridge. Ellen had not yet stirred from her slumber. The air had that cool late summer morning moisture that would soon be burning off when the sun popped over Moody Mountain. The morning fairly begged for summer to end. This was the time of year to absorb some of the last warm rays of the season. Ellen would soon begin her day, preparing the end-of-harvest fruit for canning. He must decide which of the hogs to slaughter and see that the wood was stacked in ample supply by the smokehouse. It would take quite a bundle to supply the smoke to preserve their winter's supply of ham. The squash had grown well, some over twenty pounds. Elmer Sprague had told him to plant Hubbard squash on the manure pile, and that's what he had done, more to humor Elmer than with any confidence that fruit would be produced. Elmer was a sharp young man, so Daniel had planted seeds as suggested, even though he felt sure they would burn up and fail to sprout, let alone, yield. But there they were, the best he had ever seen. He had washed them in the brook before he took them to Ellen, since she was inclined to be persnickety at times, (a trait she had seemingly passed on to Adelene), and she had been elated with the size and quality of the fruit.

There on the porch, leaning on the upright that held the overhead, Daniel breathed in the morning air and thought, "Autumn does have its rewards." The harvest was always joyful, and as the sugar maples turned gold and the white maples changed from red to russet, the golden birches dropped their coins to cover the last green blades of summer. One could almost hear the first howl of winter working it's way from the North. The honkers were already winging their way south, and he knew he should be working on preparations for the coming bad weather, but for now, he would just savor the morning. There were promises in the air, and the building of Adelene's house would start in early spring. With a chuckle he thought about how feisty she had become when he called her summer home her "Oakes Mansion." She had railed, "As long as I live it will be the Sullivan Mansion. When I am gone, they can call it anything they want, but for now, the name is "Sullivan"!!

He and Francis had both laughed, and then she started to giggle. "Well, Papa," she declared. "When I come back next summer I will bring you a black suit, a top hat and white gloves, like all the fancy men in New York City wear to the opera, and we will ride through town in a carriage, and the townspeople will say, "Oh, look," there goes Daniel Sullivan from the Sullivan Mansion, and with his lovely daughter, the actress, by his side!" "Won't that be fun Papa?"

Daniel had shaken his head,—that girl and her grandiose plans. What could anyone do but let her have her way? He recalled the time a moose had ambled through the pasture and was eating the flowers Adelene had tied in bunches to the fence, drying them to use as decoration for her bonnets. She had flung a piece of stove wood at it, hollering, "Papa! Come kill it!" And at the moose, "I'll eat you, I'll eat you for supper, you son of a bitch!"

"Papa! Papa!"

Daniel sighed. Adelene hadn't changed a lot. She could go from sweetness and light to blazing anger in seconds. It made him wonder. Was the real Adelene the darling she portrayed most of the time, or was that an act? Over the years he had stopped fretting over Adelene's ability to take care of herself. When a crisis or difficulty arose she would either handle it her own way or find someone who would. Yes, Addie was not as fragile as she looked. She had strength of character underneath that tender exterior that would serve her well. He recalled that when she was only twenty, Ulysses S. Grant had visited Maine and they said Grant took North

Haven just like he took Richmond, but with charm rather than force. She had been upset and frustrated that she was unable to meet the celebrated General and President due to having the distemper, but being indisposed was not the only reason she didn't attend his celebrated arrival and reception. She also did not wish to be seen in her less than glowing condition. She had announced to the family that a future actress should only be present at gala functions when she was at her best, and that week she had certainly been at her worst. "Hang it," she had declared, "When I am a famous actress I will send him tickets to a performance along with my regrets at having been unable to attend his reception at the time of his visit to Rockland." It was his fault, she had audaciously decided, for coming at the wrong time, but she would make it up to him someday.—Now how could a father worry about a girl like that being able to take care of herself?

Adelene was his baby, but she was grown and married now, and she wanted to build on to his house. She said she wanted him and Ellen to be comfortable, but the two rooms already added were plenty for them. He knew it was more for her personal comfort and prestige, but whatever she wanted was fine with him. If her rich husband wanted to fulfill Adelene's ostentatious plans, he saw no reason to thwart them. He realized his life was slowly ebbing, and if building a mansion made his daughter happy he would rejoice in her desires. Life is for the living, he surmised, and he had lived his. Now Addie must live hers.

CHAPTER 17

September, 1895, New York City

Francis wondered how Mr. Fisher would react to doing business involving a woman, especially a very opinionated one. Francis was accustomed to Adelene's ways, but he was also accustomed to dealing with many different types of personalities through his business contacts. Adelene had certainly prepared a pleasant atmosphere for the meeting. Gleaming silver tea service filled with choice of tea or coffee, iced raisin buns and tiny muffins filled with blueberries, fresh country butter pressed into small buttons with circles of leaves imprinted on the tops, bowls of hazelnuts and mints and pitchers of cream, along with honey and sugar for sweetening.

He observed Mr. Fisher's obvious pleasure as they consumed the elegant mid-morning repast, and he was sure the architect was impressed with Adelene's show of domesticity, probably a surprise since she was better known as an actress than a hostess. They soon settled down to business and Mr. Fisher loosened the ribbon on the roll of plans he had brought with him.

"I appreciate the information you sent, Francis. Knowing in advance what problems we might encounter were of great value."

"I didn't expect you to have anything ready at this meeting—may I call you "Adam?""

"Of course, Francis. I always make an attempt to have drawings ready for inspection at a primary conference. It enables me to have a base from which to make any minor changes you might desire. See here, I have designed a country cottage that should be comfortable on a ridge such as you describe. It is built of logs we can obtain at a very reasonable price in that area. The house is built all one story, so that it will lie low and be unobtrusive in the surrounding area. It will rest snugly on the hill, keeping it out of the path of winter wind. I'm sure it will be all you desire."

"Adam, I think you have the wrong impression of our tastes. Maine is farming country but that does not mean the populace is bourgeois. The community is quite sophisticated, and my wife desires a summer home befitting both the social ideals we hold here and the comforts to which she is accustomed." Turning to Adelene, Francis, (with a wink that only she could see), calmly said, "Darling, please show Mr. Fisher your drawings, and don't forget your written requests."

A look of consternation passed over Adam Fisher's face. His jaw tightened as he leaned over the desk where Adelene was spreading out her papers. Francis turned his back, retrieved a cigar from the humidor on the stand by his easy chair, removed a straw from the hearth broom and leaned over the fireplace. Lighting the straw he continued to face the fireplace as he lit the stogie, took a few puffs, and then rested his back against the carved mantle. This was going to be fun. It was easy to see Mr. Adam Fisher was not pleased to find his plans were not going to be accepted, and Addie's elaborate plans were going to knock him for a loop. He hoped he could keep a straight face. Most men were not accustomed to women having opinions on architecture, let alone having the wherewithal to carry them out.

"Here is what I have planned. I've written it all down and drawn a diagram. Of course, I'm not a professional draftsman, but I think you will be able to accommodate my wishes."

"Mrs. Oakes, I will do all I can to conform to your desires, but I do have a reputation to uphold."

"You will use these plans within your design if you want this job. I am very particular that my mother and father be comfortable. They are accustomed to their farmhouse and I do not want it changed. It must be a part of the mansion. Francis, please explain to Mr. Fisher why the original house must be incorporated into the design."

"As you can see, my wife if very determined. I will pay what you ask, but I insist that my wife be satisfied with this house and all the outbuildings she requests."

Adelene continued her explanation of her plans with—"and I must have three floors. The top floor should have a linen room as well as servants' quarters, the second floor must have rooms for my mother and father. I need a bathroom on every floor, complete with porcelain bathtubs, pedestal sinks and commodes. I think you would do well to build the carriage house right away, that carpenters and masons might use the upstairs quarters made for livery persons while the house is being built. I'm sure you realize a cistern needs to be built in the basement to make it possible to pump water to all floors. Later you can put in a water tower to facilitate gravity feed. When you return I presume the new plans will follow these suggestions for Tudor styling. We do not want a country cottage. You are being hired to design a house more fitting to our station."

A very confused and somewhat deflated Adam Fisher replied, "Mrs. Oakes, I will study these requests and make sure the original farmhouse is part of the new dwelling, and I will find a way to blend it into the structure as gracefully as possible. I feel sure we can obtain an amicable result. It will take several weeks, Mr. Oakes, to incorporate your wife's ideas into the design, but I'm sure it can be done. I will work up a new diagram and present it to you in three weeks, along with a cost estimate."

"Very well. I look forward to that, Adam," and shaking hands, the architect went on his way. It did not escape Adelene that her hand had not been shaken, a slight she would not soon forget.

Francis had thoroughly enjoyed Mr. Fisher's first encounter with Adelene. She never failed to excite Francis, she was so full of life and ambition. She wanted to do everything, control everything, and he enjoyed indulging her. She was both a child and a woman, wanton and demanding yet capable and artistic. Her drawings and listings of requirements for her summer home were complete and well organized. She had a clear head for business as well as her professional talent. She was a woman to be admired as well as desired.

Reading the "Times" as was his habit over his morning coffee, the news of the progress on the assembly of the statue on Bedloe's Island gained his attention. He decided they should take a day of relaxing sightseeing and check out the work. It would make Adelene happy to be one of the first to tour the statue. He was sure a few dollars here and there would gain them access to the site, and his popularity as a New York businessman would not be a hindrance. Yes, they would be among the first to make the tour of the new monument. His wife's performance as an architect certainly deserved some sort of reward, and she usually enjoyed spectacular events. He would take her to the Statue of Liberty. If they planned to dedicate it sometime in the next year it would be nearly complete, except for the final touches and all the cleaning up and landscaping. The trip up the channel by boat, lunching on the deck in the cool September air would be just the thing! She enjoyed wearing furs, and crisp air seemed to stimulate her, probably because of living through frigid Maine winters for so many years. Yes, the day trip would be full of excitement!

CHAPTER 18

"The newspapers said thirty people could stand in the head, Francis," Adelene exclaimed. "They must have meant very skinny people." Pressed closely together they stood for a moment on the small landing at the very top, peering through one window after the next, from smaller to larger, then tapering to smaller again as they began their descent down the narrow winding stairs. She thoroughly enjoyed gazing through the windows of the crown, the shining city on the mainland beyond the glistening water of the harbor spread before her. What a marvelous gift from the French! She felt some plaque should be attached to such a great monument, some eloquent passage to welcome those entering the harbor. Maybe someday it would be done.

Francis took her hand as they walked toward the ramp to the ferry for the trip back to Manhattan. Suddenly a wave of nausea hit her and she nearly fainted. "Oh, no, not sea sickness! Please, God, don't let me be crude and vomit," she whispered.

Francis eased her onto a bench and held her hand until the urge to expel her lunch passed, the fresh sea air reviving her for the moment, then helped her to the ferry that was still docked at the slip. Pale and a bit unsteady, she clung to her husband's arm as they made the journey back to the pier on the waterfront where their carriage waited. She couldn't believe she could be so seasick from such a short voyage, but it had passed, and aside from the humiliation of becoming ill in public, she was fine. However, she would be glad to get back home and rest. It was time for her monthly curse and she shouldn't have laced her corset so tightly, but she had wanted to look her best in the event she was recognized. It was important to keep up appearances.

Adelene's days were peaceful. Her career was as fulfilling as was her all-consuming love for Francis. Pleasant days passed and then suddenly she felt very ill. It brought back the fear of her bout with the mysterious crippling sickness that had left her exhausted for months, the long hours of struggling to walk again and the panic she felt when she would awaken in the night that only Francis' tender touching could calm. Now she really was frightened. It was not the middle of the night, it was not a bad dream. She was ill and violently so. It was the same feeling she had suffered on the trip to Bedloe Island three weeks ago, only much worse. She barely made it to the bathroom in time for the return of what seemed to be all she had eaten for days. Alice heard her retching and was soon by her side, wiping her face with wet towels, and when the storm passed she helped her to her bed.

"Oh, Alice. I can't stand to think I must go through that awful illness again. I just can't bear it!"

"Bear it, Miss Adelene? You will bear it all right. As I look after your personal needs I have been expecting this, or rather, you are the one expecting. Your misery is long overdue. You carry a child for Francis!"

Now Adelene really felt faint, whether from the upheaval of her stomach or the shock of Alice's announcement she didn't know, but the tender manner in which Alice pulled a fresh sheet over her shocked body, (with a warm smile on her face), convinced Adelene it was true. A baby, and at her age!! It seemed impossible, but in her heart she knew it was true and her love for Francis welled up anew. She could scarcely contain herself she was so bursting with emotion.

Alice bustled about the room, laying out a fresh gown and underthings. "No more corsets for you, Miss Adelene, not until after the young one arrives. As soon as you feel stronger, bathe and wear this pink day gown. It will reflect color in your cheeks. You want to look your best tonight. This will be a special night for you and Francis."

"Oh, Alice, what would I do without you? You are so like my dear sister Sarah, who always cared for me." And whether to please herself or Alice or eventually Francis, she stirred and slowly rose to begin her toilette in preparation for the evening, pausing by the dresser where a tintype of Francis Junior looked steadily back at her. Resting her gaze on the smooth cheeks of the young man in the picture, she thought, "This is how Francis must have looked as a young man, before the war, before Eliza, before Louella." The slender build, dark wavy hair, a youthful lock having fallen carelessly across a smooth forehead, the same chiseled features as his father. The softness would disappear from his cheeks with maturity.

Adelene loved Francis' children, their exuberance, their love for one another, and she could sense what a wonderful mother Eliza must have been. Louella never seemed to have warmed to Francis' children, rather, she had usually ignored their presence. Adelene knew Louella had missed the pleasure of being part of their camaraderie, the camaraderie she herself now enjoyed since they all lived close to the home. She wondered where Louella was and if she were all right. No one had heard from her since the settlement, so she could only assume she was somewhere happily spending it all on her favorite drink. Poor Louella, no one to love her, no children of her own and she had turned her stepchildren away with her selfishness. Her name was never mentioned in New York or in Maine, not to her anyway. She hoped she was happy wherever she was.

Picking up the picture of Francis Junior she hugged it to her bosom. She hoped her son, (at least she had it in her mind that it would be a boy), looked like Francis and Francis Junior. It might be an old wives tale, but she had heard it said that the higher the passion at conception the more likely the infant would be male, and who ever had higher passion than she and Francis enjoyed? Yes, it would be a boy, and she would name him "Paul."

—1896—

In the moment of transformation, the journey from one world to the next, in total orgasmic glory, glowing, free from pain, free from the tie that held him to his mother, he struggled toward the light, as we all reach for the comforting light that releases us from earthly fetters, and a new life emerged. Paul Sullivan Oakes entered the world and was placed in the loving arms of his mother.

CHAPTER 19

Motherhood was frightening. The children Adelene had been in contact with through her teaching in Maine were all at least five years old, but this tiny being looked so fragile it took time to become accustomed to his size, his needs, his dependency. For weeks she remained on the very edge of hysteria. If it hadn't been for Alice she would have given in to tears and become a blubbering, slobbering fool.

By the time Paul was a month old she decided she could handle things. Any thought of returning to the stage was out of the question. If Barney Oldfield could switch from racing bicycles to racing motorcars, she could become a calm and loving mother. The loving part was easy. As she gained confidence Paul became a laughing, gurgling healthy little being, absorbing all of Addie's time and attention. His adoring father spent evenings with them both, beaming with pride as his wife sang sweetly to this child of his later years, a living storybook family.

Spring was rolling quickly into summer and Adelene was anxious to see how the summerhouse was progressing. Mr. Fisher had drawn up marvelous plans, with all her requests considered. He had even found a builder in Rockland he felt confident could handle the job, having made the trip to Maine himself to find the right contractor, and felt Mr. Goulding was the man for the job. He had originally thought perhaps the locals might be unable to handle the work from his drawings, but found their ability surprising. Making several visits to the site, he was pleased to report to Francis that all was going well, and the project should be completed in two years.

As for Addie, she was anxious to show off her darling Paul to her parents. She could barely contain herself thinking about seeing her son in his grandmother's arms.

July, 1896

It had seemed an eternity, waiting for Francis to have the work at the manufacturing company caught up and running smoothly, so that he would feel comfortable in leaving it with the foreman in charge. Adelene knew it had been wise to wait until Paul was four months old before taking him on a trip. Francis had wanted her to bring a wet nurse for the child but Adelene insisted on caring for him and feeding him herself. If God hadn't planned for her to feed him he wouldn't have given her such ample breasts, she reasoned. Sometimes she thought Francis was jealous of the time she spent with little Paul. Perhaps she was taking motherhood too seriously but she never dreamed she would ever be a mother or that being one would bring her so much pleasure. Her pleasure was further heightened by the joy she saw in her father's eyes as he took the baby in his arms, walked to the porch and from there across the road to the higher ground above the house.

Daniel looked back at the house. It was so changed. The familiar farmhouse had been turned and was now just an addition to the large mansion being built. The contractors had blasted a cellar from the solid ridge rock and upon that base the mansion was quickly taking shape. He wondered if he would live to see it completed. The livery stable and the apartments above it were as fine as any home, with its windows looking down on the valley and the polished hardwood floors fit for any gentleman, let alone the hired livery hands for which it had been built.

Surveying the land with a glance, Daniel then held the baby high in the air. Little Paul gurgled and cooed with delight. "Pay attention, young man," Daniel exhorted. "You see my little house becoming smaller and smaller beside that great building of your Ma's. She's a little above her raisin', but that's all right. All things come to an end to make way for new beginnings, and you, my boy, were born into a different world from mine. Just remember, this is where you came from and even though I'll soon be gone from this earth, this is your heritage. You may be an Oakes, but you are also an Irishman and a Mainer, and this ridge is part of you."

Paul had looked wide eyed and serious as his grandfather spoke, until Daniel gave him a little toss and the baby's blue eyes sparkled and he chortled and grabbed at his grandfather's nose.

"Get serious, my little man, and look about these fields and hills. Keep them in your heart as your mother does, and always remember that you came from hardy stock. You can accomplish anything you want, you just have to go fer it!"

Adelene took the opportunity for some personal time, seeing how happy her parents were to be spending time with their youngest grandchild. She hadn't seen Borden for years, and the new one horse shay Francis had ordered built in Union had been delivered. It was shiny and new and even though it would have been easier to have someone drive her, (and certainly more dignified and befitting her circumstances), she didn't want to present any more of a financial superiority to Borden than was absolutely necessary.

The trip out to Guinea Ridge road was quite rutted and bumpy from the spring rains, so she guided the horse to the side, attempting to keep half the carriage in the middle of the road where the grass grew on the center hump, and still keep the right hand side from going into the ditch. She would have been mortified if she became stuck or broke a wheel or axel on the new shay, so she was careful, lest she humiliate herself. The trip was slower than she planned, but she knew Paul would be fine with her mother and father. Francis was also there with his son, and she had prepared several sugar-tits to soothe him if he should suddenly decide he missed his mother. She had carefully wrapped clean cotton cloth around balls of sugar and tied them tightly with twine, a trick that nursing mothers had learned ages ago. Sometimes he seemed to enjoy them even more than his mother's milk. Perhaps it was because he could bite down as hard as he wished without being scolded.

Adelene prepared herself for an unhappy visit. She hadn't visited Borden, hadn't ventured out to her farm since leaving Maine for her stage career. Knowing it would be painful to see her old friend, she had waited each year, believing she would visit, and each year stalling until it was time to return to New York. Her mother had sighed when Adelene casually inquired about Borden. Borden had lived a life of poverty and had been spared none of the difficulties of that state. And now it was time for Adelene to make the call. She dressed as simply as she could allow herself and drove the five miles to the brokendown farmhouse. Wretched looking dogs lumbered about the dirt yard and two small children paused in their play and stared as she drove up, then bolted for the house as though she were some stranger about to do them harm. Even the dogs cowered as she approached.

Stepping onto the rickety porch she was about to knock when the door opened just a crack, then wider, until an elderly woman stood before Adelene.

Oh! Oh, Adelene! It is you! You have come to visit me at last!"

With shock, Adelene realized that the toothless woman before her was her old friend. Emotions raged through her being as they embraced. Tears began to stream from their eyes, Borden's with happiness that her childhood friend cared enough to visit, and Adelene's from sorrow that she had neglected her friend for so long. She could hardly believe they were the same age. Time had been merciless in its ravaging of Borden. Her shoulders were stooped, her stomach and hips were largely disproportionate to her upper body, and her wispy gray hair was gathered in an untidy bun at the nape of her neck. Poverty and endless childbearing had taken its toll. How welcome would loss of fertility be for Borden! Eleven children and scarcely enough to eat and clothe the brood was enough to kill most women.

Borden put the teakettle on the front burner of the black iron woodstove and soon it was steaming. She prepared tea and they sat at one end of the long rough board kitchen table. It was a warm kitchen, and even in its worn state held a certain charm. The woodstove warmed the room, the steaming kettle adding a comforting moisture. A pan of freshly baked biscuits sat on the back of the stove. Borden placed one in each of two saucers, brought a pot of honey from a corner cabinet, and their afternoon "tea" was a very pleasant homecoming affair. Years melted away and their childhood bond returned, with tales of their children's antics and foibles, the impossible nature of men and the dread of advancing age.

"Being a woman doesn't mean you have to be weak," Adelene had declared. "They are finally finding ways to keep a woman from conceiving, and someday we will be able to vote!"

"Oh, Adelene, you always were strong. I'm so proud of you. And you even have a rich husband, you are my hero!"

The visit had to come to an end; Paul would soon tire of sugar-tits and the arms other than his mother's, so with hugs and tears they said their good-byes. Driving away, Adelene thought, "Borden's life should have happened to Heralda."

Adelene hurried the horse back towards the ridge road. She was anxious to get back to Paul, but she tried not to think about it too strongly lest her milk leak and stain her clothing. The Medomak Stream caused some soggy spots in the road but she maneuvered the shay quickly towards the turn as the sun was beginning to sink low in the pale sky. She began to feel a chill so she urged the horse to a trot. Finally reaching the ridge road she reined left and started the uphill climb.

As she approached the slight bend in the road just before reaching the Sullivan property the nearly completed building suddenly popped into view. She flushed with excitement. She had not realized how magnificent it was going to appear when approaching from the South. Imagining the finished bays with leaded glass glistening in the sun brought tears to her eyes. The breezeway was in place so she drove the carriage through the arch and reined up. Yes, this was exactly what she had wanted. A mansion. Some dreams did come true.

CHAPTER 20

New York, January, 1897

Something in the air disturbed Adelene. She had everything she wanted, but today something didn't feel right. In sudden panic she grabbed the arms of her chair and dashed to the French doors that led to the balcony outside the sitting room where she had been reading. Flinging open the doors she stepped into the evening chill and looked up at the sky. Blue gray, with dusk quickly falling, and she felt a chill, not so much from the cold air as from an eerie feeling that was creeping upon her—a foreboding she did not understand. Large soft flakes of snow began to drift down from the darkness, resting on her eyelashes until she blinked them away, the gathered flakes clinging to one another and then as she blinked, resting on the curve of her cheeks. She felt them melting on her face and then realized they were mingled with tears. Finally she turned and re-entered the sitting room and closed the doors against the snow and darkness. She stopped before the chair where she had been sitting and stooped to retrieve the fallen book when she heard Alice answer the bell at the front door at the end of the hall.

"Yes, I'll give it to her right away. Yes, Sir, I'll see that Mrs. Oakes receives it immediately."

The outside door clicked shut and Adelene met Alice in the hall.

"It's for you, Miss, it's a telegram."

The news of her father's death struck such a blow Adelene walked stone-faced back into the sitting room and sank into her chair and did not move until Francis entered when he returned from the factory that evening. She was inconsolable and nothing Francis could do or say stemmed the tears until finally Francis mixed a strong drink, poured it down her and carried her to bed. He held her until she calmed and exhaustion overtook her and she finally slept. He eased from her side, tucked her in with a quilt snugly about her and then sought out Alice in the kitchen.

"Here, Sir, I've warmed your supper, chicken stew, your favorite. How is she doing? I've never seen her in such a state."

"She'll be all right, Alice. She's not half as delicate as she looks. She was very fond of her father and we must go to Ellen at once. The family has lost so many, but those remaining thought Daniel was indestructible. Pack what you think we will need. Remember, it is colder in Maine so be sure there are extra robes to take on the train, as well as our warmest clothing. We will leave in the morning as soon as we can be ready."

"But Adelene is in such a state, Sir"—

"Never mind her state, Alice. She will be full of fight by tomorrow and be planning some elaborate memorial for her father."

Francis knew his wife well. As soon as the train left New York and they settled into their private car she busied herself making little Paul comfortable, arranging the suitcases, checking the food and drink Alice had prepared and putting her hat away in the top tier of her three tiered leather bound hat box. Pulling the pins from her hair and letting it fall about her shoulders, she retracted a small tablet and a lead pencil from her purse, and with a sigh, began to write.

Francis hid behind the newspaper he had been reading to keep Addie from seeing him smile. It was a sad day in her life and he sympathized, but he couldn't help being amused by the way she bounced back from any hit she took. She was a fighter, a survivor who just would not let any adversity keep her down for long. He realized the "planning" was her way of coping. He could tolerate her wild ideas much better than the heartbreak he had tried to ease last night. And now she would spend the rest of the trip planning her father's funeral. Heaven help anyone that tries to get in her way, he mused. He was sure she would have every minute detail written by the time they left the train at the depot of the Georges Valley Railroad in Union and Fred Burkett secured a carriage to take them to Appleton Ridge, and he was equally sure it would be as grand a send off for Daniel Sullivan as any the town of Appleton had ever seen.

Arriving at the Sullivan homestead exhausted from the bounce of the train and carriage, they sat by the fire and tried to console Ellen. They were glad they had brought little Paul in the summer. Daniel had so delighted in spending time with his grandson, and now this pleasant little child seemed to be of some solace to Ellen. As some go on to their heavenly reward, new life arrives on earth, and never had it been demonstrated more poignantly than in this exchange. Giving birth at age forty was not exactly uncommon, but to birth a first child at that age, quite rare. It was almost as though a divine plan was being executed.

Francis noted that the ground was solidly frozen and the sky an ominous gray, that steel gray cast that usually preceded bad weather. He hoped any storm on its way would hold until after the funeral.

They dressed Paul in his nightclothes after giving him a warm bath by the fire, and then they all settled in for the night. They could not sleep in the mansion as the bedrooms were not yet finished. Besides, they felt it was better for Ellen if they stayed in the old homestead. After all, their summer house was too spacious to try to heat in the winter. If he knew his wife (and he did), she would be over there early wanting it made warm for the relatives who were on their way to the sad event of her father's funeral. Tomorrow would be a chaotic muddle of food, friends, relatives, tears, tales and bustle. Francis planned to stay out of it as much as possible. Perhaps it would be best if he lit the fires in the "cottage." It would please Adelene, make more room for the visitors to socialize and might enable him to stay out of the flow of traffic. It was not exactly what he would have planned for a housewarming, but if there was a master plan, perhaps the Higher Power was right. He just hoped it didn't snow.

There had been several big snows in January and with the arrival of February the threat of snow was worrisome. Anything over eight inches would make travel on the ridge nearly impossible. They road crew would come to the ridge with the horse drawn rollers to pack the snow flat on the ridge road as soon as they finished in the Mills, but if the snow would only hold off a week they could be through with the funeral and be ready to leave for New York. The windy ridge had been swept bare of snow in places where the ledges jutted from the ground, a familiar landscape that Adelene had not seen in years, having made her visits in summer since she began her stage career. She felt a quick walk in the frosty air would clear her head so she bundled up, folding a newspaper and placing it over her chest beneath her sealskin coat. One needed all the protection available for even a quick February walk.

Ellen held little Paul by the fire and Adelene felt they were good for each other at this grave time. Paul did not see his grandmother often and every minute they spent together would firm a bond between them.

Leaving the warmth of the Sullivan kitchen, Adelene stepped out into the blustery cold of Appleton Ridge. Contemplating the difficult event of her father's funeral to take place in the afternoon, she couldn't help thinking about her own eventual death. It wasn't a pleasant thought, but she accepted it as something about which she could do nothing. She considered that perhaps she would like to be buried on a hill overlooking the ocean, where the gulls and peregrines would sing by day and the oceans soft rolling would croon all night. She could see in her mind's eye the stars blinking their approval as the moon made its golden path to the horizon. She could imagine herself floating over the water on that mellow way, on and on through the ages, on to where time stands still. But—her father was tied to this land, he would want to rest here, looking up to the ridge and down on the town, his adopted homeland. Pine Grove Cemetery would someday have tall pines shading the hill, and cool breezes, not as strong as those on the ridge, but restful peaceful air stirrings that would rest the hearts of the bereaved. Probably she would someday rest on that hill beside him.

With a sigh she settled herself on the cold ledge, her gloved hand fingering the fragile fluted lichens that held tenaciously to the cold slate. Year after year it held, through rain and snow and the ever-blowing winter winds. Maine tough. She, too, was Maine bred, and like the lichens on the cold stone, she would survive this latest heartbreak.

CHAPTER 21

"When is the bossy witch leaving? We don't need her supervision!"

"Remember who is paying your wages. Mrs. Oakes has a right to change anything she wants. You evidently have not noticed that some of her ideas may be new, but they are hers and it is her prerogative to insist they be used. Some of her notions are an improvement over the old ways. She also has an eye for style in building, as well as her style as a woman.

"But Mr. Goulding. She is a woman! How can she have any knowledge of building?"

"She can read, and she has studied. It would behoove you to pay attention. You never know when you might learn something!"

"I'd rather she kept to her style of dress, but I'll try to remember my wages and be polite."

"Be more than polite, be attentive. The death of her father has been quite a blow for Mrs. Oakes, and she could be easily upset. She is normally very particular, and right now she is more meticulous than ever!" With that, Mr. Goulding left his workers to their tasks and returned to the farmhouse end of the building to converse with Adelene on the next phase of building. The main floor was completed, and the exterior finished. The blue delft tiles for the parlor were set and Adelene had been pleased with the effect. The two upper floors and the porch were not ready for occupancy and it would take another year of finish work to complete the paneling and woodwork. Mr. Goulding saw no need to tell the workers that the Oakes would be returning to New York the following day.

The funeral was behind them, and Ellen seemed settled. Though sadly bereaved, she was handling things well. The support of her family would make the transition to widowhood as easy as such a life-altering event could be made. The workmen would be there every day and they would not only keep an eye on her, but their presence would be a help as she took her responsibility of preparing food for them very seriously. Adelene and Francis made sure that every possible kind of foodstuff was available for her use, with standing orders at Gushee's store that anything she requested should be delivered at their expense. They also hired a local girl to help Ellen, admonishing the girl to be sure Ellen did not lift heavy items and that she should be watched for fatigue. It was the girl's job to be sure Ellen did not cross the line from staying busy doing the cooking she loved and overdoing. Adelene was sure the nights would be difficult for Ellen, but it was something most women went through, and she was sure she would find comfort and sympathy from family and friends. Whatever the difficulty, Adelene had to leave for New York with Francis and that was that.

Packing her clothes in preparation for the train ride to her winter home, Adelene looked out the window at the slope of the land that faced the river valley. The rock walls would soon be covered with the deep snows of February. The spotty covering of white on the windswept ridge would be heavily blanketed and the rocks would disappear, the rocks that her father had placed on the perimeters of his land. And what a magnificent accomplishment it was. It had been an amazing sight, watching her father move rocks. For a man of small stature to have moved so many and of such size was amazing. He used only a steel rod and smaller rocks for fulcrums to move great slabs of stone. Driving the rod in the earth at the edge of a large fieldstone, he would find the most vulnerable spot, place a smaller stone under the bar, and then quickly "pop" the rod with his foot to loosen it from the clutch of the earth. If it were too heavy to carry or even budge enough to jack it onto a sledge, he would continue to sink the rod under the edge and then roll it to the place in the wall he had designated for that particular rock. He could work for hours with the fieldstones, and the fences he had created were a monument to his diligence. He had even built a stone settee for Adelene when she was young, placing a rectangular granite slab on level smaller stones for the legs. "Here, my little princess," he said. "Here is your throne." She had spent many a happy hour on her throne, reigning over the valley. The only thing that outshone her father's strength and diligence was his love and thoughtfulness. It took more than size to make a man, and he would always be with her, in her heart and mind. Daniel Sullivan was the gauge by which she measured all men, and it was not an easy template.

The trip back to New York was not altogether miserable. She mourned her father and she was distressed that her mother would not even consider a visit to New York. Perhaps her mother would have a difficult time going back to Maine and a visit would only postpone the adjustment to living without her husband. The funeral, though sad, was a fitting tribute to her father, but she had a memorial working in her mind. The town had turned out for the service but the ground had proven too frozen for burial. She would return in the spring when he would be taken from the crypt and properly buried. She had spoken for the highest spot in Pine Grove and she planned to speak to Francis about the gravestone.

She was just beginning to recover from the whole affair. It had been disconcerting to see some of the townspeople younger than she, looking so old. They just hadn't taken care of themselves as they should have, and even some of her former students were in their early twenties now, with wives and families. She felt only twenty, herself. Life was strange. Borden seemed as old as her mother, and looked it—acted it. She felt somehow separated from her former life in Maine. When she first went to New York she felt it was a nice place to visit, but she wasn't sure she wanted to live there. Although McLain's Mills had become the place to visit, it

would always be home. As one Texan who had married a Maine
girl had said to Francis, "What's with these Maine girls? You marry
them and give them everything they want, but you still have to
take them back to Maine every year or there is no living with
them." Francis had no answer beyond, "Nothing's free."

With the comforting arms of Francis about her every night
Adelene was soon settled back into city life. One evening as they
sat by the fire in the study after Paul had been fed and bathed,
read to, sang to, and cajoled to sleep, Adelene broached the subject
that had been plaguing her mind.

"Francis, the summer house is coming along fine, and I just
love it. The porch with its tall arched windows gives a view of
Sennebec and Alford Lake, as well as the fields below on the ridge.
It gives the feeling of being outdoors without the wind or insects.
It is truly a wonderful design. The delft tiles of the parlor fireplace
are all I had imagined, and the workers are doing a beautiful job
on the interior details, but there is something else I would like
done, not about the house. Papa's resting place is in the place I
wanted, a large family plot on a nice knoll. I feel Papa was an
important man in Appleton and I would like a statue made. Those
who respected my father will find it appropriate, and those who
didn't can be reminded of their failure to appreciate him. What do
you think?"

"Well. My dear, if it will comfort you and also make Ellen
proud and be of consolation to her, I will say it is a good idea."

"Oh, Francis, you are so good to me. No wonder I love you so."

"Adelene, you are the light of my life, and little Paul my star. I
can never give you anything that compares with this child you
have given me in my later years. Order whatever you wish. By the
way, there will be a soiree at the music hall on 57th Street tomorrow
night following a concert. There will be many celebrated guests."

"Why of course, Francis. It should be a wonderful evening. Will there be dancing?"

"There will be dancing, and feasting and socializing. I will understand if you feel it is too soon for you after your recent family tragedy or if you feel you are too busy to attend."

Adelene felt slightly confused. Was there a hint of sarcasm in his voice? Had she neglected him too long? He had just professed his love, but yet she felt his invitation was tentative, and tentative was not like Francis. She decided to look her very best for this special occasion. She would wear the blue velvet gown that always brought compliments, and the sapphire necklace. She would make it a night he would always remember, at the Music Hall—and after.

The ballroom was filled when they arrived, not only lawyers and city officials with their partners and wives, but actors and singers and showmen from her professional world. As they danced slowly about the room with Francis' hand at her waist she felt the same thrill she had always experienced at his touch and he held her hand tightly as they whirled about the room. She knew they were a handsome couple. Francis had aged well. A little heavier than his younger years, and his hair was turning white, but still thick and curling above his aristocratic countenance. She was sure she could never be happier than she was at that moment.

PART IV

CHAPTER 1

The loss of her father had diminished Adelene's joy over the completion of her summer home. He would not be there when she journeyed north for her summer respite, not be there to play with Paul and show him all the stars at night or teach him bird calls as he had done with her in her youth. Her mother's health was failing and there was nothing she could do to stem the tide of time.

At least the mansion was exactly as she had planned. The grand staircase with its elegant balustrades wound majestically to the upper rooms and the polished hardwood floors and all the accouterments would have made comfortable a Carnegie, a Clemmons, or even General Grant.

The artesian well, drilled some three hundred fifteen feet into the solid rock of which the ridge was comprised, had yielded an extraordinary amount of clear, fresh water, eliminating the necessity of using the cistern built previously in the cellar, but the cistern's presence would supply water in the event of problems with the elaborate new water system. The filled water tower provided the gravity feed for the bathrooms on every floor, as well as the kitchen.

A great crystal chandelier in the reception room glistened brightly, making rainbow patterns on the walls and ceilings whenever the sunlight cast its rays on the prisms, and sparkled at night from the wind-charger powered electricity. The kitchen help marveled at the carbide gas stove, and learned how to prepare meals with the new heat source. Every modern convenience had been installed, even to a bell button near Adelene's chair in the dining room, enabling her to ring for the servants housed on the third floor should she need them.

Woodwork glowed in light diffused by Venetian blinds by day and was enhanced by the steady illumination provided by the electric lamps and sconces by night. Fine Persian rugs softened footsteps in the study and dining room, silver and crystal filled glass fronted cases throughout the main floor. Heavy velvet drapes, festooned with gold tasseled cords, suspended their soft folds at the windows.

A furniture suite with fleur de leis patterned carvings of rosewood sat grandly in the formal living room, its black, satiny horsehair covered cushions buttoned tightly in symmetrical rows of fabric-covered studs. Her mother's cherished love seat, with its slightly worn crimson velvet upholstery was placed among the newer furniture, a bright accent among the somber fabrics of the suite.

The portrait of Adelene painted by Uriah Dyer hung above a marble-topped console, (her mother had insisted it be included in the furnishings of the mansion). Porcelain figurines, depicting heroes and heroines of the classics stood impressively on small pedestals, giving a feeling of opulence and wealth throughout.

Two bedrooms on the second floor were furnished with lace-canopied beds where an abundance of chintz and velveteen cushions rested on sparkling white matelasse' bedspreads, gilt framed mirrors and silver dresser sets on the dressing tables awaited use by guests.

Her mother's suite had, (on Francis' insistence), its own private bathroom and private sitting room. Every convenience Adelene and Francis could provide for her, they did, and no expense was spared in the furnishings. A rose satin spread covered the cherry framed bed that was so high with feather-bed mattresses that a small step stool was placed beside it to facilitate her safe trundle into its softness. Matching satin curtains graced the windows and pictures and memorabilia sat familiarly on the dresser. In the sitting room the chairs were covered with brightly flowered ruffled chintz and near a rocking chair placed by the window her sewing basket sat with her hoops and embroidery thread, needles and scissors, along with lengths of new quilting material. It was in this comfortable room that Ellen spent many an hour looking out over the Georges River valley.

Paul's room was on this floor, and there were more toys than any small boy could play with in one day, books and games, puzzles and stuffed toys, balls, pistols and wagons. Next door was the summer sleeping room in which Francis and Adelene slept, with the ever-present breeze cooling them at night. Ruffled curtains graced the windows, the sheer panels drawn back delicately to invite daylight to enter through the leaded panes. The highly carved oak headboard of the bed was the color of pulled taffy, and rose marble topped the twin dressers whose fronts bore the matching design. The woolen braided rug by the bed was the only furnishing that marked the room as being outside Beacon Hill.

The servants' quarters above were dignified and comfortable and the linen closet was filled with carefully folded cases, towels, spreads and ironed sheets. Scented soaps filled crystal bowls in the bathrooms making them as sweetly scented as flower gardens.

If one arrived at the Sullivan mansion blindfolded, having traveled from afar, it would have been difficult to imagine it a home in the country, as every metropolitan convenience had been employed. It was as any grand residence of the rich and privileged in New York, Boston or Baltimore.

Adelene hoped her mother was enjoying the mansion, and not just pretending for her sake. She had tried to incorporate the old homestead into it to make it as familiar and comfortable as possible. Francis was as fond of Ellen as she, calling her "Mother Ellen," and he wanted her to enjoy the leisure he and Adelene had provided. She seemed to appreciate the luxury, but he, too, was not sure whether it was honesty or indulgence. Since Daniel's death her attitude was of such resignation it was difficult to decipher if she at any time entertained true joy. She had, in a sad moment, stated that her "poor ol' heart was broken as a dropped shortbread," since Daniel had gone on to his reward, spoken in the thick Irish brogue of her childhood, (as all old people tend to return to the familiar and beloved with advancing age.)

When summer was over Adelene and Francis vowed to return for Christmas. They hired a livery man to remain throughout the winter to care for the livestock and take Ellen anywhere she wished in the large new coach, as well as hiring a live-in maid and cook. Even though Ellen preferred to cook her own meals the maid would be there to help. The full staff of six would be necessary only in the summer. It was easy to find help for a week or so over the Holidays. There were always eager young people willing to put in a good days' work for a dollar a day. Francis had a policy of paying well for hard workers.

And so, summers and winters rolled around. Francis had been unable to spend the whole summer in Maine in 1901, and Alice had been ill in the spring. It looked as though she would not be with them much longer. Her illness did not seem to be improving and Francis felt he should return to New York early to make sure everything was all right. Addie and Paul bid him good-bye at the Union station in early August with plans to follow in September. The house was complete and the hired help absolutely satisfactory. Finding good workers in Maine had not been difficult. They not only appreciated the good pay, they were anxious to work with the modern equipment. The running water was of great fascination and the glamour of working "at the mansion" had kept a line of workers on a waiting list.

Adelene was relieved when a letter came from Francis.

August 20, 1901

My dear Adelene and son, Paul,

I miss you both with all my heart, and anxiously await your return to New York in September. All is well here. Though Alice continues to decline I have hired her niece to assist in her care and train as our housekeeper. It pleases Alice to know her kin will be working for us. She seems to be a sturdy girl and well suited to the position.

With all my love, sweet darlings,

Francis

"Well," Adelene thought, "things in New York are going well. Alice is failing, but a plump relative of hers should work out fine." She could relax and enjoy the remainder of the summer. She was considering a return to the stage for a short run of 'I Pagliacci," so she decided to spend some time with her music. She wasn't sure she wanted to spend a lot of time performing, but a guest performance might be fun. It would give Paul a chance to see his Ma on stage, and might lead him to consider theater in his own life. Sometimes she worried about him. He was just a bit too dare-devilish, always jumping off things. First it was footstools, then chairs, and now he had taken to leaping off ledges, always facing the valley with his arms extended like a bird.

"I'm flying," he'd call, and she'd admonish him with, "Paul, you are not a bird. Come down here this minute!" It was beginning to require constant vigilance lest he hurt himself. She would be glad when he outgrew this stage. Still, it was her greatest pleasure to be with Paul. He was nearly six years old and his zest for life was contagious. His active mind brought forth questions that sometimes took great thought to answer, but his inquisitiveness was always welcomed. His eager desire to learn was of great pride for Adelene. To her, he was the most intelligent child that ever lived, and as a former schoolteacher, she felt herself a good judge of mental ability. In New York, she had taken him to libraries and museums and every art gallery. He was overly intrigued by the mystery of flight but she felt his imaginings would do him no harm. And now, here he was in Maine, where he could spend time with the animals and learn all about country living first hand. Also, it was an education to spend the summer with the barrage of visiting relatives, and he enjoyed helping to serve doughnuts and lemonade to visitors.

They had attended the fair in Union where Paul delighted in the many animals, the horse and steer pulling and all the food and festivities. The only part of the fair Adelene didn't like was the traffic over the ridge road. The waving fairgoers didn't realize how much dust their carriages were creating. It meant a lot of work for the hired help and Adelene didn't want her curtains soiled, so it had been necessary to close the windows to protect her furnishings. Fortunately, it had been a cool summer so the situation didn't cause too much discomfort, and by the time she was ready to retire, the travelers were past the mansion on their way home and she could again let in the summer breeze.

The summer of 1901 was nearly over and soon it would be time to return to New York and her waiting husband. The blueberries had been canned, the potatoes were dug, and the root vegetables were stored in their bins in the cellar, as were the apples. She made sure the winter's larder was filled and that the store in the village would deliver whatever her mother might need or want.

Adelene made a decision. They would return to New York a week early. Francis would be so surprised and pleased! With Ellen settled and plenty of foodstuffs having been delivered and put away, Adelene felt comfortable leaving her in the competent care of Angie Kimball. Kind and affectionate, she seemed not so much a servant, but a companion for her mother. Adelene herself did not like to "cross the line" in her relationship with hired help, although she understood her mother's reluctance to be authoritative in that respect. Ellen had always done her own work and it was easier for her to work with a friend than give instructions to a servant. Angie seemed to understand both Ellen and Adelene and worked well with either or both.

When Adelene told her son of their eminent trip to New York his reaction was, "If we could fly like a bird we could get home to Papa quicker, Mama."

"Yes, Paul, but birds sometimes don't see things and they crash into windows. We want to arrive safely, so we will just take the train as usual."

Adelene's idea of returning to New York early was due to her intense yearnings to be with her husband, and making it a surprise made it even more exciting. They would arrive a full week ahead of schedule and she would hire a carriage when they arrived at Grand Central, rather than call for the house carriage for the short jaunt home. She and Paul would sneak in and throw their arms around him and he would be so pleased! Oh, she could hardly wait to see his face!

Taking a compartment, Adelene read to Paul and played games, then they ate the lunch Ellen had prepared for their trip, biscuits with ham, sugar cookies and fresh cider. Soon Paul became sleepy so she tucked him securely in his bunk with the retaining curtain preventing any mishap from the jolting and swaying of the transit.

Adelene herself was not sleepy, so she sat near the window cuddled in a lap robe and watched the countryside slide by. Autumn was such a wonderful time of year. The colors were so vivid; warmly glowing yellows, flaming reds and burning fuchsias, deep rusty browns adding their warmth to the flames, all shouting with joy against the constant evergreens as though they were taking their last stand before winter's onslaught. Finally she dozed and let her mind wander, half remembering, half dreaming of the day they met with the architect to plan her summer home in Maine. She had been brushing her hair, sitting before her mirror at her dressing table. She remembered saying, "Francis, I know young girls look for love while young men look for sex, and now that I'm older I still want love. I want to be held and shown that you love everything about me. When you look at other women with a gleam in your eye it is a sexual attraction, as the gleam comes before you have even spoken to each other. The object of your random desire could be mean and hateful and deceitful for all you know, perhaps a torturer of small kittens, or even have a hidden disease, but none of those conditions are a consideration of your roving thoughts. Am I a substitute for all your true desires?"

"Adelene, I swear to you, glances mean nothing. When I admire other women it is only a game. Sort of like pondering over fancy cupcakes before eating the main course," he had answered.

Her straight body had hidden the turmoil dizzying her mind. Was this the way men were? Was sex behind everything? Well, not to her. She valued herself above being a mere sex object, for what would happen when beauty was gone? Certainly Papa had loved Ma. He had always spoken tenderly towards her. Could it have been only because he had sex with her when they were young? He hadn't seemed to love her any less as years rolled by. And Francis' own fondness for her mother, certainly that was not sexual. No, there was more to it than that. Either she was failing Francis or he had a character flaw, a weakness towards sex. Perhaps he had a harem personality, or should have been a Mormon and moved to Utah, but if that had happened she would not have been a part of it, and she would not have Paul.

Turning it over in her mind she considered that perhaps Eliza had been the truest love he'd ever had, and she had died before ever knowing his weakness. Probably better that way. She had held him during his most ardent years, and Louella had been the first substitute for that love, and now it was she. She was glad she had him in his mid years, for most of the time she felt very loved, and he had given her everything she had ever wanted, fame, riches, a magnificent home, and she had been his equal in every way. Love, what a strange and mysterious concept!

Perhaps there was no such thing as true and lasting love, perhaps the books and stories she had read were just made up dreams, fantasies, wishful thinking, or maybe love only grew to be true if it were fought for, suffered for, as her parents had. Their love had withstood the hard work and deprivation of an immigrant carving out his place in a new land. They had endured backbreaking, grueling work with many mouths to feed and it had taken years before their lives had reached a comfortable stage. But hadn't she and Francis fought to be together?

She remembered how Francis had held her and said, "I love you with all my heart and you mustn't place any importance on a moment of instinctive foolishness. To be honest, Adelene, I think men are stimulated by looking at women just to get their wagons loaded, but I assure you that when I am with you my whole being is consumed with my love for you and you alone. Your eager spirit stimulates me as much as your perfect body, and my heart jumps when I look at your dear face. No, Adelene, do not put any importance on any flickering glance at another. You are the flame of my heart."

"Oh, Francis," she had replied, "Perhaps I am all wrong. I waited so long to find you I cannot bear the thought of losing you."

"Let's talk no more of this. We have an important meeting to attend, so clothe your lovely self and we will speak with Mr. Fisher about your summer house plans."

Sometimes she felt she was being bought off, but oh, how she loved creature comforts and she adored fine clothes and jewels. She knew she was not without flaws herself and had no right condemning Francis for his small flirtations.

She felt the train slow. Rousing herself, Adelene realized she had finally fallen asleep in her seat and the trip home had neared its end. Pushing aside the small blanket she had drawn over herself when she had settled by the window, she rose. Holding onto the rail by the bunk where Paul slept she woke her sleeping child, dressed him in his coat and cap and they eagerly anticipated their homecoming as the train pulled into the station. Any thoughts and dreams that had raced through Adelene's mind during her fitful sleep had dissipated and she felt anxious and exhilarated with expectation.

Their bags were quickly loaded and secured on the back of a small carriage and the driver helped them to their seats, closed the door and off they went. The reunion was so near Adelene almost cried with excitement, and Paul was so thrilled he was a handful to keep in his seat, wanting to stand at the window. They should provide some sort of restraining ribbon in seats for children, she thought. If the carriage should lurch a child could fall forward and be injured. If only women designed carriages, a lot could be improved. Even baskets tied or fastened tightly in a seat could be provided for babies so a mother wouldn't have to hold them in their arms on trips. Men never thought of such things, only of the design and mechanics of the things they built.

Pulling a string that had tied a wrapped biscuit sandwich from her purse, she played cat's cradle with Paul until they arrived at 73rd street, had the driver quickly place their bags on the stone steps at the doorway, paid him and quietly pressed the thumb latch on the door. Placing her finger to her lips to caution Paul to silence, they stole into the hallway. Hearing no sound they quietly peeked in the study, found no one, then the dining room. Still no Francis or servant was found so they stealthily crept up the carpeted stairs and down the hall towards the bedroom suite. She hoped Francis wasn't ill. He was usually in his study this late in the day.

Hearing laughter, she flung open the door to their bedroom.

Grabbing Paul, whose eyes were as big as saucers, she backed out of the room in horror.

"Go to your room, Paul, I'll be down shortly," she told the stunned boy, and as he ran down the hall she turned back to the room, where a girl was frantically snatching her rumpled clothes and began covering her naked body.

Adelene could not cry, she could not scream. Her mind, her heart, her very soul was shattering with such pain she could scarcely breathe.

"I think you should pull your pants up," she admonished a horrified Francis, "and I think you should send this girl home. I will speak with you later."

With head held high she sedately walked down the hall to Paul's room.

"Here, darling, let Mama give you a warm bath. We have had a long trip and we need to relax.

"But, Mama, can't I play with my toy soldiers? I haven't seen them all summer long. And what was Papa doing, and why can't I talk to him?"

"Papa was playing a joke on us and it wasn't very funny, so we will forget it and not speak of it again. As for toy soldiers, I'm afraid the South would win tonight so let's have a bath and some supper instead. We will play with the soldiers in the morning.

As she drew the water for his bath Adelene felt her body tremble. "Don't faint now," she admonished herself, "you have a child to bathe."

Lovingly, she bathed her son, dressed him in his flannel nightshirt, and let him play while she went down to the kitchen. She returned with cold sliced beef and biscuits, milk and cookies.

"Darling, we are going to have a picnic in your room. Isn't that exciting?"

"But can't Papa come and eat with us?"

"No, Dear, Papa is busy. You can see him tomorrow."

After their meal, (with Adelene nearly gagging but managing to pretend enjoyment), she reached into the bookcase and retrieving his favorite storybook, read to him until his eyes began to droop, then put him in his little bed.

Adelene pulled the rocking chair close to his bedside, the rocker she had rocked him in and nursed him as a baby. It wasn't fair to Paul to make him go to bed when he was so excited to be home, but it was the only way she could handle the situation, and she hoped the excitement of the trip and night's sleep closely following would make the whole incident seem like a dream to him. She remembered that Francis had wanted to hire a wet nurse for him when he was a baby, but she had insisted on feeding him herself. She had thought then that Francis had been jealous of her attachment to her son, which was ridiculous to her. Love of a child and love for a man were two different things.

She told her son a fairy story, one where everyone lived happily ever after, then crooned softly all the lullabies she could think of until slumber overtook him and his breathing softened. Gently, she kissed him on the forehead, and gave thanks that children usually forgot adult problems if they ever even realized what was happening outside their own worlds.

Quietly slipping from the room she walked to the room she had occupied when she first visited the Oakes residence years before, entered and closed the door. The quilt her mother made for her had been folded and placed at the foot of the bed. She slowly removed it from its resting place, sat on the bed and raised it to her eyes. Tears streaked and matted the velvet squares and dripped from the fluted lace edges. Every dream that had been fulfilled was now replaced with the worst imaginable nightmare. Utterly and completely crushed, she remained in the darkened room.

She had only one consolation. The calmness she had displayed to Paul had been her best performance ever.

After finally falling asleep from exhaustion, Adelene awoke to a knock on the door. She didn't answer, so Francis opened it slowly.

"Adelene, I'm sorry, Adelene. Please forgive me. I beg of you, forgive me!"

"Francis, how can I even speak to you?"

As tears threatened to blur her vision, Adelene fought them back. There was no way she would show weakness, no matter how much pain she suffered as her heart was breaking. The resolve she had made to never let any man dominate her had been pushed aside in the years she had spent loving Francis, but now it had returned. She would not allow herself to be betrayed and then run whining and crying in an attempt to restore what had been lost, and she had, in this realization of his betrayal, lost all. Losing all was one thing, but allowing the loss to crush her was unthinkable. The tears waiting in the wings could just stay where they were, they belonged to a performance she would never allow to debut.

She hated to be seen all disheveled and puffy-eyed, but she drew herself together and sat up, turned, and smoothing her rumpled traveling dress she stood before him.

A contrite Francis implored, "Adelene, I'll give you anything you ask, you must forgive me!"

"Francis, you will give me whatever I ask if I stay with you, but you will also give me whatever I ask if I leave you!"

"Leave me! You wouldn't leave me! Not over a mere dalliance!"

"I accept your difficulty in controlling your physiology, but when you act with no restraint, you prove yourself thoughtless as to my feelings. How can I ever feel loved again, how can I retrieve my broken trust in you under these circumstances? I will be publicly humiliated, as illicit trysts never remain secret. Everyone will soon know, if they don't already, that you have sought out a younger woman behind my back. They will laugh at the poor wronged Adelene. I will not have it!"

"Well maybe we should just end it all, Adelene. There is no use going on the way we are now. I've had enough misery in my life, and if you can't believe in me again we may as well go out right now. I have the cure for this problem right down in my factory, and it can end it for both of us. That is, unless you want a public divorce. If you decide on that course you will not be able to keep all the sables and jewels you prize so!"

How she hated this tack he was taking. He should have known better than to try to threaten her into submission.

She retorted, "Take my love, take all I possess, leave me nothing and think you have won, but my soul, my self, my very being will still remain, because I am me, and those things are and always will be mine, mine, MINE! As for doing away with our lives, why would you want to do that when if I were gone you would find an immediate replacement! After all, your fidelity didn't last a month. You seem to have done very well for yourself in that short span, so don't try to coerce me into thinking you are so devastated that you feel suicidal. But if you insist, Francis, bring home your poison, and if you think a suicide pact is called for, let's go ahead with it. But when it comes to swallowing it, you go first!"

With that, she stormed out of the room, leaving a stunned and defeated Francis Oakes absolutely speechless.

Moments later, Francis sighed. "Bitch! Bitch! Uncontrollable Bitch! That's what she is. Unforgiving, uncontrollable, selfish bitch!"

But he still loved her. She was the most amazing, thrilling, spirited woman on the face of the earth. He should have known she would find out about his meaningless fling. Why couldn't she understand it was only a substitute for her, that it was mere physical pleasure, and meant no threat to their love. And now he had lost her simply because she couldn't understand the difference between men and women. Women wanted love and fidelity but men needed sex. But, oh, he needed Adelene. He needed her touch, her fire, her ambition and determination.

Sinking to a chair he leaned forward with his elbows on his knees and his hands on his face until the tears flowed and wet his shirt cuffs and trickled beneath the linen to his elbows. His remorse was overwhelming and he couldn't see any way to repair the damage he had done. Their love had gone from smoldering coals of great anticipation to a raging, all consuming inferno, and now it had burned itself out, with nothing but ashes remaining, ashes that were blowing away with every breath they breathed.

CHAPTER 2

In the following days Adelene slept in her old room and she could not bear to even speak to Francis. She could not overcome the pain by day and her sleep at night was fitful, thoughts and longings tearing her apart, remembering the nights he had left her body glowing with ecstasy. Then as she became fully awake anger wracked her mind and body.

"I'll kill him, she thought. I'll just kill him." But then, prison garb would not be becoming and the thought of living in a jail cell, eating meals with low-life prostitutes and murderers didn't appeal to her finer sensibilities. The frustration of her position was almost more than she could bear.

Adelene had wanted no love in her life but when she met Francis that had changed. Then she wanted to be cherished by someone, if not Francis, then someone else who would be oblivious to any slight imperfections she might have, and she would be oblivious to his. They would laugh together and watch sunsets and embrace before a warm fire in the hearth, and they would make love the whole night through. Now she realized a dream like that rarely came true and if it did, it was not lasting. Perhaps completeness in love could be realized by a very few, and then only because they had lesser expectations than she. She felt as though she could figure it all out if only she could get back to the ridge and watch the orange fireball setting over the Pettingill, making orange rivers of light flowing across the sky until they slowly faded into the dusky clouds where the setting sun cast bright edgings on their billows. The evening light would slowly burn the ridge in the east to lavender, causing purple patches to slowly fade into darkness as the last glimmering of light succumbed to night. Stars would move closer and stud the sky with diamonds. But she could not go there now. She would have to figure it out here.

The Mystery

Why must I read about happily ever after?
Why are stories written of everlasting love?
It's all a fantasy.
Happiness is a moment,
A stolen smile,
A comforting hug,
A tender touch.
Not lasting forever, but just for an instant.
To build hopes on,
To form dreams from,
To look back on.
And perhaps even pretend
It will last forever.

Looking for a way to piece her life together, Adelene called the shipping lines. She would go away for a while and think things over. She informed Francis of her intention to take an extended trip to Europe and they could discuss their marital situation upon her return. It was never good to make rash decisions in the heat of the moment. Francis appeared stricken, but she felt he should stew in his guilt and think about his transgressions. She would take Paul with her. Francis fussed about the time of year being dangerous, but the steamship would be both warm and safe as far as she was concerned, and her need to get away overwhelmed any caution she might have employed. She and Paul would leave on the first of November.

Adelene could have left earlier on the S.S. New York, but she wanted everything connected to that city out of her life for a while. There was thinking and planning to do and decisions to be made.

She bought passage for herself and Paul on the steamship "Philadelphia." British built, the staterooms would be Victorian and well suited to her temperament at this critical time in her life. She needed dignity and order. She needed to be pampered and soothed, and if providence would have it, an enchanting, soul-refreshing tour of Europe. She called Randolph and cancelled his visit with them that had been planned for the Holidays, and told him that she and Francis had some differences to overcome. He asked for more details of the problem but Adelene refused to elaborate, promising to explain all when she returned. By then she planned to have her life in order again. She would reminisce about Maine and the Novembers she had spent there, the pain free years before she had known love.

> On a gray November morning, the silent fields are waiting,
> Their flaxen blades are waving under skies of somber chill.
> No birds find cause to flutter, no cheerful call to utter,
> Expectantly they're waiting, quietly waiting, waiting still,
> For the magic of the morning when it settles without warning
> And covers all with blankets, every tree and rock and hill.
> All covered in the softness, asleep in silent wonder,
> And dream there in their resting of the warming winds of spring.

The voyage from New York to Liverpool began when Adelene stepped onto the deck with her son. She breathed a sigh of relief. The six weeks waiting for this day had been difficult. She had pretended things were normal for Paul's sake, and they had been able to get through meals with stilted formality. She was sure her son realized that something was wrong, and on the rare occasions when he asked why she didn't sleep with Daddy anymore she had been able, or at least she hoped she had been able, to satisfy his curiosity by feigning fatigue on her part or Francis' part. She didn't want to upset her son in the event they were able to work things out. She would never take Paul away from his father, at least not very far and not for long. She had told him that his father had arranged this trip as a special treat.

It was a new world they were entering, and Adelene inhaled deeply. The crisp autumn air was tinged with the salt breeze of the ocean, and she held her son's hand tightly. Francis had finally agreed to her traveling with Paul, (as though he had a choice). He was struggling to keep Adelene and he was ready to agree to any request she might make. And now they were on their way, the last blast of the horn had sounded and the loading ramps had been withdrawn. The chubby red tugboats were chugging and muscling into their positions to pilot them out of the harbor.

Paul was very interested in these small harbor workers, their mighty engines pushing and pulling the huge steamship into the open waters of the Atlantic. Everything was new and exciting for Paul and Adelene realized that if nothing else were accomplished from this trip, Paul was going to learn at lot that would not have been available through regular schoolbook studies. Anything she could do for her child, she would, and this was going to be a great experience for him.

Making their way to their cabin Adelene felt the recent past fading from her mind. She would enjoy this adventure and settle her New York problems when she returned. The less she dwelled on them now, the better.

"Mama, is Papa coming to France to see us?"

(Leave it to a child to bring one back to reality.)

"No, Darling, we will return and see Papa in the new year."

"But, Mama, why can't Papa come? Uncle Rand is here so why can't Papa be here?"

"Uncle Rand is not here, Paul. What makes you say such a silly thing?"

"But, Mama, he is. I saw him when we got on the ship. He was by the rail, but then he went away. Does he have a room like

ours, Mama, and will he play cards with me like he did when he
visited us in New York?"

"Paul, you are mistaken, let's not discuss it. If Uncle Rand
were here I'm sure he would play cards with you. It's late, so get
into your nightshirt and into your bed. Look at the lovely curtains
that close so your bed is like a little tent. Play with your little
soldiers for now. We will read a story when I find your books in my
bag. We will be hardy old sailors by morning!"

With that she helped him into his sleeping alcove and began
to unpack a few things. Singing softly she unfastened the strap of
her trunk and opened it, laid out her own nightgown and was
unpinning her hair when she heard Paul murmur sleepily, "But,
Mama, he really is here."

The imaginings of her child amused Adelene. One never knew
what a six year old would think of next. She was glad they boarded
late in the day and with Paul tucked snugly into his bunk Adelene
sat on her bed with a sigh. Lifting her gown from the bed she
placed it on her lap. It was the smooth pongee silk she loved to
wear, so soft against her skin, and the matching quilted robe was
warm as only silk could be. Suddenly she pushed them aside onto
the pillow and snatched her seal coat from its hanger by the door,
pulled the hood over her head and softly stepped through the door,
locking it behind her. She would have a breath of fresh air before she
retired, and the rail was only a few feet from her cabin door. She could
hear any sound Paul might make, as the sea was calm and the gray
November sky was a windless coverlet over the ocean and all on it.
Leaning on the rail with the coolness of the night enveloping her she
let her mind rest, only absorbing the quiet of the evening.

Footsteps on the polished deck caused her to turn from her
seaward gaze and before her in the evening light stood her friend.

"Rand, is it really you?" As she threw her arms about him in a
tender embrace she cried, "Oh, my dearest friend in all the world,
why are you here?"

"Adelene, I thought you might need a shoulder. Knowing you, you are not looking for one, but if you decide to break precedent, it's here."

"Oh, Rand, of course," and as her eyes filled, she leaned against the trusted shoulder, and the tears poured down her face. He gave her his handkerchief and held her as her heartbreak burst forth.

"Adelene, I know you are hurting and I understand, but don't burn your bridges. Wounds have a way of healing, even the worst ones are not always fatal."

With his arms around her they stood at the rail in the evening shadows until Adelene was calm and once again in control of her emotions. Whatever the future might hold, Adelene hoped Rand would always be a part of it.

CHAPTER 3

As the Philadelphia steamed towards Liverpool in calm waters, the ease of the crossing was interrupted by a small problem for the captain when the ship's steward approached him.

"Sir, there is a gentleman who wishes to speak to you."

"Is it a complaint, or praise for the smoothness of this journey?"

"I don't know for sure, Sir, but he seems quite agitated, so I assume it is a complaint."

"Very well, send him in."

Upon entering the captain's cabin the man glanced about the room. The large cabin contained leather upholstered chairs, a marble stand where a polished brass sextant gleamed, a smaller stand on which a compass was secured, and an iron bound door which he presumed opened to the captain's sleeping quarters.

The captain sat militarily at his desk with the ship's log to his left and a quill pen and writing paper on his right.

"And what can I do for you, Mr. Richeau?"

"Sir, there is a problem with dinner seating. I request that the actress and her friend be eliminated from your table. Their presence makes my wife very uncomfortable."

"Why should they make her uncomfortable?" Miss Syloane is a famous actress and her friend an accomplished musician. Those who sit at my table are chosen for their merit."

"But, Sir, can't you see that he is definitely colored? It is a shame to all womankind that she travels with him. I understand that she is a married woman, making the shame even more intolerable!"

"I think you are overstepping your position, Mr. Richeau. They do not share a cabin, she shares a cabin with her young son, and she is married to a very wealthy man who could buy this ship if he so desired, so take it in good grace. Perhaps he is her bodyguard. I do not question the intent and position of my passengers."

"Then I dine at your table under protest. It makes my wife uncomfortable to dine at the same table as darkies."

"It is up to you, you are free to dine elsewhere, but many of my passengers are on the way to France, where color is not an issue. I suggest you study your itinerary carefully, or your trip will prove to be a great disappointment to you."

"Sir, we have heard the boy call this man, "Uncle Rand." Doesn't that prove some kind of liaison?"

"He has a private room. She and her son have their own cabin on this vessel, and even though actresses sometimes live under more relaxed conditions than that to which you are accustomed, these two have done nothing to warrant dismissal from my table. You, on the other hand, are very close."

"Sir, this is our honeymoon. I would like for my wife's feelings to be considered. She was raised with every care lest her purity be stained. This situation upsets her. She needs to be calm and unruffled at this delicate time in her life."

"Young man, your wife's delicacy and purity are not my concern. Eat where you wish. The courtesy of dining at my table was offered to you, and though I now realize it was a mistake to include you and your wife, I will not withdraw my invitation to you or anyone else. We are at sea, and as in Europe, differences in culture are accepted. By the way, you might like to know that there are several complaints about you. Arrogance is difficult for some people to tolerate. Perhaps you are unschooled as to the fact that Europeans consider all Americans to be Yankees and fail to distinguish Northerners from Southerners, as with one breed of monkey from another."

Redfaced, the man backed from the room, closing the door behind him. He grasped the rail for a moment and then hurriedly returned to the passenger deck. Now he had to face his wife with his failure. He had the feeling his honeymoon cruise would not be as romantic as he had anticipated.

CHAPTER 4

London was enchanting, the theater, the cathedrals, the palaces. Everything was exactly as she had imagined. The short ferry over to France amazed her, and they found a hotel on the Rue de Rivoli that was clean and comfortable and served marvelous food. Even Paul was happy, as chocolate was everywhere. She loved it herself so she indulged with him, explaining that they would have to give it up when the vacation was over. Every pastry shop was an adventure and they spent many an evening reading and eating bread and butter and drinking hot chocolate. It was a wonder they ever slept but they enjoyed every minute. Many nights Rand came by and they played cards and shared the day's pastry finds.

The wide street of the Rue De Rivoli housed many shops, and the youthful atmosphere took Adelene to another world, away from the trouble she would have to face upon her return to New York. She and Paul visited the Louve, toured Notre Dame with its statues tucked neatly in their niches, and marveled at the vastness of the cross shaped cathedral. She said her rosary and asked for guidance, wondering if she really received it or if her enlightenment was merely her mind's confirmation of what she had already decided.

Paul was more intrigued with the parks and zoos, both at Bois de Vincennes and Bois de Boulogne. He loved the many animals he had never seen before and the friendly children in the great playground. The adjoining museums were of less interest but Adelene hoped he would remember some of what they had seen. He did become intrigued with Da Vinci's sketches on flying machines. She surmised that small boys always seemed interested in the amazing world of impossibility, probably not a recent development.

A rested and determined Adelene Oakes prepared for the trip back to New York. She vowed that never again would she give her heart away so completely. No one would ever possess her soul as she had let Francis. Now her folly had come to light. For many years she had been blinded, even obsessed by him and the power of their passion. In her innate optimism Adelene assessed the situation. She would keep a home in New York, her estate in Maine and enough money to care for her mother. Her career had blossomed and faded, and she had her son. Paul, fruit of the great love many only dream of, her darling, beautiful boy. Someday he would inherit the house on the hill in Maine, and everyone would marvel at the lord of the Sullivan mansion. But for now, she would return to New York and maybe even take a character part in a play. She could play a beautiful older lady who hadn't lost her beauty to age. She was still in good voice and there was nothing to hinder her performing again. Everyone would be pleased to see her returning to her career, and Paul would love it.

This trip was the best thing she could have done to calm down her situation and make plans. Having Rand close by had been comforting. He was such a dear friend. He always seemed to know when she was troubled. No one in her life had been as constant as he and she loved him for it. Not the burning passion of lovers, but the confidence of familiarity. She knew Francis had been jealous of her relationship with Rand, but he had also been jealous of her closeness to Paul in his early years. Perhaps males needed undivided attention and since they were incapable of platonic relationships with the opposite sex themselves, they assumed that women, also, were incapable of true friendship with men.

Perhaps that was what she really needed, a friend as a companion, not a passionate lover, and then all the problems created by such a consuming relationship could be avoided. It might be better to have less passion and more understanding. If Francis could philander, she, at least, well, she could come to an understanding with Rand that they could marry after her divorce.

Rand had most certainly had opportunities for permanent relationships, she was sure, but no liaison had lasted. Their friendship, however, had endured over the years. She had never thought much about Rand beyond his loyalty. She had always admired his talent but he was such a dear friend she had neglected to really consider his feelings. This had been her first opportunity to think of him as an escort and companion. Paul loved him, and she loved him. He was completely trustworthy and reliable.

Of course she had always felt his attraction to her, now that she thought about it. Her career had totally absorbed her in the beginning, and then Francis, but now her heart was free. She had not been alone for years, and it would present an adjustment unless her heart found a replacement. It wouldn't be a wildly romantic liaison, but it would be comfortable. Oh, Randolph was going to be so happy!

Yes! She would tell him she would soon be available. What a life they could have together, and the world would see her once again defy convention! He would be accepted in Maine as he was in France, and the rest of the world be damned!

'How opportune it was, that she and Rand were to meet for dinner that evening. Paul would be in the care of the Belgian Nanny she had hired for her stay in France, and Adelene was filled with anticipation. Rand had called the day before and invited her to meet him for a "special occasion." She knew what he was planning. They would feast on escargot, drink wine and dance, and then he would tell her he loved her and wished to marry her when she was free, and that he had loved her since the first day they met. She would fall into his embrace and say, "Yes, yes, my beloved. I will be yours." It would be a night of nights!

Adelene laid out the most glamorous gown she had brought with her for the occasion, the lavender silk. Its soft folds shone in lamplight and framed her face with romantic pastel. After kissing Paul goodnight she wrapped her fox fur cape about her shoulders and took a carriage to the restaurant. Usually Rand came for her, but he had been busy working with other musicians since they arrived in France and she understood his meeting her at the restaurant rather than at her hotel. Arriving early, she was seated, glowing and relaxed when Rand entered.

On his arm was a girl she had never seen before, and as the couple approached the table Adelene couldn't help noticing what a striking pair they were.

"Adelene, I would like you to meet my fiancée, Mademoiselle Aurora Bolenoux."

With all the grace she could muster, she rose, took the girl's hand, and bowed her head. "Enchante`, so very pleased to meet you," and as her plans, her pride and her confidence crumbled she embraced Randolph for the last time.

Somehow, the evening became pleasant. Realizing she had given her mind over to weakness, revenge and desperation, Adelene quickly regained her balance. She was so genuinely happy for Rand. He glowed with delight with every glance he and Aurora exchanged. How could anyone doubt that his happiness was deserved? He would be forever in her heart where he belonged, and seeing true love blossom in her darkened world gave her faith in her future. She had achieved so many of her dreams, she could not complain. She thought of all the people over the ages that had lived through wars and famines and acts of God that stripped them of all their earthly possessions, leaving them naked to the elements, robbed of all pride and self worth. Some fought their way back to dignity and well being, while others perished. Perished not just from the terrible deprivations inflicted upon them, but from soul starvation. No matter what, she would never go down easily. Her inner self would still be glowing and she'd find a way to control her destiny. That is what counts, she knew, the fire within. She knew her fire would be like the hearth at home. It might seem to die as the night descended, but would awaken in the morning and burn brightly again. After all, she still had Paul.

CHAPTER 5

When Adelene planned her European trip she had been anxious to spend time in Ireland, to see the hills and cliffs and streams of the land from which she had sprung. She had dreamed of looking up her Irish relatives and absorbing all the ambience of her father's homeland she could, but when Randolph appeared she had altered her itinerary. Now she was happy with the way her situation had evolved. This trip to Ireland was to be shared with no one but Paul.

Rand was happily ensconced in Paris and she was free to pursue her adventure to the land of her heritage.

Instead of stopping in London, they remained on the ship and disembarked at Cork, having not left their cabin for the entire voyage across the English Channel on the way to Cork Harbour. Adelene did not want Paul to become ill from the winter weather on the last leg of their journey.

Bundling in furs against the winter chill, they took a carriage to a pleasant village just outside the city that offered comfortable lodging and traditional Irish fare. The smell of stew and corned beef and cabbage was reminiscent of her mother's cooking, and they consumed more at their first meal in Ireland than any since they left the States.

After a good night's sleep they arose refreshed. Making several inquiries, they began their sojourn through the southern Ireland countryside, finding plump cousins that reminded her of her mother. Their laughing blue eyes and round noses splattered with freckles, dark hair pinned into prim pugs with fringes at the nape curling from steam rising from tea kettles boiling in the hearths. Short sturdy Irishmen whose gnarled and calloused hands declared their hardworking lives, their jolly smiles showing acceptance of their lot, only asking a mug of ale and a rousing song or two with their comrades in the nearest pub at day's end.

Children played at bowling and throwing sticks for their scruffy terriers to fetch, much to Paul's delight. The charm of the extended Sullivan family and the comfort of their hospitality captured their hearts. Adelene had searched for one or two relatives and found a whole family of loving cousins.

Paul was ecstatic with the finding of his "folks", as he put it, and ran about the barns and petted the sheep, fled from the honking geese and gathered eggs from the chickens, all the while chattering about his home in Maine and all the ways things were the same.

Adelene found it strange that there were no snakes or skunks, but plenty of rabbits, (or hares as they called them), and her favorite little arbutus that she searched for in early spring grew to tree size on the Emerald Isle. And emerald it was, at least the parts she had seen, covered with lush forests of hardwoods where moss and ferns formed a dense mat underfoot. The leaves were gone from the trees for the winter but she could envision the dark canopy that would return in the spring. The ferns would sprout green again and the moss would drink the early rains and swell into a luxurious carpet.

Ireland's woodlands were much like the forests in Maine, though with fewer evergreens. No wonder her father had chosen Appleton. It was so reminiscent of all she had found in his homeland.

Their ten days in Ireland took them from Cork to Lismore, where the Knockmealdown Hills rose in the distance, to Mallow, north from Midleton to Fermoy and on to Dungarvan, following the Blackwater River that still bubbled and sang as Daniel had described, the green hills and valleys displaying all the beauty she had anticipated. The cool winter wind was not bitter as in Maine, but moist and soft as an Irish lilt. The temperature had never dipped below forty degrees even though it was January.

As her visit came to a close the Sullivans gathered to give them a homecoming and bon voyage, and to the pleasure of all who gathered she sang all the old Irish ballads her father had taught her in her youth. Tears came to the eyes of all those attending, even Adelene's.

She was presented with a fine hand knit cardigan of softest ivory Irish wool, knitted with a pattern of cables and ladders of intricate detail completely covering the garment. Emotionally accepting the gift, her thoughts immediately sprang to her mother. She would give this wonderful bit of Ireland to her. She had been so absorbed with herself she had neglected to find her a gift, so fate had done it for her.

Too soon it was time to meet the Philidelphia for the return home. She was sad to leave, but so refreshed that forgiveness was forming in her heart. Perhaps, just perhaps, her absence this time had given Francis a taste of loneliness. Perhaps he was sincerely contrite and had consumed a good dose of sorry. It might be possible for them to form a truce until she could heal her heart and they could make a new start. A truce would at least make it possible to conceal the riff from her mother. Ellen loved him so much and Adelene hated to break her heart by revealing his infidelity. Yes, this trip had settled a lot in her mind.

Perhaps she could accept his weakness as long as it didn't happen again. She would never wholly trust him, but she had her son to think of. She would have to stay with him and not let him be tempted to stray. And Paul, he should not be deprived of his father's love, so somehow she would work things out when they reached New York.

CHAPTER 6

The reunion at 73rd Street was stilted. Paul ran to his father, bursting with news of their exciting voyage and Adelene steeled her heart against the emotions that were attempting to surface. She knew she would never stand between Francis and their son no matter what their own estrangement entailed.

When dinner was over and Paul was finally asleep Adelene refreshed herself in the guest room where she had requested her trunk be placed. No point in completely unpacking, she thought, until she made a definite decision on her future. Donning her gown and robe she sat at her dressing table and unpinned her hair, then carefully brushed it smooth. Turning in her chair she started to rise when she heard a knock on her door.

"Come in," she answered.

Francis entered and he was noticeably agitated.

"Well, Adelene, how was your trip? I understand you were not lonesome! How could you subject Paul to such reckless behavior?"

With shock, Adelene realized what Francis was saying.

"Spit it out, Francis. Tell me what it is that I have subjected Paul to."

"I checked the ship's manifest after you left and I know what you have been up to! I've always known about you and Randolph!"

Adelene's mind raced. The nerve! The very nerve! He was accusing her of having an affair with Rand! What did he expect her to do, sit and grieve over their lost marriage? Give up on life completely? And she had taken Paul with her. He could as well have called her a whore!

Francis' face reddened when she stood and slammed her fist on the table, with, "Rand! Rand! You think I slept with Rand? He is my friend,—has been my friend and business partner for years and it has never crossed my mind to sleep with him! (a slight fib, but not far from the truth). She felt the rush of words coming faster than her thoughts could keep up and she had no control over the words vehemently spewing from her mouth. So violent was the rush from her betrayed body that her lungs felt both restricted and explosive simultaneously. "Oh, I do not think I can forgive you for this, Francis. Perhaps Randolph had thoughts of me, as many, MANY men have, but it was never reciprocated. I am ashamed of you and proud of Randolph."

"You were on that ship together and you spent a month in Europe with that—that—"

"Don't say it, Francis. If you do you will be destroying the last shred of respect I have for you!"

"You were probably sleeping with him when you were performing in Providence!"

"And you, Francis, have you slept with the hired help everywhere we have been? Should we have hired only old, fat, ugly women as servants to keep you faithful? I was not with Rand on the trip. I didn't know he would be on the ship. He journeyed to Europe because he was worried about me, as I had called him before I left, telling him you had broken my heart. Thank God he has remained in Paris where color matters to no one, where he has found the life and love he deserves. He is happily married in France, where no one will ever call him less than a gentleman, which he is, and that is more than I can say for you. The only male I truly love, as I did you in the past, is only six years old! So draw up the papers, Francis, and be sure you are generous, and I will never tell the world what an undisciplined lout you are!"

"Wait, Adelene, hear me out. I didn't mean to be unfaithful. You must understand. I couldn't help it. It was all her fault. She pursued me, and she was so sweet and pure, a virgin, and I just couldn't control myself! I'm sorry, but it was more than a normal man could stand.—and, and Adelene, she reminded me of you!"

"Reminded you of me? Give me a break, Francis. I fought to save myself for the man I would marry someday, and I was untouched until I became involved with you. How many virgins are you planning to spoil? How many virgins do you plan to rob of their purity? Certainly you are not finished. Of course, you will leave a lot of men with no virgins at all! How will they satisfy their lust for purity? I can no longer look at you and feel respect. I may never respect any man again, for I will always remember this night and your ridiculous excuses for unpardonable behavior. I trusted you with all my being and I have been betrayed.

I will find new quarters as soon as possible, and I presume you will take care of the expenses. Isn't that the way it is done? I want my own dwelling before you decide I am crazy and send me to Connecticut! Leave my sight, I cannot abide this!"

"Adelene, you stayed in Maine and I was defenseless. It was a physical thing and doesn't mean I don't love you. If you had been here it wouldn't have happened. You are behaving as though this is all my fault."

"Throughout history men have blamed women, when it is their own lack of control that brings about their downfall. I am not a naïve little country girl, though country Irish, I am. You men may have the vote and control the courts, and perhaps you think you deserve to control your women and get away with it, but it won't always be this way. Someday women will vote and sit on juries, perhaps even hold public office, and male control and abuse will stop. Until then, I accept no blame for yours or any other male's philandering. It's indulgence, it's cruel, and it is a death knell for true love. You could have kept your fly buttoned, you could have summered the complete season with me. Mama loved you so. It was your choice to return to New York before me, and your choice to be unfaithful."

"You are being very unreasonable. You know I love only you, it meant nothing, a dalliance means nothing. You are my only true love. Why else would I have married a woman nearly forty years old if not for true love?"

The words hung between them like a guillotine poised for release, then with a crunch the severance was accomplished.

For a moment, Adelene stood perfectly still, her heart racing so violently she thought it would burst from her bosom. Without a tear she stood her ground. Francis turned white with the realization of the impact of his words. His eyes quickly darted from side to side as his mind searched for the words to undo his execution. Beads of sweat formed on his brow and the muscles of his cheeks twitched beneath his moustache until the whole situation became a stalemate.

Adelene spoke calmly. "Do you think I couldn't have lovers, with those Lotharios mooning over me after every performance? You may have all the virgins you wish, Francis. As soon as the papers are signed I will move into my own apartment. Fortunately, you can afford all I will ask of you."

Adelene turned, feeling she had put forth a great performance. She ached for their marriage to be as it had always been, but knew it could never be.

Looking over her shoulder, she quietly spoke. "I charge you, Francis, to financially support Paul and myself, that Paul may grow up in the atmosphere that is his birthright. When you show me papers ensuring his upbringing as well as full ownership of my Maine residence, I will sign. Until then, Good Day!

Having the last word always gave her a good feeling, and it lasted until Francis left the room. With her bedroom door closed and tightly latched, she poured her tears again on her quilt. She had not imagined the pain that would be hers.

CHAPTER 7

Neither Adelene nor Francis attended the funeral. Alice was dead and to her it would not matter. Adelene would not face Alice's niece and Francis did not dare. A sad Nathan, the butler, went to the service and took flowers from the Oakes family.

Adelene hoped the girl's time with Francis had been worth losing the lifetime of well-paid employment she would have had if she had kept her legs together. If any employer asked for reference from Adelene the response would read, "unsatisfactory performance." She was not required to lie and Alice would never know. Neither Francis nor Adelene mentioned the reason her niece left their employ, as Alice was so very ill. She had been a faithful and beloved employee and they did not wish to increase her pain. No ripple of scandal ever reached her ears.

Adelene herself selected the replacement housekeeper; a very plump dark skinned Puerto Rican. She was a wonderful cook and Paul loved the stories she told of the islands, even the wild scarey ghost tales. He was such a daring child he seemed to enjoy the thrill of being frightened. They never mentioned their problems to Paul, and the passing of Alice was an event that easily masked their marital dysfunction. With Rand married and out of the picture Francis had concentrated his efforts to destroy any association she enjoyed with male friends. Albert Soler became the victim of Francis' attempt to erase his own transgressions. The wonderful kindness he had exhibited in his business management and the thoughtfulness and patience he had shown to all his family, seemed to have dissolved. In his anger over their broken marriage he had lashed out at Albert, seeking to find Adelene at fault rather than accept his own guilt.

Poor Albert, he was her friend, as Rand had been, just a fellow musician in the theatrical world. Perhaps he would have liked it to be more, but Adelene did not want, nor was she ready for, a new liaison. Men seemed to have difficulty accepting the possibility that a woman could think of a man as only a friend, however dear, probably because they are unable themselves to refrain from thinking beyond friendship with a woman.

In time, it was settled, and Adelene found her own apartment. Paul adjusted to spending time with both parents. His adventurous spirit found no problem with having two homes as long as he had the love of both his parents, and he was never aware of his mother's pain.

CHAPTER 8

1919

Francis lay motionless in the large four-poster, his children by his bedside. "Strange," he thought, "I can't seem to open my eyes." Trying to raise his arm to signal to his eldest son, he found himself unable to make that gesture, also.

"Good Lord, I must be dying. I don't feel any pain, I feel good!" He tried to call out, but no words came forth. He felt strangely warm, with a floating sensation. "ADELENE!"

CHAPTER 9

1923

News article:

January 18, 1923. Cheyenne, Wyoming: Pilot Paul Sullivan Oakes, along with mechanician W. R. Acor, were killed when an air mail plane which they were testing crashed at the local field at 2:15 o'clock this afternoon. The plane fell 500 feet and instantly burst into flames. Both bodies were burned.

Oakes and Acor left the hanger where the machine had been overhauled a few minutes before the crash. They took off in a high wind and circled the field, attaining an altitude of about 500 feet.

Oakes was transferred to Cheyenne from the New York—Cleveland air mail division about three months ago. He was twenty-seven years old and unmarried.

At her apartment on West 47th street, the telegram fell from Adelene's hand and she staggered slightly. Words from the past filled her mind as the room darkened and faded. She would never remember finding her way to the rocker by the window.

"Adelene, they are going to make machines that fly, and everyone will go everywhere without harnessing a horse, whiffletrees will be a thing of the past. Anyone with a big field will be able to have their own; there will be shows with flying machines performing tricks, and they will deliver mail by air!"

"Oh, Dennis, you always tell Ma that I put on highfaluting airs and you're no different. Tricks with flying machines and delivering mail! Anyone would be killed when the machine fell down from the sky!"

She rested her head against her hand. "Oh, Paul! You were the love of my life!"

As the sun sank and the room gloomed she still did not move, her mind reaching back to savor the life of her son, reliving all the happy moments—the sweet smell of his curling hair against her cheek, the grasp of his baby hands around her finger. His toddling days, flying kites in central park, then his teen years, so exuberant, so alive, now all gone.

She and Paul had survived the war to end all wars, and they had survived the influenza. She had grieved for Angie Fish when she heard of Kenneth's passing and for all the other mothers who had lost children to the swift killer. Her heart had ached for all those who lost sons and husbands to the Kaiser's hateful siege, but only now did she fully understand their grief and anger. Angie had nine other surviving children, but her only child was gone and all the reasoning and blame in the world would not bring him back.

Her suffering was so deep that she thought she might die. What evil thing had she ever done to deserve the horrid losses she had suffered? Betrayed by Francis, who was gone, but had even remarried before she could forgive him and take him back. She had planned to let him suffer a few years and then swallow her pride and allow him to beg her to return, but no, he had to show her she could be easily replaced. She was positive it was a vindictive marriage and when her own plan for a possible reconciliation was dashed her anger overtook her humiliation. She wondered if Francis had ever thought of her, perhaps in his last moments, but never mind. She had him those glorious years, had shared his life and for a time had been all he had needed. She understood his weaknesses, not knowing if it was physical or mental, but he had slipped and she had been unable to forgive him then. If only he hadn't turned against her and continued his frivolity. He had been like a little boy caught with his hand in a cookie jar, and then claiming the cookies were the best ever as an excuse for the pilfering, blaming the stolen item rather than the thief. All water over the dam, now. Francis had gone to his reward, but Paul, joy of her heart, how could he be gone? How could she go on without him? For days Adelene struggled with the pain, silently screaming in the night and hardly leaving her bed by day.

February came and went, March blustered in and roared out and the April rains came and washed the panes with soft healing sounds. "I'll go to Maine soon, I'll breathe again and find comfort. I'll not accept pity from anyone, and I will not mention his name again. I will forever hold him in my heart; it is the one love that will not be taken from me!"

Mayflowers. She needed to smell mayflowers!

"Stella! Stella," she called to her maid. "Fetch my trunk! I am leaving for Maine early!"

Perhaps she could get there before they were gone. Her mother and father wouldn't be there, only Sister Ella was left, but mayflowers came back every year!

CHAPTER 10

Summer, 1928

Adelene hated the thought of selling any part of her furniture to keep up the mansion. Much of her jewelry was already gone. She decided the oak sideboard in the hall could go. She had stubbed her toe on it many times on gloomy days when she was tired, so it was no heart wrenching decision to part with it. It had brought enough money to heat her Manhattan apartment for the winter. Two small oriental rugs were no sacrifice, either. She loved hearing the sound of her footsteps on the polished floors; she didn't need rugs.

The black horsehair parlor set she would never sell. The slick satiny button-tufted coverings were still a delight to see and touch and the carved rosewood arms were smooth as satin. But the extra furniture could go. The faded tapestry loveseat that had been her mother's would remain as her favorite piece. The raised embroidered roses still felt the same under her hand, each stem and leaf and petal still distinguishable to her touch even in the dark. They could auction everything off when she was dead and gone, but these would remain with her until then. She sat in the rocker and looked about the room. Her gaze fell on the furniture arranged so one could sit in any chair and look through the arched windows of the porch and view her cherished Sennebec. Sennebec, her precious jewel of comfort in her greatest times of sadness, her talisman when she needed to be encouraged, her charm when she needed to call upon luck to help her, her dream when nightmares attempted to prevail.

As her eyes returned to the elegant parlor she wondered who would own it when she was no longer living. Hopefully someone who would love it as she did, someone who would put a hand on the carved rose behind her head and say, "Adelene," and perhaps some spark of her being would be kindled in that person. The thought comforted her.

The chickens and livestock had been sold, as Helen didn't need to be burdened with their care. She thoroughly enjoyed having Helen with her as summer help. She could cook and clean and keep the house running smoothly, and she was only a young girl. They had some good times together. Just last week they had written a poem to Della McCorrison as Della had complained that there was "trouble with the line" dividing their property. Helen had delivered it with a straight and serious attitude, then came running back to wait with Adelene for Della's reaction. The poem, which they titled "To the Wall!" read,

> See the rocks where primrose bloom,
> Bright and pink to chase the gloom
> Of fog and setting sun.
> The rocky trail will mark your way,
> Where you must walk, where you must stay.
> To the Wall! To the Wall!
>
> And when you pick the berry blue,
> Be careful where you place your shoe.
> The rocks will show you where to go
> In sunshine, hail or falling snow.
> To the Wall! To the Wall!
>
> There is no fight, for there you'll see,
> The rocky wall twixt you and me.
> Let not our line cause unjust wrath,
> Just stay beyond that rocky path.
> To the Wall! To the Wall!

They waited for an answer but received none, so Adelene assumed the problem had been settled, but sometimes when they discussed any upheaval in the household either Helen or she would shout, "To the Wall! To the Wall! Then they would laugh again.

It was strange what a few years could do to change one's life. Feeling as mentally youthful as ever one had to deal with the ravages of time on one's face and body. When one was young eccentric acts were cute, interesting, intriguing; the same behavior by an old person was considered comical and silly.

That evening as she prepared to retire she reached for the large hatbox on the top of the armoire and lifted it down and placed it on the bed. She removed the round damask covered lid and slowly untied the faded ribbon that kept the lid closed on the container. Raising the cover she pushed the protective tissue aside and carefully lifted a flower-covered hat from the box. Turning her body that she might see herself in the mirrored door of the standing closet, she placed it on her head.

Laughing, she crawled into bed and pulled the covers up to her bosom.

Propped there on the pillows she continued to smile. Helen was getting ready to turn in for the day in the room opposite Adelene's and she glanced through the door at Addie before turning away.

"She must be thinking I've gone crazy," Addie thought. She realized Helen was too young to understand how quickly youth flees. Laughing, she closed her eyes. Her spirit was no longer in her aging body, but once more strolling the streets of New York.

Finally, Helen knocked on the door casing. "Is there anything I can get you before I retire, Mrs. Oakes?"

"No, Helen, I'm just reminiscing a little," and they both found the moment amusing.

As daylight faded into night she continued to think about her life and all she had done. It had been all, no, more than she had expected. All the sages had pronounced life to always be less than one's youthful imaginings, but she had found the opposite to be true. Even her moments of utter despair and of great heartbreak were of the greatest intensity. She had loved deeply, sorrowed unfathomably, but the joys and accomplishments had far outweighed the sadness.

She realized that everything changes. People were moving buildings around until one never knew where a barn or a house would be located next. She wouldn't be surprised if the schoolhouse were carted off and made into a house in the valley. And the horseless carriages! They were an affront to good taste! They were always getting flat tires and running out of gas and causing all manner of trouble, getting stuck in the roads and holding up traffic. Now they were even building "trucks," but they hauled such a small amount of cargo they seemed worthless to Adelene. If one had to make several trips with one of their little trucks to haul what a good team of horses or steers could pull, what was the point? Of course, if they built a much larger vehicle with a big storage compartment, they might have something, that is, if they improved the roads. It seemed like quite an impossible project to her. Things would have to improve a lot to convince her the whole idea was going to work.

But change was coming, actually had come. Styles were changing. Girls were engaging in sports: tennis, basketball, softball, and even wearing trousers, making their movement less restricted. Wouldn't it be something if women were allowed to compete with or against the male dominated sports world! Someday. Someday perhaps someone living in her very house would do all those things. She could envision the house ringing with their laughter, giggling and singing in the rooms, racing up and down the staircase. Perhaps someone living in her mansion would do all those things. And boys, playful spirited boys, running through the woods and berry fields, playing at the frog pond as Dennis had as a child. Life would go on in this house, longer, fuller lives than her Paul had enjoyed.

Before sleep overtook her consciousness, Adelene planned. She would return to her apartment in New York for the winter and in June she would sell all the furnishings and return to Maine. She still had time to dream!

When morning came, she arose with a happy heart. She began to pack her trunk and Helen was readying the house to close it for the winter. She turned from her packing when she heard a carriage pull into the portico. She had not expected company, but a visitor would not be unwelcome on this, her last day on the ridge this year.

"Why, Mr. Wentworth. Won't you come in? Helen, please find some lemonade and doughnuts for Mr. Wentworth. What brings you here today?"

"I'm sorry, Miss Adelene, I cannot stay for refreshments. I'm afraid I have brought you bad news. I'm sure it is just an oversight, but your taxes are long overdue. I understand you are having financial difficulties and the selectmen have agreed that if you could just fill in the ruts for about a quarter mile here on the ridge, we would forgive your taxes this year."

Adelene stiffened. "You need not worry, Mr. Wentworth. You will receive either the tax money or I will have the ruts filled promptly. Thank you for reminding me, you are correct, it is merely an oversight!"

As the carriage left for the valley Adelene walked into the parlor. She was weak with fury. Didn't the selectmen realize that women had the vote and she could hold meetings and vote them all out of office? When she returned in the spring she just might do that, have political meetings with the women of the town and make a few changes!

Plopping down on the red upholstery of her mother's loveseat, she leaned back, her cheek against the rose design of the covering.

Tears of anger rolled down her cheek. Her hand slid from the arm of the sofa and into the crack between the seat and the chair arm and rested on something soft and smooth. She pulled herself erect and reached down and extracted a small piece of gray leather. Her glove! Her lost GLOVE! So many years ago, and now it was found! Clutching the glove to her breast she leaned back and closed her eyes, tears squeezing from the corners and resting on her cheeks. Then a smile began to play on her lips and she shifted her position on the couch and rose to her feet.

"Taxes! Drat the taxes! Fill the ruts for a quarter of a mile and they would "forgive" her taxes! How generous, after all she and her family had given the town!" She would sell the rest of her jewels when she returned to New York and pay them, but first she would show the townspeople how low they were. She hoped there would be lot of traffic going to Union today!

Hurrying upstairs she went to the closet in her mother's bedroom and found a pair of her father's old ragged trousers and a faded shirt from years ago, pulled them on and found a shovel in the stable. Walking to the road she shoveled some loose dirt in one of the ruts made by the fairgoer's traffic, then another. She did not look up as folks drove by, she did not speak, she did not wave. Sweat trickled down her face in front of her ears and pooled in the hollow of her neck. As the salty moisture from her forehead became too voluminous for her brows to divert she used the bundle of her rolled sleeve to wipe it from her blearing eyes. She decided enough people had seen her performance so she was about to return to the mansion when she suddenly grasped the shovel and thrust it straight down into the earth with all the force she could muster, and there it stood. Leaning on the shovel handle, Adelene lowered her head and rested it on the shovel handle. Her whole body began to shake as though a convulsion wracked her body, and then she threw back her head and her silvery laughter rang out over the valley. "What a trip my life had been! What a great, scary, exciting, wonderful trip! AND IT ISN'T OVER YET!

There's a chestnut tree in the meadow, sturdy and straight and tall,
Its growing years never were easy, but it vowed never to fall.
Not from winds that tested its branches, not insects invading its bark,
Not the drought, not the floods or the snowstorms,
It stood firmly in daylight and dark.
Oh, pestilence came, and it threatened to ruin its stately design,
But the chestnut learned not to falter as adversity threatened to malign.
It bent, but never was broken, steady patience kept it alive,
It outlasted the fray that stood in its way,
Its persistence kept it alive.
So look to the tree in the meadow, when threatened with life's darkest hour.
Just bend with the wind and you'll find you can win,
And rob adversity of all of its power.

And though the storm rages 'round you.
You don't have to surrender and fall,
You'll be able to beat it,
Your strength will defeat it,
With victory yours, after all!

EPILOG

Adelene Sullivan Oakes died June 2, 1929 at her winter home on West 47th Street in New York City. She was returned to her beloved hills of Maine where her body was laid to rest on a knoll in Pine Grove Cemetery overlooking the Saint George River.

What was that Willow-the-wisp?

That pale flutter of light leaving Pine Grove for the heights of the western ridge above the Georges? Was that a moonbeam?

Was that haunting laughter the call of a loon heading for the cool waters of the Sennebec?

And that song whispering in the conifers—Is it the wind?

Printed in the United States
45582LVS00002B/442

9 781413 491586